"A second welcome appearance of Conan Flagg, many-talented detective."

The Columbus Dispatch

"Conan Flagg looks good for a long career in the ranks of fictional sleuths. . . . [*A Multitude of Sins*] adds up to good news for whodunit fans."

Amarillo Sunday News-Globe

"In *A Multitude of Sins,* M.K. Wren gives mystery lovers an unbeatable combination of favorite sleuth and damsel in distress."

Lewiston [Maine] Journal

"*Curiosity Didn't Kill the Cat* was good and the second book is even better. It confirms . . . that Flagg was a character who would be as durable as he was intriguing."

The Seattle Times

"This cozy thriller is full of goodies: a sinister but blind stepmother, a wicked trustee, iniquitous testamentary arrangements, drug addiction. Exciting!"

Library Journal

Also by M. K. Wren
Published by Ballantine Books:

CURIOSITY DIDN'T KILL THE CAT

A MULTITUDE OF SINS

M. K. Wren

BALLANTINE BOOKS • NEW YORK

 Published in the United States of America by Ballantine Books, a division of Random House, Inc., New York, and simultaneously in Canada by Random House of Canada Limited, Toronto. Originally published in 1975 by Doubleday & Company, Inc.

Library of Congress Catalog Card Number: 74-18839

ISBN 0-345-35001-4

All characters in this book are fictitious, and any resemblance to actual persons, living or dead, is purely coincidental.

Manufactured in the United States of America

First Ballantine Books Edition: May 1989

FOR L.A.T.—who somehow made room for one more

CHAPTER 1

Meg stretched herself, obliterating most of Harney and Malheur Counties in a gray fog, then she smiled her Mona Lisa smile, blue jewel eyes half closed, and challenged him to do something about it.

He did, with a resigned sigh, closing his calculations of day's marches and encampments inside the leather-bound tome, then devoting his attention to a gentle, systematic rubbing, working down from her ears to her tail.

Conan Flagg knew himself to be a sucker for blue-eyed females, and this blue-point Siamese was totally female. But being also very much a lady, she was seldom overdemanding. She indicated her satisfaction with a thrumming purr and after a few minutes lapsed again into catnap.

He leaned back and rested his eyes, strained with fine print and illegible topographic markings, with a long look out the window to his right. Past the chimneys and roofs of the village, the Pacific Ocean lay shining in the April sun, gray-green, dappled with lavender cloud shadows.

To his left, through the one-way glass on the door, he

could look into the bookshop and across to the front entrance. His view included the end of the counter and Miss Dobie, her determinedly auburn hair in close-ranked curl. She was contending with a horde of youngsters with her usual inertial efficiency, circling the dour square of her face with a benevolent smile. Beatrice Dobie had no great fondness for children, but she thoroughly enjoyed the dinging clank of the ancient cash register registering cash.

He was spared that sound as well as the clamor of exuberant youth; this small sanctum which he called an office was soundproofed. Satisfied that Miss Dobie needed no assistance, he lit a cigarette and took a moment to savor the Ravel *Quartet in F* playing on the tape deck hidden in the Louis Quinze commode, his dark eyes focused on the opposite wall. The Leonard Baskin woodcut was new and deepened the shadows at the corners of his mouth with a smile of pleasure.

But a few seconds later, the smile vanished when Miss Dobie knocked and hastily opened the door.

"Sorry, Mr. Flagg, but I just found this on the counter." She handed him a long white envelope. "Looks like somebody's trying to save money on postage."

He frowned at the address. It was printed with a rubber stamp; the one available at the counter.

THE HOLLIDAY BEACH BOOK SHOP
AND RENTAL LIBRARY
BOX 73 HOLLIDAY BEACH, OREGON
CONAN JOSEPH FLAGG, PROPRIETOR

His name was underlined in red, probably with Miss Dobie's pen, also available at the counter. The letter inside the envelope was typed on quality bond; a modern typeface, possibly an Olympia electric portable. There was no letterhead, signature, or name on it.

"Who left it, Miss Dobie?"

She shrugged, her mouth a thin, nonplussed line.

"I don't know. I was upstairs looking for that Kathleen Norris book for Mrs. Hoskins, then the school bus dumped the kids just as I got back downstairs. I didn't even notice that letter till I got rid of most of the little—" She turned and sighed at one of the youngsters. "Danny, please stick to the children's section."

"Can you remember who was in the shop when—" The bell on the counter clanged for attention. "Never mind. I'll read it first and see if it's worth the questions."

"Probably a fan letter," she said, closing the door with an arch smile. "Or a *billet doux*."

"Typewritten?" But she was gone. He took a short puff on his cigarette and began reading the letter.

Dear Mr. Flagg,

Forgive me this unorthodox approach, but I find myself in an unusual situation. I need professional assistance of a kind I know you're qualified to offer, although your private investigator's license seems to be a well-kept secret.

It isn't so secret that you're majority stockholder of the Ten-Mile Ranch Corporation, and as such, I realize you can well afford to turn down any cases that don't excite your interest. This is one reason for my reluctance to commit either my problem or my identity to paper. There are other reasons, but they're part of the problem.

All I'm asking is a chance to explain the problem to you *in private*. Please believe me, that is imperative. I've formulated a plan to assure the necessary privacy. If you're willing to grant me an interview on these terms, you can indicate assent simply by carrying out your part in the plan. If you don't do so, I'll accept that as a refusal, and I assure you, won't bother you again.

I would like to meet with you at your house. There's a path leading from the beach to the patio south of the house, and that will be my avenue of approach. I know your housekeeper, Mrs. Early, is there on Mondays and always leaves promptly at four. I mention this because you may wish to have her transmit a message to me. I'd prefer to have no one else involved, but I'll leave that decision to you.

I'll be on your patio at four o'clock. If you aren't there, or I don't receive a message from you by four-thirty, I'll understand you aren't interested in my case.

Thank you.

His first response was annoyance—at the letter, its writer, its method of delivery, the school bus and its contents for delaying Miss Dobie's discovery of it, and even Miss Dobie for reasons he couldn't define beyond that coy *billet doux*. It was now only five minutes until four.

He reached across Meg for the phone, then waited impatiently through five rings for an answer.

"H'lo? Flagg residence?" The thin voice was underlain with wheezing.

"Mrs. Early. I was afraid I'd missed you."

"Oh, Mr. Flagg? Well, I was jest about out the door, and Chester's outside leanin' on the horn waitin' for me."

"Sorry to keep him waiting, but I'm glad I caught you because I . . . ah, forgot my house keys this morning."

That produced a bemused cackle. "Oh, I swear, Mr. Flagg, if you ain't the most absent-minded man I ever did know. Why, if your head wasn't—"

"But it *is* firmly attached, fortunately. As for my immediate problem, you can solve it very nicely by leaving the patio door unlocked for me." Then he added, "Just leave the door open. Air the place out a little."

"Leave it open? But anybody could jest walk right up from the beach and—"

"The path isn't that obvious, and you can't see the door from the beach. Anyway, I think I'm coming home soon."

"Well, all right, but it jest don't seem right to—"

"Mrs. Early," he said carefully, "leave the door open. Please. Oh, and if you don't think Chester will get too impatient, would you mind putting on a fresh pot of coffee?"

"Sure, Mr. Flagg. Chester's used to waitin' fer me. He's been Early all his life." She paused to appreciate her threadbare witticism with a gleeful chuckle. "Oh—don't fergit to look in your fridge. Had some spare ribs left over yestiddy. Didn't want 'em goin' to waste."

Conan laughed. "To throw away your spare ribs would be more than a waste; it would be a crime. Thanks, Mrs. Early."

He looked at his watch again, then at the letter, not yet fully convinced he should answer the anonymous summons. Perhaps it was only reflex that induced him to tell Mrs. Early to leave the door open, literally and figuratively.

The incidence of neatly corrected typos suggested he wasn't dealing with an experienced typist, but the writer was obviously educated; the letter was literate and even rational in tone despite its unusual content.

The writer was also very familiar with some aspects of his personal life, but only the reference to his private investigator's license concerned him. That *was* a well-kept secret. But not perfectly kept; he had a file of anonymous inquiries from obvious cranks or paranoids. He was also aware that certain people regarded Conan Flagg, private investigator, with some animosity, and wouldn't be above setting a lethal trap for him.

The latter consideration he dismissed. The letter was too well written for any of the potential Flagg-killers he knew. He was also inclined to dismiss mental aberration.

Still, he wondered at the repeated references to privacy, the insistence on meeting at his house, and the approach through the patio, which like the path, was heavily screened by trees. And the path began in a small cove hidden from view except in a narrow arc directly west. Jane Doe's "problem" included a pronounced fear of observation.

Then he frowned. Why was he thinking in terms of *Jane* Doe rather than John? Something about the syntax, perhaps. He began rereading the letter, but stopped himself and returned it to its envelope.

He was procrastinating. As if he still had a choice to make. He *would* keep this appointment. At least, he'd find out about the problem. And the writer. But it rankled, this feeling that he'd been pushed into a decision before he had time to think it out.

He rose, pausing to give Meg a brief rub.

"Wish me luck, Duchess."

CHAPTER 2

She was late.

Isadora Canfield looked at her watch, finding it hard to focus. Ten minutes past four.

What if Conan Flagg came for this appointment, and finding the patio empty, left in disgust? Should she leave another letter? Sorry, Mr. Flagg. Couldn't meet you today because it took fifteen minutes for me to muster the nerve to walk up this path. How about tomorrow?

It was so hot for April, even under the dense shadow of jackpines wind-cast over the rough footpath. A creek chattered nearby, hidden in the impenetrable cover of salal.

No, it wasn't that hot. Her palms and face were damp with perspiration for the same reason her throat was dry.

Isadora Canfield had never walked this path before, and realized now she was a fool to think she could without being reduced to a state of quivering terror. The child on the beach last week had been so nonchalant. Sure, it goes up to Mr. Flagg's house. Jeremy—so he called himself—cheerfully admitted to frequent trespassing and provided a detailed description of the path and the Flagg residence, including the patio and sliding glass door opening onto it.

The path was easy. A couple of minutes.

But Jeremy wasn't afraid of . . .

Oh, Lord, don't *concentrate* on them. The clay was slick; she placed her steps carefully, occasionally reaching out for a tree branch, but only after examining it closely.

How much farther?

She wouldn't take her eyes from the path, the hiding shadows lacing it, the dark, festering worlds under the salal. If she slipped and fell into it—fell *through* it . . .

She made herself stop and take a long, deep breath.

What's the alternative to this path? The office at the shop with its door in clear line of sight through the glass-paneled front entrance to Highway 101? And the red Ford that always parked directly across the highway?

This couldn't be explained in five minutes. The faithful watcher would wonder if she spent too long in private conversation with Mr. Conan Flagg. *She'd* found out he was a private investigator; the man in the red Ford could, too.

Or could she enter this house by way of the front door? It was only a few yards from the beach access at the foot of Day Street where the red Ford was waiting near her silver Stingray. He was bound to be suspicious if he knew she was having a long talk with Flagg in his own house.

Isadora resumed her cautious course up the path, a little calmer. Nothing like a larger fear to put a lesser one in perspective. Hold on to that. Thank God for the sunlight; it helped somehow, even if it deepened the shadows.

She'd come this far. This far on the path, this far with her diurnal and nocturnal watchers. She *knew* they were watching her, but they didn't know she knew . . .

It was ridiculous; crazy. Maybe Dr. Kerr was right.

A shingled wall and the top of a glass door lurched into view through a tangle of branches; her steps quickened.

The watchers must not know she knew. If they did, they

might send someone else, change the situation somehow, so she could never learn the truth, never find out why . . .

Something brushed against her ankle.

She heard her own choked scream as she stumbled onto the stone paving of the patio, pounding across it toward the open door. She didn't stop until she was inside, the glass barrier closed behind her.

For some time, she stood gripping the door handle, forehead pressed to the cool glass. Probably nothing more than a tendril of vine had precipitated this panicked retreat. The fear always seemed foolish when the danger was past.

Danger. There wasn't even that to justify it.

She remembered her father sitting down with her in earnest consultation one day. Years ago. She'd been twelve; it was . . . yes, at the beach house at Shanaway.

"Dore, honey, just remember, there aren't any poisonous snakes west of the Cascades. These little grass snakes can't hurt you. They're probably just as scared of you as you are of them . . ."

She felt the aching behind her eyes. Not now. Don't think about that now.

Then she became aware of her silent surroundings, and was both embarrassed and apprehensive. The patio was empty. So was this room. A narrow room with a disproportionately high ceiling, the west wall a solid span of glass looking out on the ocean. Straight across from her was a heavy wooden door with carved panels. It was closed.

If Conan Flagg weren't here . . .

But the glass door had been open. Didn't that constitute a message? An assent?

She squared her shoulders. That's how she would interpret it. Mr. Flagg could argue the point if and when he arrived. He might also argue her decision to wait here in his house, but she wasn't ready to return to the patio just yet.

She took off her sunglasses and put them in her handbag. A library. A proper library, the walls lined with shelves and solid with books except for the numerous spaces left free to display a collection of paintings remarkable for its diversity. Her steps were silenced by a rich brown carpet that made velvet for the jewels of five Navajo rugs. There was little furniture; a desk near the patio door, a contemporary armchair and reading lamp by the windows. A very personal room, and although the decor was quite different, it reminded her of the library at . . .

Not *now*. Can't you keep your thoughts away from that?

She turned, something glimpsed but not yet consciously recognized drawing her eye to the east wall; the corner at the left end of the wall. A painting hung there. The shelves were built around it to form a deep vertical niche exactly the size of the canvas.

With recognition came shock, all the more stunning because it was unexpected. She knew that painting. A life-size figure of an armored man, a knight. But the armor was of a peculiar design, equivocally anatomical; it was bone and muscle as well as armor, the head both helmet and skull, empty sockets staring out with blind sight. The psyche armored against pain in a bronzed sheath of fear.

The painting was Jenny's.

But something more than years had come between this painting and Jennifer Hanson.

That was what made it so bewildering. It wasn't so surprising that it was here; Conan Flagg was obviously a collector, and the early works of Jennifer Hanson could be found in many Northwest collections.

The early works.

Isadora stared at the painting, shoulders sagging. Not an hour ago, she'd left Jenny in her studio at the cottage facing a naked canvas, a palette knife in her hand, slowly, incessantly marbling the pigments into muddy grays. And she'd wondered if Jenny would get as far as daubing some of those sickly, blemished mixtures on the canvas before she wandered away to the window or down to the beach.

Where are you going, Dore? When will you be back, Dore? What about supper, Dore?

Yet she always accepted Isadora's vague answers with an indifference that never made sense.

Have a good time, Dore.

And five, six—how many years ago?—this was an early work of Jennifer Hanson. There was power and conviction that sprang from the soul in this haunting image.

She wondered bitterly if Catharine remembered the Knight; remembered her daughter's early works.

She turned to the wooden door. She couldn't stay in here. Breaking and entering, invasion of privacy—she didn't care. And where was Conan Flagg? Perhaps the open patio door was only a coincidental accident.

With the library door closed behind her, she caught her breath, finding herself in a long corridor ending in the distance with another door. That must be the front entrance. On the left, spanning half the length of the hall, was a wash of light. The living room. An intricate wooden grille maintained the semblance of a corridor.

She paused before taking the single step down to the living-room level. On the south wall was a bar decorated with Haida motifs. At the west end of the north wall was a stone fireplace; at the other end, a pass-through into the kitchen. There was a hint of voyeurism in this secret inspection of someone else's house that made her uneasy; something unreal and dreamlike. But no more unreal than the situation that brought her here.

Her abstracted gaze traced the spiral of the staircase to her left; the low ceiling of the hall was a balcony that must give access to the bedrooms. The living-room ceiling vaulted above it to the west wall, which, like the one in the library, was solid glass; solid sea and sky.

She almost smiled, thinking that no decorator had ever touched this room. It was immaculately kept under Mrs. Early's aegis, but immensely cluttered and furnished with abandoned eclecticism. Mr. Flagg was definitely a collector and paintings were only the beginning.

But only one thing here could hold her attention for more than a few seconds.

A concert grand.

It was in the center of the room, turned so the pianist could look out over it to the windows. She walked toward it, drawn as if by an offered hand of solace, finding in its familiar lines a remedy.

The name over the open keyboard was Bösendorfer, and her eyebrows came up at that. She wondered how many years had gone into the warm, satin gleam of the wood; how many hands now dead had touched the yellowed ivory of these keys, and how many yet unborn would make music with this instrument crafted out of exalting genius and exacting pride.

That Conan Joseph Flagg, owner of this piano, was absent, might appear for an appointment she'd asked of him, or might *not* appear, was forgotten. The watchers, the coiling shadows on an innocent path, even the grief was forgotten.

The piano was in perfect tune. The decision to begin playing occurred with the same absence of conscious consideration that let the testing chromatics glissando into the Paderewski *Minuet in G*, shift capriciously to Saint-Saëns's *Swan*, form a collage of Beethoven, Liszt, Chopin, Bach, Rachmaninoff; music born in the minds of men who defied mortality on barred sheets of paper and in succeeding generations of memories. In these sounds, in the intricate, instant interplay of muscle and nerve, she was out of reach of fear or even time. A familiar paradox; music exists in one dimension, time, yet obliterates it.

She didn't know what made her stop.

She only wondered how long she'd been playing, and when she'd ceased to be alone.

He was standing by the staircase, watching her.

Her first impression was shadow; whip-lean, relaxed as a

cat, flashes of bronze in the sunlight. And she didn't recognize him.

Yet the face was quite familiar; dark skin drawn in angular contours, straight black hair, black eyes with an almost Oriental cast. But there was none of the polite friendliness a "proprietor" displays for his customers in those eyes. They were opaque as stone, yet she could all but feel the rapt tension in them, and her only coherent thought was: What in God's name am I doing here?

CHAPTER 3

It was a short walk. A block south to Day Street, then two blocks west to its terminus in a paved beach access. The house lodged into the wooded hill south of the access was always a joy to his eye; an angular structure with great spans of glass set in slabs of satin-shingled walls.

But Conan walked past his own front door, ignoring it. The cars parked in and around the access included the usual assortment of stationwagons, VWs, and campers. A silver Stingray was the only sports car, and only one car was occupied, a red Ford.

It had the anonymous look of a rental. The driver had a similarly anonymous look; average build, indeterminate age, coloring a mean drab tan. His air of indifferent patience alerted Conan for the same reason it made him invisible to the unpracticed eye.

The sand made squeaking sounds under his rubber-soled shoes. He stayed close to the bank, absently frowning at the number of people on the beach; a preview of summer. But there was no one lurking suspiciously near the foot of the path. He looked at his watch: 4:15. Jane Doe would be waiting on the patio. Supposedly.

But when he reached the patio, it was empty. That didn't especially surprise him, but finding the patio door closed did. If Mrs. Early had taken it upon herself to . . .

But the door was unlocked. His faith in his housekeeper was restored. Not, however, his faith in Jane Doe.

Music. His first angry assumption was that someone had the temerity to touch the stereo console without his permission. But when he heard the *Emperor Concerto* shift with a nice improvised chord transition into *El Amor Brujo*, he realized he was dealing with a more heinous crime. Someone had presumed not only to touch but to *play* the Bösendorfer.

His anger lasted until he reached the step down into the living room, and there died an unresolved death. He had no right to anger. This young woman belonged to that piano, possessed it as he never would; he only owned it.

He was stunned, like a skeptic in the presence of a miracle. She played with the passion generally ascribed to youth, yet with the restrained precision of a Rubinstein. It was chilling to hear her; an atavistic response to extra-human powers, witch or wizard, magician or saint.

When at length she became aware of him and the music ceased, he felt in some sense cheated, and at first he didn't realize how badly he'd startled her. Then he relaxed into a smile.

"If you've come to steal the piano, take it with my blessings."

Her eyes widened in embarrassed surprise, and he thought to himself they were exactly the same shade of sapphire blue as Meg's.

"Mr. Flagg, I—this is really unforgivable of me."

"Don't apologize. This piano hasn't enjoyed musicianship of that caliber since it's been in my possession."

She rose, smiling uncertainly as she started to close the cover, then seemed to remember it had been open; still a little off balance, but recovering remarkably fast. He leaned on the piano with one elbow, automatically making surface observations, noting that the gold-mounted ring was jade and possibly Imperial; the casual, off-white slacks and tunic with the matching sweater had probably set someone back several hundred dollars.

"I'm not sure I'd be so gracious if this were my piano." She touched the keyboard reverently, smiling to herself. Her nails were unfashionably short but perfectly manicured, and Conan doubted her long, sable-colored hair ever went a week without professional care.

She looked up at him. "Do you know its history?"

"Oh, I was given a rather colorful account when I bought it—from a Hungarian gypsy in Paris who claimed to be a descendant of the last Czar Nicholas." He also noted—again automatically, perhaps—that she had the kind of tall, lithesome figure that evoked envious glances from women and long stares from men; a fine-boned oval face with fair, perfect skin, and with the reserved smile, her mouth had a particularly sculptural quality. Bernini. No, the hands were Bernini, but the mouth was Houdon.

He sighed. His objectivity was going to hell.

"But it's a long and probably apocryphal story. May I offer you a cup of coffee—or something else, perhaps?"

"Why, yes, thank you. Coffee would be fine."

"Sugar and cream?"

"Please, if it isn't too much bother."

He retired to the kitchen and after a brief search in the cupboards, took out a tray and a pair of porcelain cups and saucers. Somehow, mugs didn't seem appropriate. While he prepared the tray, he took advantage of the pass-through and her momentary interest in the Netsuke case to study his enigmatic guest, a nagging memory refusing to come into focus. He'd seen her before. Not at the bookshop, although he was sure she'd been a frequent customer, lately. Sometime before that.

He was still frowning in pursuit of the memory while he poured the coffee, but when he carried the tray into the living room, he offered a reassuring smile. He put the tray on the table between the Eames Barcelona chairs facing the windows, and when they were seated, made a diversion for himself in lighting a cigarette while she stirred sugar and cream into her coffee. He looked around finally to find her studying him over the rim of her cup, to all appearances perfectly at ease; she seemed privately amused at something.

"You know what they say in the village, Mr. Flagg?"

"In this village, a great deal is said."

"They say your mother was Chief Joseph's daughter."

For a moment, he was stopped by the sheer incongruity of that; then he laughed aloud.

"Is *that* what they say? Well, there's a flaw in the chronology of several generations. Chief Joseph met his Waterloo long before my mother was born. But she was Nez Percé; she gave me my middle name in honor of the old chief."

"What was she like?"

"Thoroughly 'civilized.' But I don't remember her too well; she died in one of Pendleton's bad winters, of pneumonia, when I was thirteen." She looked vaguely startled at that. "Didn't they tell you about that in the village?"

"No, I mean, it just occurred to me that I was thirteen when *my* mother died."

"That isn't a pleasant thing to have in common." He paused, watching her. "You know, it's disconcerting thinking of you as 'Jane Doe.' It doesn't fit you somehow."

She put her cup down, centering it precisely in the saucer, and with that seemed to shift mental gears, an underlying tension exposed in her retrained composure.

"Does Isadora Canfield fit better?"

"Yes. You have identification, of course?"

That apparently surprised her, but she reached into her purse, which she'd put on the floor by her chair, took out a billfold, and handed it to him without hesitation.

"My driver's license and some other cards are in there."

As she reached across the table, her sleeve pulled back, and he caught a glimpse of a thin, reddish scar across the inside of her wrist.

The driver's license told him, among other things, that she was twenty-one years old. There were membership cards for the Young Republicans Club, Sierra Club, Portland Symphony Association, and a student ID from Willamette University in Salem. The address on all the cards was Mission Drive in Salem, the Oregon state capital.

At this point, the "Canfield" began to register.

He turned over the last plastic folder and found a faded snapshot. Three people, obviously mother, father, and daughter, seated on a porch ornamented with elaborate Victorian gingerbread. The child was Isadora Canfield at about ten years old. The woman was smiling down at her, while the man, broad-shouldered and vigorous, but already graying at the temples, was looking directly into the camera.

"The late Senator John Canfield," Conan said quietly. "You're his daughter."

She nodded once. "Yes."

Finally, the nagging memory came into focus.

"Now I remember where I've seen you."

"The Canfield name always rings bells."

He ignored her sarcasm. "You did a concert with the Portland Symphony two years ago. The Tchaikovsky *Concerto #1*, wasn't it?'"

"Why, yes. Don't tell me you were there?"

"Actually, I was coerced into going since I expected nothing better than a parlor pianist of the Senator's daughter. You see, sometimes a name rings the wrong bells. But I was forced to eat crow, and gratefully."

Her eyes were a warmer blue when she smiled.

"And I'm grateful you'd remember."

Conan looked down at the snapshot again.

"This was your mother."

"Yes."

"She was a beautiful woman, and you favor her."

"Thank you. Yes, she was beautiful. She was a dancer. I mean, she studied ballet until John Canfield swept her off her *en pointe*. That's why I was named Isadora. Mother was a great admirer of Isadora Duncan."

"It's a beautiful name."

"A little unwieldy. Most people just call me 'Dore.' Dad started that; he said 'Dora' sounded so old-maidish." There was a wistful sadness in her eyes; something that made her seem achingly vulnerable.

"I'm sorry about your father."

"So am I. It was so unexpected. But perhaps it was better for him; no long illness."

"A heart attack, wasn't it?"

"Yes."

"That was only a few months ago, as I remember."

"January. January fifteenth."

She spoke the words with dull, weighted portent; a date she would carry in her memory until she died. And Conan's memory of John Canfield—the public image, at least—was revived. A vibrant, intelligent man, passionate in his convictions, articulate, and graced with a fine sense of humor.

He returned the billfold to her. "I'm sure this isn't a subject you wish to pursue. Perhaps you should tell me about this 'problem' of yours." He watched her as she picked up her cup before replying. She was much too pale.

"Well, it's very simple, really."

"I find that hard to believe."

She smiled bitterly. "I mean, the basic . . . situation. You see, someone is following me. Closely and constantly. I'm never free; I can't set foot out of the cottage without an escort. That's why I was so insistent on a *private* meeting with you."

He blew out a stream of smoke, allowing himself no change of expression.

"Do you know this 'someone'?"

"There are two of them. No, I don't know them, and I've been very careful to ignore them. I don't want to alarm them into changing the status quo. Mr. Flagg, I have political connections and a good memory." A slight, uneasy pause at that. "In some areas. Anyway, *I* found out you're a private investigator without too much difficulty. *They* could, too, and if they knew I was seeing you, they might guess why, and—well, I was afraid it would make it that much harder to get at the truth. And that's why I'm here. I want to know who they are, and most of all, *why* they're watching me."

He hesitated, then said drily, "Well, your curiosity is reasonable enough."

"Reasonable?" She put her cup down, suddenly defensive, then seemed to catch herself, even calling up a brief smile. "Reasonable, but not a very interesting problem?"

"No. Surveillance is usually quite interesting; it's so often a symptom of something more serious."

"Whatever it's a symptom of, I must know. It just doesn't make sense; it's so pointless. I *must* find out what it's all about, or I'll go—" She stopped abruptly.

After a short silence, he asked, "I assume you've considered going to the police about it?"

She shook her head. "No. I mean, I've considered it, but I couldn't cope with the publicity if the reporters got hold of it. That's one disadvantage of being the Senator's daughter. You're always good copy."

"All right, but before we go on, I'll be honest with you—I must be sure you actually are being followed."

She looked at him sharply, again on the defensive.

"You think I'm imagining things?"

"That's a possibility, but I wasn't suggesting it. I've had some experience with tailing myself, and I'm good at recognizing it, but I've also fallen into a series of coincidental meetings and come to the conclusion I was being tailed when a little checking proved me wrong."

"There've been too many 'meetings' to be coincidental. *Or* imaginary. That . . . did occur to me."

His eyes narrowed. He had the feeling she'd considered that possibility seriously, and he wondered why.

"All right, then. Tell me more about it."

Her breath came out in a long sigh of relief.

"Well, as far as I know, there are only two men. One I call the day man, the other the night man."

"They seem to maintain regular shifts?"

"Yes. The day man must be staying out at Shanaway somewhere. I'm living there now; we have a cottage up on the ridge. Anyway, every time I drive into town that red Ford shows up before I reach the highway. From then on, he follows me everywhere I go."

He tensed at the words "red Ford," but didn't comment on that, asking, "Does he leave his car to follow you?"

"Yes, I'm sure of that, but I've never had a really close look at him. He seems to prefer staying in his car as long as he can keep me in sight."

Careless, Conan thought; but he'd seen the man in the red Ford, and that in itself was indicative. A good operative wouldn't be seen without an intentional search. Certainly his mark shouldn't be so aware of him.

"Can you describe the car?"

"Oh, yes. Dark red Ford; a new model, two-door sedan. Oregon license plate AMK510."

That cool and competent observation definitely took her "problem" out of the realm of the imaginary.

"What can you tell me about the *night* man?"

"Well, I know *him* by sight, but I'm not sure of his car, although I thought I saw him getting into a light blue Ford one night."

"How is it you know him by sight?"

"I see him where I work." Then she explained with a crooked half smile: "I'm playing evenings at the Surf House bar, much to Catharine's consternation."

"Catharine?"

"Oh, I'm sorry. She's Dad's—I mean, my stepmother."

"And she disapproves of your job?"

"Oh, my, yes! A *Canfield* performing in a bar? It's a blot on the family escutcheon." There was a nearly ferocious undercurrent in her sarcasm that surprised him.

"I gather you aren't too fond of your stepmother."

"Not very subtle, am I? No, I'm not fond of her, and the feeling is mutual, although we both kept it under wraps for Dad's sake. But that's only family in-fighting." And obviously, she thought it of no interest to him. "The job at the Surf House is just cocktail piano, but I . . . I needed something to do."

He nodded. "Tell me more about your night man."

"He was the first one I noticed. He'd come to the bar every evening about eight when I began playing and nurse a few drinks along until closing time. He didn't talk to anyone, or dance, or even drink enough to show it. I couldn't believe my music glued him to that bar stool for six hours every night. Max—that's the bartender, Max Heinz—didn't know anything about him, and if anyone comes into the bar more than twice, Max can usually give you their life history. Anyway, I ran a few tests. Once, on my night off I drove to Westport for dinner, and another time I took in a movie at the local theater, and the night man showed up both times. I even went down to the Surf House on my night off once, and he wasn't there, but he arrived within ten minutes.

"When did you first notice him—and the day man?"

"I started working at the Surf House on March first, and I noticed the night man three or four days later, then after another couple of days, I spotted the day man. I ran my tests during that first week, but when I was sure I wasn't—I mean, I was sure they *were* following me, I stopped that. I didn't want them to know I'd caught on to their little game."

He smiled at that. "Amazing."

"What?"

"Most people would panic in a situation like that."

"I don't—well, I don't *usually* panic easily."

There was something hidden in her eyes. He remembered the glimpse he'd had of the scar on her wrist.

"And your next step was to find a handy private eye?"

"Yes. Mr. Flagg, do you believe me?"

Both the question and the intense plea reflected in her eyes caught him off guard, and he realized that again he'd made a choice without being fully aware of it; the decision made when he first saw her—or rather, first *heard* her. Anyone possessed of talent of that magnitude should be spared the natural shocks to which lesser flesh is heir.

"Believe you? Is there any reason I should doubt you?"

Her cheeks went red, and the question seemed to have deeper meaning for her than he intended. He didn't wait for a response, but rose and went to the cabinet by the fireplace and took out a Polaroid camera.

"Miss Canfield, come into the kitchen a moment."

She hesitated, nonplussed, then followed him into the kitchen. He crossed to the high windows on the north wall and looked out into the beach access. The red Ford was still there, its driver still waiting.

Conan motioned her to the window.

"I think you'll find the view interesting."

CHAPTER 4

Isadora Canfield's blue eye were glacier cold.

"That's the man." Then she looked up at Conan. "You *knew* he was here. But, how—"

He smiled and focused the camera on the man.

"Are you asking me to reveal trade secrets?" He concentrated on the camera until the finished photograph was ready, eyed it critically, then put it on the window sill. "Now, give me a smile."

He got a quizzical frown instead when he turned the camera on her.

"Why do you want a picture of me?"

"This won't be a one-man job." He paused until the photograph was developed. "Doesn't do you justice. I'll have to call in reinforcements. I need a picture because I may not have a chance to make formal introductions."

"Then, you—you *will* help me?"

He laughed. "Have I a choice? At least, I'll try."

"Oh . . . thank you . . ."

She was on the verge of tears, and he said tersely, "Thanks aren't in order yet. Come on, we've work to do."

"Work?" She frowned in bewilderment as he guided her back to the living room. "What do you mean?"

"Isadora, I have just begun to question." He waved her to her chair and seated himself, eyes narrowed intently. "You want answers to two questions *re* your watchers: who and why. The *who* we'll ignore for now; they're probably hired professionals, and their identity is only important if it leads me to their employer. The question that concerns me now is *why*. Have you any theories on that?"

She shook her head. "No. That's what's so unnerving about it. There's no reason for it."

"There's a reason; every effect has a cause. It might be something very personal; something out of your past."

That called up a faint smile. "Some skeleton in my closet rising up to haunt me? The trouble is, there's never been time in my life for anything but the piano; I've never been involved in anything remotely illegal or even immoral, and I'm too egocentric for the kind of personal involvements that might lead me astray. Believe me, there's nothing in my past interesting enough to attract this kind of attention."

He believed her, but *something* about her had attracted someone's attention.

"How long have you been living at Shanaway?"

"We came down February twenty-fifth."

"We?"

"Jenny and I. My stepsister; Catharine's daughter." Her eyes narrowed. "The faithful watchdog."

"The what?"

But she only laughed. "Don't mind me. That's just more family in-fighting."

He hesitated, then: "So, you discovered the tails within . . . what? About two weeks after moving to Shanaway? You're sure you weren't under surveillance before that?"

"As sure as I can be. Before Dad died, I was at Willamette

University. It's a small school, and these two, or anyone like them, would stick out like sore thumbs."

"You've graduated from Willamette?"

"No, I have a year to go, but after Dad died my . . . doctor suggested I sit this quarter out."

"So, as far as you know, the tailing began when you came to Shanaway?" Then at her nod: "What about the time right after your father's death? It was over a month before you moved down here."

"No," she answered, too quickly. "I'm sure I wasn't being followed then."

"You were at home in Salem?"

"I . . . yes, I was in Salem."

He considered her constrained tone. There were restricted areas in every life, and however vital they might be to an investigation, they were still jealously guarded.

"There's one obvious explanation we should discuss."

"What's that?"

He reached out and caught her left hand. At first, she resisted, but only until he pushed her sleeve back.

"This," he said. "There's a matching scar on the other wrist, and the wounds are fairly recent. Probably acquired around January fifteenth."

Her eyes closed, her hand trembling in his.

"Dore, are you ashamed of those scars?"

"No," she said dully. "Not . . . ashamed."

"Then what?"

She pulled her hand free, shaking her head.

"It's just that I don't remember . . . doing it. I've *lost* a week. The week after Dad died."

Amnesia. Not such an unusual response to grief, yet he found it in some indefinable sense more disturbing than the scars.

"My point is, if you made one attempt on your life, someone might be concerned that you'd try again, and that might explain why you're being watched."

Her head fell back and she laughed.

"Oh, I thought about that. Conan, you said yourself those men are hired professionals, and they're costing someone a lot of money. So, who cares that much if I cut my wrists again? Catharine? Not on your life. And who outside the—the *family* would be remotely interested?"

He made no reply, silenced by that potent antipathy.

Then she sighed. "Sounds like the old Cinderella bit, doesn't it, mean stepmother and all."

"Or a distaff Hamlet, *sans* ghost. Or murder."

She shivered, then covered it with an uneasy shrug.

"Anyway, you can forget that theory. For one thing, Jenny's here to make sure I don't take a razor to my wrists again; she's cheaper than hired detectives."

"Jenny? Your stepsister? Tell me about her."

She hesitated, the bitterness more equivocal.

"Jennifer Hanson. It was decided I couldn't stay here alone, so Jenny was elected to keep me company."

"Hanson? Her married name?"

"No, Catharine's name before she married Dad. But the name should be familiar to you. She paints."

"Oh, of course." He laughed with the pleasant shock of finding the familiar in an unfamiliar context. "The Knight."

"I saw the painting in the library. It was a surprise, to say the least."

"It's always a surprise; that's why I like it. But I haven't heard anything about Jennifer Hanson for years. Where's she exhibiting now?"

"Well, she isn't showing many paintings lately. She was quite ill for a while, and after that . . ."

He waited for her to go on, but she seemed at a loss for an explanation and uncomfortable with the subject.

"I'm sorry if her painting suffered because of her illness. Has Jenny said anything to suggest *she's* being followed?"

"No."

"Would she tell you?"

"I think so. She worries about burglars and that sort of thing. Too much city life, I guess. She's very careful about locking the doors at night, and even keeps a gun by her bed, although I doubt she knows how to use it."

Conan rose and went to the window. The beach was still crowded, and that was to Isadora's advantage; crowds served to conceal both presence and absence.

"Did your father confide in you about his private political affairs? Is it possible you know something incriminating or damaging to someone?"

"No. He used to pass on some of the political gossip, but nothing that wasn't more or less common knowledge. He was very careful about that."

"You're sure the tailing began only after you came to Shanaway?"

"Yes, I told you that." The strain was showing, more in her voice than her face.

"I know, but the time when the surveillance began is crucial. It was triggered by *something*, Dore; some event of importance to someone, and it was probably important to you, too, since you're the object of it." So far, he knew of only one event in her life that might fill that bill.

He turned to the window again. "Your father was quite wealthy, wasn't he?"

"Yes, he was. That's one reason he was such an honest politician. He could afford to be."

"That doesn't always guarantee honesty in politics. What were the terms of his will?"

This called up a questioning frown, then a shrug.

"Well, I don't know exactly."

"You weren't at the reading?"

"No." A flat, wary response.

"That occurred during the week you lost?"

"Yes."

"But weren't you informed of the terms later? I'm not interested in details; just the general outlines."

"I couldn't give you the details anyway. The estate is out of my hands. I'm not eligible for my inheritance until I'm twenty-five. Dad didn't believe maturity comes automatically at twenty-one."

Conan returned to his chair, smiling faintly.

"So, he thought an extra four years would insure the onset of maturity? What *can* you tell me about the will?"

She pushed her hair back over her shoulder nervously.

"Why do you want to know about that?"

"I want to know about many things, most of which will have no bearing on your problem, but I have no way of sorting it out yet. What was the total estate, by the way?"

"Oh . . . six or seven million dollars."

"I admire your cavalier attitude." He couldn't repress a laugh, but she didn't respond to it.

"I suppose you're wondering what my share of it is?"

"Among other things, yes."

"It isn't an exact amount; the left-overs, so to speak. Somewhere between three and four million." She turned to the window, eyes clouding. "Words. That's all it is."

Words that could be dangerous. "To you, perhaps, but three or four million might mean more to someone else."

She frowned at that, but after a moment looked out to the horizon again.

"I'm not being honest. The money *is* important to me since I'm in such an expensive business. I began studying piano when I was four, and played my first concert at fourteen, but I've still just begun, and there isn't much chance I'll ever actually make a living at it." She laughed with a twist of irony. "No one goes into this business for the money, but the trouble is, once you're in it, you can't get out. Not—not alive. Not with your mind and soul intact. It's a trap, but that's the price, and I can never really explain the compensations; a kind of . . . power. Insights and highs no drug could ever touch. That's why I've never been interested in drugs. I don't need them. I don't need anything except my hands, my mind, and a piano."

Conan found himself staring at her hands. Beautiful by any standard; long-boned, slender, nicely articulated. The brute strength that would be a product of the years of hard training wasn't evident, but there was a power residing in them, even in repose, even away from the keyboard.

Her soft laugh recalled his attention.

"I'm sorry, I've gotten us off the track. Where were we?"

He took a deep breath. "Money. Your father's will. Were there any other major beneficiaries besides yourself?"

Her laughter had vanished. "No. Just the family."

"You mean Catharine, Jenny, and you?"

"And Jim."

"Jim?"

"Oh, you haven't met the full cast of this so-called family yet. James Canfield. Catharine's son."

"Canfield? Your half-brother?"

"No, but Jim was only fifteen when Catharine and Dad were married. You can be sure she got him fully adopted."

"But not Jenny?"

"She was already of age then. I think some sort of guardianship was set up."

"How do you feel about Jim?"

She sent him an amused sidelong look.

"You'll be happy to know there's someone in the family I like. I kid him and say he's just like a brother to me, and he really is." She frowned slightly. "He has a reputation for being—well, quite a swinger, but you have to understand, his father deserted Catharine before Jim was born. It was hard going when he was a kid, then suddenly, at fifteen, he was wealthy *and* the Senator's son. I guess he didn't adjust too well."

"That would test any adolescent's emotional equilibrium. How old is he now?"

"Twenty-two. My big brother by six months. He's a senior

at Willamette, and making lousy grades; he'd always rather party than study.'' She sighed, smiling ruefully. ''I just hope he'll finally get his fling over and settle down.''

''Have you discussed the surveillance with him?''

''No. You don't take your troubles to Jim if you're looking for answers, but he always has a good shoulder ready for crying on. I don't know what I'd have done without him after Dad died.''

''A ready shoulder negates a multitude of sins. What else can you tell me about the will?''

He knew her answer concerned Catharine Canfield before she said a word; the cold bitterness was in her eyes.

''One more thing. The house in Salem—the old family house—will be mine, which means in four years, I'll have the option of throwing Catharine out.''

He let that pass without comment.

''Who's executor of the estate?''

''Oh, it's divided somehow between the Ladd-Bush Bank and Bob Carleton.'' Then she added caustically, ''That's *C.* Robert Carleton, the family attorney.''

''You mean Judge Carleton?''

''No, I wish it were. The judge handled Dad's affairs for years, but he died five years ago. This is his son.''

Conan didn't pursue her feelings for C. Robert Carleton. They were obvious.

''Did your father have a history of heart disease?''

''No. Not even a hint of trouble. No warning at all. He was only fifty-five; he loved hiking and still played tennis and skied—'' She stopped suddenly, a trembling hand coming up to hide her eyes. ''Conan, please—why all the questions about Dad?''

He waited, giving her a little time; she was dry-eyed when her hand fell away from her face.

''Dore, before we go on, you must understand two things. First, I can't work in a vacuum; I must have information, and that means asking questions. Secondly, you've hired me to find some answers for you, but if I'm successful, you may regret it; the answers could be extremely painful.''

She nodded. ''Conan, I have no choice. I *must* know.''

''All right. As for the questions about your father, remember the tailing began only after his death. The demise of a man of wealth and power usually changes the course of other people's lives; it's inevitably a catalytic event.''

''But I don't see what it could possibly have to do with—with those men.''

''Neither do I, now, and the surveillance may have been triggered by something that happened *after* his death. It was a month before you moved to Shanaway.''

It was a question, and she seemed to recognize it as such, but she turned away, hands clasped tensely.

''I can't think of anything that happened since his death that could explain it.''

That was probably true. Still, there was something about that month she *could* tell him. But that was a restricted area, and he'd have to find out why eventually.

''I'll spare you more questions now; we've kept your friend waiting long enough. But we have some plans to discuss. Like they say, we can't go on meeting like this.''

One eyebrow came up. ''How can we go on meeting, then?''

''I have a plan which will require some Thespian skill, but since you grew up in politics, that should be easy.'' He gave her a slow smile. ''Isadora, tonight will mark the beginning of a beautiful, or at least, plausible romance.''

''Ah. Just what I've been waiting for.''

''No doubt. Anyway, It'll give us an excuse to see a great deal of each other in the future. I'll have dinner at the Surf House—you *are* playing tonight?'' Then at her nod, ''I want to be sure your night man is there when we 'meet.' We'll need a signal. The Chopin *Fantasy Impromptu*, you know it?''

''Of course.''

"When he arrives, play the *Fantasy*, as written, but only the—well, the 'I'm Always Chasing Rainbows' theme."

She laughed delightedly. "A musical code—marvelous."

"Almost inevitable in this case. When I get your signal, I'll set up our introduction with Max. This won't be love at first sight, but make it clear you're at least interested."

"I think I can manage that. You're considered Holliday Beach's most eligible bachelor, you know."

"Mrs. Early has been trying to remedy that for years. Now, I want you to memorize a telephone number: 779-7070."

She reached for her purse. "I'd better make a note—"

"I said memorize." He repeated the number, and she hesitated, then closed her eyes, concentrating.

"779-7070. Right?"

"Right. That's only for emergencies. It's a special line. A while back I had some trouble with bugs in my phone, so a friend of mine, who happens to be an electronic genius, put in the special line. But, Dore, if you call me, be careful. Your phone at the cottage is probably bugged."

She nodded wearily. "I was afraid it might be."

"I'll check it as soon as possible." He looked at his watch and rose. "You'd better get back to the beach now. Your friend might go looking for you if you're gone too long." He felt her tension at that, but assumed it was only the reference to her watcher.

But as he walked with her out onto the patio, he began to realize her strained silence had another source. She glanced almost furtively into the low brush near the path, so distracted his voice startled her.

"What's wrong, Dore?"

"Oh, nothing, really. It's just that—well, your back entrance is a little primeval." When he made no response except a level gaze that demanded further explanation, she sighed. "I have sort of a—a thing about . . . snakes."

He felt strangely relieved; perhaps because her willingness

to explain meant this wasn't a restricted area. But he didn't dismiss it lightly. Her tone might be casual, but her eyes were telling a different story. Phobia.

"Does company help? I'll walk you down to the beach."

Her quick laugh brimmed with relief.

"Yes, it helps. Thank you. Oh, I forgot to ask—I mean, about your . . . fee, or whatever."

"I'll expect carte blanche on my expenses. I warned you I'd be calling in reinforcements."

"But, what about—"

"As for *my* fee, it's beyond price."

She studied him skeptically. "And what is it?"

"Something money can't buy me. A private concert, with you at the Bösendorfer."

A smile curved her lips, giving her eyes a warm light.

"That hardly seems fair; it would be so much my pleasure. But it's yours, whenever you want it."

"I'll have to earn it first. Come on, I'll blaze the trail down to the beach."

CHAPTER 5

It promised to be one of those clear, spectrum-shaded sunsets, but the sun was still a good twenty degrees above the horizon, reflected in a molten glare from the ocean. Conan stood at the library windows, watching the waves smoothing the dimpled pattern of footprints in the sand.

Isadora Canfield had already made her exit from this scene, but not unattended. Her silver Stingray left the beach access just thirty seconds ahead of the red Ford. Conan was only surprised at the negligence.

He went to the desk, reached for a scratch pad, and tore off a single sheet. This was nearly reflexive; he'd found too many "lost" messages indented in second sheets. Then for the next half hour, he scarcely moved except to light a succession of cigarettes while he mentally reconstructed his conversation with Isadora in sequence and detail. By the time he finished his mnemonic exercise, the light in the windows had a reddish cast, and he'd covered the paper with cryptic notes and big-looped question marks.

Finally, he swiveled around to face the bookshelves and

pressed a concealed lever. A section of shelves opened, revealing a compartment containing a radio transmitter, four two-way radios, an assortment of minuscule monitors, a Mauser 9 mm. automatic, and a telephone; the special line.

He put the phone on the desk, then opened his address book to the D's, surrendering to a reminiscent smile as he focused on one entry: *Charles Duncan, the Duncan Investigations Service, San Francisco.*

That name always called up a crowd of memories whose sharp edges were blunted by time, polarized on the twin axes of G-2 and Berlin. He'd called on Duncan for professional assistance many times since Berlin, but when he thought of him, he always thought first of that grimly divided city.

He glanced at his watch; it was after office hours, but that had an advantage; he was spared contending with a receptionist. Duncan himself answered, his terse formality dissolving when Conan identified himself.

"Hey, Conan—I'll be damned!"

"Probably. How's life in the city?"

"Beautiful. Just great. Shirt-sleeve weather and sunshine. Uh . . . . you *do* remember what sunshine is?"

"The sun shines in Oregon regularly twice a year."

"Glad to hear that. Wouldn't want you to lose your tan. Say, I tried to get hold of you a couple of months ago. Had a nice little case on; the Campina murder."

"Yes, well, I gathered from the headlines you did all right on that one even without my help."

"We try. What the hell were you doing in Teheran?"

"Some research on the Medes for a collector in Miami. He picked up a cuneiform-Aramaic tablet in an estate—"

"One of your 'consultation' deals? Don't bother. Cuneiform's Greek to me. You got something on your mind, or you just running up a phone bill for kicks?"

"I have something on my mind, Charlie. A client."

"Uh-huh. So, how many men do you need this time?"

"Three. Two for surveillance, and another for some background research."

"What's the problem?"

"A lady asked me to find out why she's being tailed."

"Sounds a little tame for you, Chief. Ask her husband."

"She isn't married. I haven't much information yet, but I do know this much: her father died recently, and she's an heiress to the tune of three or four million. It may have no bearing on the tailing, but large, round sums like that seem to bring out the worst in people."

"Yeah. What about her father—how'd he die?"

Conan laughed. "Charlie, you were always a suspicious soul. Heart attack. Apparently."

"Sure. Who was he?"

"One of our U.S. Senators."

"You mean *Canfield*?"

"I see his fame reached beyond our borders."

"Well, he *did* shoot off his mouth on a lot of hot issues, you know. So, your client's his daughter?"

"Yes. Isadora Canfield."

"Isadora? Sounds like a spindle-shanked spinster."

"Well, technically, she *is* a spinster." He smiled to himself. "About five-eight, long brown hair, blue eyes, approximately 36-24-36, twenty-one years old."

"Yeah. Now I understand your interest in the case."

"She plays piano beautifully, Charlie."

"I'm sure she's rolling in talent."

"As a matter of fact, she is. But talent and vital statistics aside, the tailing raises my hackles a little with that much money involved."

"Well, you got a point there. I wish to hell I could come up and give you a hand—vital statistics aside—but I'm tied down with a subpoena."

"Can't you make a deposition?"

"No, I tried that. I may be stuck here for weeks."

"Damn. Who else is available? What about Carl Berg?"

"Carl? He's available. Just came back from his vacation. Another session with you should get him back in shape again. Hang on a minute; I'll see who else is loose."

While Conan waited, his gaze wandered to the painting in the corner: the Knight. He found himself trying to imagine the creator of that brooding image playing the "faithful watchdog" for anyone. What had happened to Jennifer Hanson? But that was one of the question marks on his list.

He picked up the pen as Duncan returned to the phone.

"Conan, I have a new man available. Done some good work for me. Harry Munson."

He made a note of the name. "All right. Who else?"

"Well, as a favor for an old buddy, I'm sending one of my top operatives. Came to me from the LAPD and CIA."

Conan noted the overtone of irony with some suspicion.

"Tell me more."

"Let's see. About five-six, red hair, blue eyes, approximately 36-24-36. *Miss* Sean Kelly."

He laughed. "Interesting qualifications."

"I figure since you're both Irish you'll have a lot in common—*if* you can get her to swallow the Irish once she's had a good look at you."

"Blood always tells, Charlie."

"Seriously, though, she's damned good at digging up information. You'd better use her for your research."

"I'll take your advice on that. Now, I need all three of them as soon as possible."

"I know. Like tomorrow, right? You want them in Holliday Beach?"

He hesitated, absently embroidering a question mark with baroque curls.

"Have them take the earliest flight available to Portland tomorrow morning. Give Carl the special line number and tell him to call me when they arrive."

"Okay. Anything special they should bring?"

"No, just the usual gear. And beach clothes. *Oregon* beach clothes; I don't want them looking California."

"That means raincoats, umbrellas, and hip boots."

"But they won't need wet suits now; we're going into the dry season. I'm sorry you're stuck in court."

"Yeah, so am I. Nobody's offered *me* a case with vital statistics like that."

Conan didn't hang up when Charlie did, but immediately began dialing again; another office number in spite of the late hour. The call went to Salem: to Steve Travers, Chief of Detectives, Salem Division, Oregon State Police.

It was answered on the first ring. "Travers."

"Hello, Steve. Are you busy?"

"Conan?" There was a short laugh, and Conan had a clear image of Travers with his lank body folded into his chair, his feet undoubtedly propped on his desk.

"No, of course I'm not busy. I always stay here at the office when there's a hockey game on TV I want to see."

"Let me rephrase that. Are you too busy to give me a couple of minutes?"

"Oh, I guess I can squeeze in a couple. I might even make it three, since you're a taxpayer."

"Damn right I am; in spades. Are you alone?"

"Sure. Why?"

"I'd like to ask you a few questions, and I don't especially want anyone to know they're being asked."

Travers paused. "I gather you have a client. Okay. Somebody get knocked off down there?"

"Not that I know of. What can you tell me, off the top of your head, about John Canfield and family?"

"Canfield? How come you're interested in him?"

"I have a client."

"And I suppose that client's name is confidential?"

"Yes, but off the record, it's Isadora Canfield."

"What's her problem?"

"So far, only that she's under surveillance and has been since she moved to the beach about a month ago."

Travers said cautiously, "Well, I suppose you know she took her father's death pretty hard."

"I know she cut her wrists, if that's what you mean. We discussed that as an explanation for the tailing, but she doesn't think anyone in the family cares enough to pay the price. Besides, her stepsister is here to watch over her."

"Mm. Well, she's probably right about nobody caring that much. Too bad; she's a nice kid. And I can understand why she fell apart since she was the one who found the body."

Conan was still struggling with the term "kid" in reference to Isadora Canfield when that last statement struck home.

"She what?"

"Didn't you know about that? She came home from the university the night he died and found him in the library."

"No, I didn't know. She said she 'lost' a week after his death."

"Well, that happens, especially with an unexpected death. You . . . you're sure she *is* being tailed?"

His response was purposely oblique. "By the way, Steve, I have a license number I'd like you to check."

"You're sure. Okay, let's have it."

"Oregon AMK510. Probably a rental, but it'll give me a starting point. Incidentally, Charlie's sending up some operatives. I'll assign one to some research in Salem, and I'd appreciate it if you'd give her a hand."

"Her?"

"Miss Sean Kelly, and from Charlie's account, she'll brighten your day."

"Send her around. My days could use some brightening."

"Thanks. Now, back to the Canfields. Anything that comes to mind."

"Well, let's see. The Canfields are old pioneer stock, very

well heeled; been in politics for generations. John Canfield was the second senator in the family."

"Has he any brothers or sisters?"

"He had a brother, but he died early; no children. Anyway, Canfield went the Harvard route, then married Anna Morrison, another scion of a wealthy, pioneer-type family."

Who studied ballet, Conan added privately; a fact her daughter considered more pertinent than lineage or wealth.

"A merger or a marriage?"

"Well, I'd say a marriage, but they only had the one child, then Anna died about eight years ago. Overdose of barbiturates."

Conan paused as he was about to check off a question on the list.

"Suicide?"

"Oh, I don't know. Officially, it was accidental, and I'm inclined to go along. She had a big drinking problem, and booze and barbiturates don't mix too well."

"Would you let me see the report, Steve?"

"Sure. Aren't you digging up a lot of old ground?"

"I have to dig somewhere. I'd like to see the reports on Canfield's death, too."

"Conan, it was a heart attack, pure and simple."

"Of course. Anything else on Anna's death?"

"No, but a year later Canfield married his private secretary, Catherine Hanson. She has two kids, you know."

"Yes, and the Senator adopted her son."

"Right. That's about all I can think of off the top of my head. Except the accident, of course."

"What accident?"

"Where were you when that hit the papers? It was about five years ago. Car accident on I-5 south of Portland."

"How bad was it and who was involved?"

"Just Canfield and his wife. He came out of it with a broken arm, but Catharine had some head injuries. Lost her sight; totally blind."

Conan felt a crawling chill, remembering Isadora's relish at the thought of one day throwing her stepmother out of the family house. Her *blind* stepmother. Then his mouth tightened in disgust. He was thinking in platitudes.

"Steve, was Canfield at fault in the accident?"

"I don't think so, but I can check with DMV. Conan, I've got a call coming in on the department line."

"All right, Steve. Thanks for the three minutes."

"Sure. Keep me posted."

"Don't worry. You'll be hearing from me."

CHAPTER 6

Conan sat at one of the window tables in the Surf House dining room watching a flock of sandpipers spinning in and out along the edges of the spotlighted waves. His table had been cleared, the check signed, and his coffee was cold, but he waited patiently until at precisely eight, he heard a rattle of applause, then a shimmering chromatic scale leading into "Ebb Tide." He looked toward the bar, but the colored glass divider revealed only a few faint lights.

He listened for a full minute before he left his table, walked casually up the steps to the foyer, then turned left into the Tides Room. There he paused, both to make sure Isadora saw him, and to adjust his eyes to the dim light.

The room was sparsely populated; Monday was a slow night. The bar ran half the length of the north wall with a narrow opening at the west end. There was a table near the opening, and to his relief, it was unoccupied.

The piano, a baby grand, was at the east end of the room. Conan made his way to the table, his attention obviously on Isadora. She wore velvet and diamonds tonight, and a sunny smile that put her audience in pleasurable thrall. He wondered how, at twenty-one, she'd attained that indefinable presence which marks a totally professional performer. The performance itself, even in "cocktail piano," was mesmerizing; that she was also beautiful seemed only an adjunct of it.

"She's really something, isn't she?"

Max Heinz was leaning on the bar, watching him with a sly grin. Conan raised an eyebrow as he seated himself.

"Yes, I'd say she is, Max. Very talented."

"Sure. How you been, Conan? Haven't seen you around."

"Oh, I've been hibernating for the monsoon season." He offered a cigarette, but Max declined with a reluctant sigh.

"No, thanks. I'm trying to quit."

Conan smiled as he lit a cigarette for himself. Max Heinz, a big, barrel-chested man fully capable of acting as bouncer as well as bartender, had been quitting for years.

"Well, what'll you have, Conan?"

"The usual," he replied with a wry smile.

Max rose to the challenge. "Uh . . . Forester on the rocks, right? Hell, it's been so long, I almost forgot."

"Max, you never forget."

"That's what I got everybody thinking," he said, pouring the bourbon with a flourish. "Truth is, I keep notes."

Conan laughed as Max brought his drink and sat down in the chair across the table from him.

"Sure you do. How's business?"

"It's always slow in the winter, but it's picking up."

Conan purposefully let his gaze wander to Isadora.

"That should help."

Max smiled. "Hasn't hurt. Hasn't hurt a bit."

"Okay, Max, since you aren't offering, I'll ask. Who is she?"

"Wondered when you'd get around to that. But you'll never believe it. That little doll is Isadora Canfield. *John* Canfield's daughter."

Conan looked appropriately amazed.

"What the hell is she doing—"

"Yeah, what's a nice girl like her doing in a place like this? I'm not sure. She's been living at the family cottage at Shanaway since her dad died. Says she wanted something to do. I just hope she stays through the summer." He turned, rising as a waitress approached. "Excuse me. Order, Mary?"

As Max went about his business, a round of applause marked the end of "Ebb Tide." Conan waited, taking a slow drag on his cigarette as Isadora turned to the piano again.

The Chopin *Fantasy Impromptu*.

That meant the night man was already here; no one had entered since his arrival. He pinpointed the loners in the room and finally picked as the most likely candidate a balding man sitting at the bar contemplating a gin fizz. He was short and stocky, but he carried no extra fat.

"Now, that's what I like about Dore."

Conan turned as Max resumed his chair. "What's that?"

"She knows how to play the old-timers, too. 'I'm Always Chasing Rainbows'—man, does that ever bring back memories."

He nodded absently. "Max, maybe you'd do me a favor."

"Uh-huh. Like maybe introducing you? Listen, I could retire on the drinks Dore's turned down." Then he relented with a canny grin. "But considering it's you, and you're just a Pendleton country boy at heart, I'll do you your favor when she takes a break. After that you're on your own."

"For once I'm grateful for my rural upbringing."

Isadora played her role well when Max made the introductions, initially hesitant, but apparently reassured by Max's attitude. When she was seated, Max brought her coffee, refreshed Conan's drink, then retired behind the bar. The bald man watched the encounter attentively. Isadora's back was to him now, but he still had a three-quarter view of her face.

"Miss Canfield," Conan said, "you're extraordinarily beautiful tonight. And a damned good cocktail pianist."

"Thank you," she replied, her eyes glinting with laughter. "Do I detect a little Irish coming through there?"

"Only the pure truth." He kept his voice low, grateful for the arrival of an inebriated and noisy party of six. "Now, where's your night man?"

Her laughter died. "At the bar; the short, bald man."

He allowed himself a fleeting smile of satisfaction.

"I'll keep an eye on him and let you know when he's looking this way. How much time do we have?"

"About five minutes."

"All right. I have a friend who runs an investigation service in San Francisco. He's sending up three operatives; they'll be here tomorrow. Two will be working here, tailing the tails and keeping an eye on you."

"What do you mean, keeping an eye on me?"

"I mean, seeing that no one makes any unfriendly moves in your direction. So, if you notice someone *else* following you, don't worry. They're on our side."

"That's a nice feeling for a change."

"I'll try to introduce you to them privately, or at least point them out, but that might be difficult at first."

"You said your friend was sending *three* operatives."

"Yes. The third will be doing some research in Salem."

She tensed at that, her tone shaded with apprehension. "In Salem? What kind of research?"

"General background information on you or anyone connected with you; family, friends, etcetera."

"But, Conan, why—"

"Smile, Dore," he said, following his own advice. "We're being watched."

She mustered a nervous smile. "This is worse than a press conference, Conan, why the research? I can tell you anything you want to know."

"Can you? Then tell me why your bald friend is straining his ears right now."

"But I don't see what connection—"

"With your past, or your friends and family? Dore, motives come out of personal history and interactions, not out of the blue."

"Yes, I . . . suppose you're right."

He studied her, wondering what restricted area she was afraid that research would expose.

"You know, hiring a private detective is like going to a doctor or lawyer. I can't help you if you won't be honest with me."

"Conan, I . . ." There was a taut silence between them, but finally she turned away, and he sighed, putting on a smile as the night man looked in their direction again.

"All right. Don't look so serious. You've just met a man who's obviously attracted to you, and you should seem something less than miserable."

She looked up, her smile no longer forced.

"If I seem miserable, it isn't the company."

'That's reassuring. Now, there's something I want to ask you about. The accident, the one your father and Catharine were involved in. I just found out about that, and my information is rather sketchy."

She seemed puzzled. "You didn't know about it? That's refreshing; I'm so used to having everything in my life public property. You didn't know Catharine is blind?" At his negative headshake, she paused. "You must think me awfully bitchy saying what I did about a poor, blind woman."

"I don't know her, so I can't judge your bitchiness. Tell me about the accident."

A thoughtful frown etched a line between her brows.

"Well, it was two years after they were married; that would be five years ago now. They'd been in Portland for some political affair, and they were late coming back."

"Your father was driving?"

"Yes. It was January, and there was ice on the highway. Dad said he just started skidding. I'm sure he wasn't going too fast; he was always a very careful driver, but the car flipped over a guard rail and down into a ravine. When he came to, Catharine was still unconscious. He wrapped her in everything he could find to keep her warm, including his own coat, then he climbed up to the highway and waved down a car. And he did all that in spite of a broken arm." She hesitated, then added wistfully, "Poor Dad."

"Why poor Dad?"

"Oh, it's just that he paid such a high price for that accident, and it wasn't even his fault."

"What kind of price?"

She regarded him with a sad, ironic smile.

"Little pitchers have big ears, Conan, and when it came to Dad and Catharine, I was willing enough to sink to a little eavesdropping. About a week before the accident, I heard them arguing in—in that room."

"What room?" Her sudden uneasiness was close to fear.

"The . . . library."

He let that pass, remembering that Steve Travers had said she discovered her father's body in the library.

"What were they arguing about?"

"A divorce." Her eyes narrowed, fear giving way to bitterness. "Dad wanted a divorce."

"But Catharine wasn't agreeable?"

"Of course not! Give up the money, the precious Canfield name, the role of Senator's lady?"

"Keep your voice down, Dore."

She took a deep breath and finally laughed.

"I guess I won't win any Oscars tonight."

"You're doing fine. Was your father prepared to fight her on the divorce?"

"Yes, but that was before the accident. That's what I mean by the price he paid. After that, he just couldn't go through with it. He felt responsible for her blindness. And she *used* it, Conan; she played on his pity and guilt. That's how she held him." Then she shook her head slowly. "But it doesn't matter. Not now."

It didn't matter because death had resolved the problem. Conan took a swallow of his drink, thinking that the investigation business fostered certain unpleasant mental attitudes. He was automatically suspicious of problems resolved by death—especially an unexpected and sudden death.

"Do you know why your father wanted a divorce?"

"Just incompatibility, I guess. He married her on the rebound from Mother's death, really. He was so lonely, and the faithful secretary was there. Waiting." Then she added: "I *don't* think she gave him any other grounds."

"Are you playing the devil's advocate?"

"Maybe." She gave a short laugh. "Or just honesty's advocate. Conan, you said something about unfriendly moves in my direction. Do you think those men—"

"I'm sorry. I didn't mean to add that to your worries. If these two had any unfriendly intentions, they've taken their time about it, considering what an open target you are. Don't look so alarmed. I'm trying to reassure you."

"It's beginning to sound like the Mafia."

"I can almost guarantee it isn't that. Of course, I can't be sure of the intentions of the person—or persons—who hired these men. That's why I want someone to keep an eye on you as well as them."

She sighed despondently. "Oh, you know, I can't even work up much fear for my life, really. It's so *senseless*."

"I doubt that. Dore, there's something else I must ask you about, and I know it will be painful."

"What . . . what is it?"

"You found your father's body, didn't you? Do you remember anything about that?"

Her first response was a quick intake of breath, and even in the dim light, he could see the ashen color of her face. He resisted the urge to reach out for her hand, regretting the question now.

"No, I . . . don't remember . . . anything."

"All right, we'll talk about it later."

"Conan, for God's sake, why do you keep coming back to Dad's death? What can that possibly have to do with—"

"Please, keep your voice down. Your audience is quite attentive."

She stiffened, visibly bringing herself under rein, after a few seconds giving him a warm smile in which the constraint would be evident only at close range.

"I'm sorry," she said.

"No, I'm the one who should apologize, and we'll defer that for now." He leaned back and inhaled on his cigarette. "Did Jenny have any questions about this afternoon?"

"No. She never asks many questions, strangely enough."

"Why strangely?"

"Oh, I guess I'm just being bitchy again, but I'm sure she reports to Catharine regularly."

"About you?"

"Yes."

"Why would she do that?"

"What do you mean?"

"You called her Catharine's 'faithful watchdog.' Why would Jenny play that role?"

"You don't believe she *is* playing it?"

"I simply want an assessment of her motives from someone who knows her. I'm not doubting you."

She averted her eyes uncomfortably.

"Well, I don't know why. I don't know why she didn't go back to art school after her illness. She was working on her Master's at the Chicago Art Institute, but she just tossed it. Dad had the attic converted into a studio for her, but she doesn't do much painting. She spends most of her time playing nurse to Catharine."

"This illness of Jenny's, when was that?"

"Soon after the accident; about a month, I don't know much about it. I was in a private boarding school, so I wasn't home except on weekends or holidays."

"She didn't go back to Chicago?"

"No, and she only had a quarter to go on her Master's."

Conan frowned as he crushed out his cigarette.

"She just quit, then, to play nurse to Catharine?"

"Apparently. I don't know of any other reason, but then I don't know Jenny very well. I was always at school, or she was at college. But I used to have a great respect for her paintings. They were . . . haunting; like the Knight. Catharine's using her, too, just like she did Dad, but maybe this is the way Jenny wants it. She's made a hermit of herself, really; no friends or outside interests. In fact, she seldom leaves the house."

"What about Jim? Is he under Catharine's influence?"

She laughed. "Jim isn't subject to coercion by guilt or pity, and more power to him. He has his weaknesses, though, and she usually gets her way when it comes to a showdown, but at least he stands up to her occasionally. Maybe that's why I get along better with him than Jenny."

"Perhaps." He looked at his watch. "Well, question and answer time is over."

She glanced at her own watch and straightened.

"Yes, it is. I'd better get back to work."

"I'll be leaving soon, but I won't be far away. I'll check the restaurant and motel parking for that blue Ford."

"I'm not really sure it was the night man I saw in that car, Conan."

"I know. Anyway, I'll wait in my car until he leaves; it might be informative. Now, we have a date for dinner tomorrow."

She tilted her head to one side. "We do?"

"Yes, ma'am. This is going to be a whirlwind courtship, and I have more questions."

"Oh. I'm beginning to see what you meant by a *plausible* affair."

"Sorry, but there isn't much romance in life these days. We'll have dinner here, then I'll stay for the evening. And be sure to mention me to Jenny—as a suitor. You might say something nice about me, but don't go overboard.''

''I'll see what I can dream up,'' she said, laughing.

''We'll have an early dinner so you can get to the piano on time. I'll pick you up at six at the cottage. Will Jenny be there? I want to meet her.''

''I'm sure she will be. Well, I'd better get to the piano *now*.'' She paused. ''Conan . . . thank you.''

He rose with her. ''Take care, Dore. Tomorrow at six.''

CHAPTER 7

The call came at 7:35—A.M.

Conan struggled across a morass of sheets and blankets, knocking a book off the bedside table as he stretched for the phone.

"Hello." But the only response was a dial tone, and the buzzing sounded again.

"Damn."

The special line. He fumbled for the control panel at the back of the table, hit the wrong switch and had his attention called to a pounding headache by a burst of Beethoven from the stereo system. He silenced that as the buzzing shrilled again, and finally found the right switch.

"Hello."

"Conan? This is Carl."

"Yes, Carl." The voice jarred him into mental focus: Carl Berg of the Duncan Investigation Service. He threw back the covers, unaware of the morning chill on his skin, and sat up on the edge of the bed. "Good Lord, I didn't think you'd be arriving *this* early."

"You said to get the first flight available. Sorry to wake you up so early."

Conan managed a laugh at that irony-laden apology.

"I asked for it. I gather you're in Portland?"

"Yes, at the airport with Sean Kelly and Harry Munson, all more or less alert and ready for your instructions."

"Well, you and Munson will have to wait until you get to Holliday Beach to be instructed. I'll meet you at the bookshop. Rent yourselves separate cars; something other than the usual economy models, but nothing too exotic."

Berg laughed. "No Ferraris?"

"I expect you to tend to business. I'll fill you in on that when you get here. Is Miss Kelly handy?"

"Sean's about as handy as they come. Just a second, I'll call her. Harry and I are on our way."

"Thanks, Carl."

He fumbled for his cigarettes and managed to get one lit before a new voice came on the line; one of those husky, child-siren voices; thoroughly intriguing.

"This is Sean Kelly."

"I'm sorry we have to meet by phone, Miss Kelly. Did Charlie tell you anything about this case?"

"He gave me your client's name and said she hired you because she's under surveillance, and you were concerned because of a large inheritance due her as a result of her father's recent death. And if you don't mind, I really prefer 'Sean.' 'Miss Kelly' sounds so damned secretarial."

He smiled to himself. "Then Sean it is. Your base of operations will be Salem. You're in charge of research; anything on Isadora's friends or associates, and particularly her family. I'm after general background now, but I have a few specific questions. You have a notebook?"

"With pen poised."

"I thought so. First, anything you can find out about John Canfield's death; second, the terms of his will; third, check out the family lawyer, C. Robert Carleton. Then I want to know where Isadora was during the period after her father's death, January fifteenth, until February twenty-fifth when she and her stepsister moved to the beach."

"Okay. Mr. Flagg, about Canfield's death—do you have any reason to think it wasn't a simple heart attack?"

Conan frowned. He hadn't answered that question to his own satisfaction yet.

"No, I don't have any *reason* to think that."

"But you want me to dig into it."

"Yes, and you'll have some help." He gave her Steve Travers's name and number. "Call him when you get to Salem; he's expecting you. And ask him to check a license number for me: LAT529, light blue Ford sedan, new model. I gave him another one yesterday, and he should have a name by now. I want the identity of the drivers; the cars are probably rentals, so you may have to follow that up."

"These are the men tailing Miss Canfield?"

"Yes. If you need to talk to me and I'm not at home or at the bookshop, I have an answering service, or you can leave a message with Miss Dobie at the shop."

"Who's Miss Dobie?"

"Beatrice Dobie. She really runs the bookshop. I'm just a figurehead. But don't tell *her* that."

Sean laughed appreciatively. "Your secret's safe as a babe in hand. Anything else I should dig into?"

"Not now. That should keep you busy. And good luck."

"Mr. Flagg, with two Irishmen on this job, we *have* to be lucky."

That's optimism, he thought pessimistically as he hung up, but at this hour of the day optimism inevitably eluded him. He started for the bathroom, swearing as he stubbed his toe on the book he'd knocked from the table. He eyed the culprit—*A History of Marion County, Oregon*—and chose to ignore it. But when he returned after a cold shower and two aspirin, he picked it up and checked it for damage.

The *History* was partially responsible for his headache and the fact that he'd been awake until 3 A.M. It contained a wealth of information on the Canfield family, beginning with their arrival in the Willamette Valley in 1851, but it had proved a waste of time and lost sleep. Any hint of skeletons in the family closet had been censored out.

But there were skeletons in some closet, if he could only find the right door.

Beatrice Dobie was just turning the OPEN sign when Conan arrived at the shop. Meg was impeding her efforts, making affectionate loops around her legs.

"Good morning, Mr. Flagg."

"Good morning, Miss Dobie." He paused to lift Meg to his shoulder. "Hey, Duchess, you're in a good mood today."

She made a gravelly Siamese comment as he took a proprietory survey, smiling with possessive satisfaction at this fusty, nooked and crannied anachronism, redolent with the dusty but pleasant smell peculiar to old books.

While Miss Dobie busied herself with counting change into the cash register, Conan retired to his office, leaving the door open. When he deposited Meg unceremoniously in a chair, she purloined a scrap of paper from the desk for a solo hockey game designed to do as much damage as possible to the Kerman. He ignored her, knowing remonstrance only made the game more interesting.

The coffeepot was in the final throes of its Plutonic cycle. He filled two mugs, put one down at the front of the desk, and settled himself in the leather-covered chair behind it. The morning's mail was arranged in two neat stacks as it always was: personal and business. He'd just begun sorting the personal stack when Miss Dobie came in, loosing one of her habitual sighs as she sat down.

"You know . . . this is the first day it's really *smelled* like spring. The daffodils have been blooming for a month, but I haven't any faith in them."

"Miss Dobie, if you haven't any faith in daffodils, what's left?"

"Flowering quince," she pronounced. "I saw the first blooms today. Thanks for pouring my coffee."

"Mm? Oh. You're welcome." He frowned at a return address, the Ten-Mile Ranch Corporation in Pendleton. Engraved discreetly under it was *Avery Flagg, Chairman of the Board*. He noted the red-inked URGENT! and swept the letter into the top drawer along with the rest of the personal stack. The business stack he pushed across to Miss Dobie.

"You can check these. The others will keep."

She raised an eyebrow. "Well, let's hope so."

He took his billfold from his hip pocket and removed a Polaroid photograph, then tested the steaming coffee.

"Miss Dobie, I'm expecting some gentlemen shortly. One of them you'll remember. Carl Berg."

Both eyebrows came up this time.

"Oh. Then you're on a . . . case."

"Yes, so I'll be in and out for a while, and I have some instructions for you." She was so earnestly attentive, he had to repress a smile as he handed her the picture of Isadora. "You may have seen this young woman in the shop lately."

"Oh, yes, that's Isadora Canfield."

He looked at her blankly. "How did you know?"

"Well, I *do* occasionally read the society section."

"Oh. Well, Miss Canfield is my client. That's strictly confidential, but if she asks for me, she has priority."

"I understand." She returned the photograph, her cool tone betrayed by the glint of excitement in her eyes.

"I have an operative working in Salem," he went on. "If Sean Kelly calls, get hold of me as soon as possible."

"Sean Kelly. All right, anything else?"

"No, except if you notice a sudden interest on my part in Miss Canfield, don't be alarmed. It's only a ploy."

"Well, now I certainly wouldn't be *alarmed* at any interest you showed in Miss Canfield—*or* surprised." She gave him a sly smile, and he felt an inexplicable, and highly annoying, warmth in his cheeks. He turned with some relief as the bells on the front door jangled.

"Here's Carl. You'll excuse us, Miss Dobie?"

"Of course." She tucked Meg under one arm, picked up her coffee cup, and exited, sending Carl Berg a conspiratorial smile as he passed her on his way into the office.

Conan closed the door behind him, noting his clothing—faded denims, a light windbreaker, and a worn sweatshirt.

"Welcome back, Carl."

Berg went to the chair Miss Dobie had vacated, his tanned face creased with a smile. Only the tan and his sun-bleached blond hair suggested he came from a sunnier climate.

"Just like old times," he commented drily.

"Don't get too nostalgic. Where's your partner?"

"Right behind me."

Conan glanced out through the one-way glass, "Coffee?"

"I could use some. I was up a little early."

"You can catch up on your sleep this afternoon." He handed him a filled mug. "I'm putting you on the night shift. Your headquarters will be the Surf House Resort."

"Pretty plush. I think I'm going to like this job."

"That's to make up for your last—" He looked around and saw a big, dark-haired man coming into the shop, his blunt features marked with a slightly flattened nose. Conan opened the door, meeting his cool, assessing gray eyes.

"Come in, Mr. Munson."

Berg pulled up another chair by his. "This is my partner, Conan. Harry Munson—Conan Flagg."

Munson extended his hand. "Glad to meet you, Mr. Flagg. Charlie's told us a lot about you."

Conan laughed at that, poured coffee for Munson, then returned to his chair.

"I hope you took anything Charlie said with a grain of salt. He filled you in on what I told him about this case?"

"Yes," Berg answered, "which wasn't a hell of a lot."

"So far, there isn't a hell of a lot to tell." He handed Munson a photograph. "That's our client, Isadora Canfield."

He studied the photograph, his only comment a raised eyebrow, then passed it on to Berg. He was more vocal.

"Well, there's plenty to see, if not to tell."

"And that's a lousy picture," Conan said. "Here's another." He showed them the photograph of the day man, then for the next fifteen minutes, recounted the scant facts of the case and answered their questions. Both men made occasional notes of names, dates, or license numbers, until at length he ran out of facts, and they ran out of questions.

"Your assignment for now is simply to watch the tails and Miss Canfield. Mr. Munson, find yourself a comfortable motel, then check out the cottage and locate a good vantage point. There's a heavy growth of jackpine on the crest, so it shouldn't be too difficult to stay out of sight. I'll be carrying a two-way radio, and I have a receiver in my car and at home. You have radios with you?"

Berg nodded. "Probably the same model you've got."

"Probably. Charlie recommended it. When you check into the Surf House, Carl, find out who's registered for unit seventeen. That's our night man. I did some tailing myself last night."

"Okay. What are our shifts going to be?"

"Long. Isadora goes to work at eight every evening, and so will you. Mr. Munson will take over at eight in the morning. I'll be with her and keep track of the tails part of the time, if the hours get too long."

Munson laughed. "Mr. Flagg, I wouldn't know what to do with an eight-hour day."

"Contending with one probably won't be among your problems here. What kind of car are you driving?"

"Pontiac Firebird, sort of tan color, RDG410."

"Carl?"

"White T-Bird, JST937."

Conan made a note of the numbers. "I'm taking Dore to dinner at the Surf House this evening; I'll pick her up at six. Mr. Munson, you keep an eye on the cottage afterwards until I send Carl out."

Berg turned to Munson. "I'd better go out with you before it gets dark to get the lay of the land. I'll check into the Surf House, then when you find a bed, call me."

"Okay." He rose, glancing at his watch. "Well, I guess the day shift starts now. Will you be here at the shop this afternoon, Mr. Flagg?"

"I'll be at home, by the special line and the radio."

"I'll let you know where I'm staying and check out the communications system."

"Good, and thanks for coming up."

As the bells on the shop door marked Munson's exit, Conan accompanied Berg to the office door.

"Carl, stay in my line of sight this evening. When the night man shows, I'll give you a signal and we can meet outside."

"Okay." Then with a crooked smile, "I hope this one doesn't get as hectic as my last go-round up here."

"It may be dull as hell, Carl." He didn't add that he doubted that very seriously.

Miss Dobie, watching Berg's departure from behind the counter, unleashed a pregnant sigh.

"Well . . . it looks to me," she intoned, "as if the battle has been joined."

CHAPTER 8

On the northern boundary of Holliday Beach, Highway 101 turned a few degrees inland, making a Y with a spur road which angled seaward to connect the world with Shanaway.

Shanaway had little interest in being connected with the world. Most of the houses scattered on the green slopes and clustered along the beach were vacation homes. Their owners cherished Shanaway as a personal refuge and preferred to regard it as a place rather than a community.

But the world refused to be excluded. At the highway junction a new shopping center glittered in the slanting sun, its regulation issue supermarket inspecting the troops of cars aligned on the field of asphalt. The open meadows to the north were subverted to a more attractive encroachment. A golf course spread its links under the spring sky, swaths of incredibly green lawn studded with red and yellow golfers.

The XK-E purred sedately along the road. This black, cat-sleek, mechanized sculpture Conan recognized as an extravagance, yet it was a sensual pleasure as gratifying as the clear

April light. The road curved into Shanaway, following the beach behind a battlement of close-ranked houses. He shifted into first gear when he turned up a rain-gutted dirt road toward a forested ridge, then swung left onto the even narrower lane that ran along its crest. The Canfield cottage—one of the oldest in Shanaway, steep-pitched roof silvered with weathered shingles—occupied the corner lot. It had grown from the central square living-room area into a U-shape with the addition of two side wings. The open end of the U faced east, toward the crest road.

When he got out of the car, he studied the wooded slope across the road; Munson was there, but invisible even to his close scrutiny in the tangled growth.

It was Isadora who responded to his knock, smiling as she opened the door for him. She looked older than her years, wearing a long-sleeved gown of black silk, her hair drawn back into a shining chignon at the crown of her head. Against the severe black, her skin seemed translucent.

"As usual, you're lovely, Dore." Then he smiled at the color that warmed her cheeks; it was so unexpected.

"Thank you, but isn't that in the eye of the beholder?"

"True, and you're quite an eyeful." He looked around the sunlit living room curiously. "Is Jenny here?"

Her smile turned subtly cooler. "She's in her studio. Come, I'll introduce you." She went to a door on the north wall and knocked. "Jen? Conan's here." Then at the responding invitation, she glanced at him and opened the door.

He surveyed the room, noting the varied accouterments of Jennifer Hanson's craft: paint-crusted palette, bouquet-like clusters of stained brushes, stretched canvases stacked against the walls. The air was thick with the resinous scents of linseed oil and turpentine.

Yet something ran false. The haphazard clutter, perhaps; it wasn't the *working* clutter he'd encountered in other artists' studios. There was the feeling of an attic here; a repository of disuse. But it was the paintings in progress that were most bewildering, and remembering the powerful and finely executed Knight, he felt almost ill.

Stylistically, Jenny's work had evolved toward the abstract, which neither surprised nor disturbed him. What he found so incomprehensible was the total lack of cohesion or content, the slack carelessness and palling indifference.

But his shock was masked with a polite smile as Jenny left her chair by the west windows, and Isadora made the introduction with etiquette-book correctness.

Jenny responded self-consciously, "I'm . . . glad to meet you, Mr. Flagg. I know your bookshop. It's like . . . like an old friend."

"Thank you. That's what it should be." Strange, he didn't ever remember seeing her in the shop. There was something purposefully anonymous about her. Under average height; lank brown hair tied back with a scrap of ribbon; a round, quiet face that was at first glance unattractive, although she had good features. But something in her attitude discouraged second glances; something in her gray-green eyes, wary, walled-in and . . .

He almost frowned.

There was something else about her eyes.

Perhaps it was only that she'd been looking out into the white glare of the sun on ocean.

A silence was growing; he glanced around him.

"You have a beautiful studio, and an inspiring view."

She turned to the windows, nodding as if to herself.

"Yes. Not that I'm interested in seascapes *per se*, but the sea . . . I guess you could never get tired of it. I mean, I couldn't."

She studied him skeptically for a moment, and he read something else in her eyes: a thinly veiled suspicion bordering on hostility. Then she smiled politely.

"Well, it's nice to meet you. I'm sure you and Dore want to be on your way, since she has to work tonight."

"Yes." Isadora agreed. "We'd better be going, Conan."

He nodded. "Miss Hanson, it was a pleasure meeting you. Next time you're in the shop, be sure to say hello."

Her only response to that was the set smile.

"Good-bye, Mr. Flagg. I'll see you later, Dore." Then she added, "Have a good time."

"A window table, Mr. Flagg? Hello, Miss Canfield."

Conan smiled absently at the waitress.

"Yes, Hazel. We may be in for a beautiful sunset."

"Looks that way," she said as she led them to the west side of the dining room. "Here you are, a front-row seat. Cocktail before dinner?"

He looked inquiringly at Isadora.

"You aren't at work *yet*, Dore."

She smiled, then lifted her shoulders in a shrug.

"All right, I'll have an old-fashioned."

"Good. I was beginning to think you had no vices. Bourbon for me, Hazel, on the rocks."

As the waitress moved away, he looked around the dining room. Neither the day man nor the night man was in evidence, but Carl Berg was.

"Conan?"

He turned. "Yes, Dore?"

"What's going on behind those damned shades? You've hardly said a word since we left the house."

He laughed and removed his dark glasses.

"I'm sorry. I was just thinking."

"About Jenny?"

His smile faded. "Yes."

"She's very shy. I mean, she never makes much of a first impression. Or much of an impression at all, really."

That wasn't what I was thinking about."

Isadora nodded, a sigh escaping her.

"The paintings."

"I was just wondering what happened."

"They're pretty bad, I guess. I don't know."

"Has this change come about since her illness?"

"I think so. I didn't see the work she did in Chicago, but I know she was showing in galleries there. She doesn't even try to show anywhere now." She paused, watching him. "Conan, there's something else bothering you about Jenny, isn't there?"

He looked out at the breakers, backlit by the lowering sun, the waves casting moving blue shadows on the sand.

Then he smiled at her. "I'm just sorry about the paintings. By the way, take a good look at the man at the table by the steps; blond hair, wearing a blue sweater."

"Oh, yes. Who is he?"

"Carl Berg. He's your new night man."

"One of the men you hired?"

"Yes. If you ever need help in a hurry and I'm not handy—" He stopped as the waitress brought their drinks, waiting until she was well out of earshot before he continued. "Your new day man is Harry Munson. He's been on duty since about noon."

She blinked at that. "I didn't see anyone."

"You weren't supposed to." He paused to light a cigarette and sample his bourbon. "I'll introduce you to him as soon as possible. He's driving a tan Firebird and looks like an ex-boxer. Harry located your day man's headquarters, incidentally. He's living in that duplex about a block north and a little below you."

"Yes, I know the house."

"He can't see your front door, but he has an excellent view of all those windows on the west side, *plus* the road."

"Have you located the night man?"

"He's staying here at the Surf House, but he probably uses the duplex as an observation post, too. He registered as Albert Hicks, supposedly working for Boeing in Seattle."

"Not very imaginative of him."

"I doubt he's an imaginative man. Carl is here at the Surf House, too; room ninety-two. Remember that."

"I'm going to get all these numbers confused."

"Here's another. Munson is staying at the Seaside Motel, room eleven."

"Okay," she sighed. "Eleven and ninety-two."

"That's only for emergencies; but don't forget them."

"I won't." She hesitated, focusing intently on her old-fashioned. "Is . . . is your third operative at work?"

"Yes. Why?"

"Oh, I was just wondering."

Conan took a long drag on his cigarette, wondering again why *she* was just wondering.

"Dore, what is it you're afraid of?"

"I'm *not* afraid," she said tightly.

"Has it anything to do with your father's death?"

She was suddenly angry, and it unnerved him at first.

"*You're* the one who's so fascinated with his death. I don't even *remember* it. How can I be afraid of something I can't remember? I told you I lost a week. It began when . . . when I—that room . . ." Now the anger was gone; only fear was left. He reached out for her hand.

"We'll talk about it later."

She seemed to relax, even managing a brief smile.

"I'm sorry, Conan. I guess I'm a little wound up."

At that, he began to relax, too, and he was entirely unprepared for the sudden change that occurred in her.

He felt it first in the trembling of her hand.

She was staring out at the breakers, their sinuous, tumbling crests washed in color caught from the setting sun. Her eyes widened, then she blinked and stared again.

"Oh, God," she whispered. "Oh, God, *no* . . ."

He looked out at the ocean and saw nothing but moving lines of foam. Yet she was seeing *something*.

"Dore, what is it? What's wrong?" His voice was low, and he didn't move except to tighten his hold on her hand.

But she was totally oblivious to him. Her hand compressed under his, and he was chilled by the conviction that he could tighten his hold until he broke the bones under that unresisting flesh, and she wouldn't even feel the pain.

"Dore, look at me!" His voice was still low, but sharp and insistent. "Turn around—this way. Now!"

Finally, she turned and there was terror in her eyes.

She blinked again, then flinched dazedly. At that, he released her hand and glanced quickly around, relieved to see only one face turned toward them—Carl Berg's.

"Are you all right, Dore?"

"Yes, I . . . it must've been the light or . . ." She laughed, a thin brittle sound. "I'm really not used to drinking, especially not on an empty stomach."

Conan leaned back, studying her with narrowed eyes. A flimsy rationale for something totally irrational.

"Isadora, don't spout nonsense at me. Something happened, and it wasn't just a couple of swallows of whisky. This isn't the time or place to discuss it, but for God's sake, don't shut the door in my face."

She nodded bleakly. "Conan, I can't explain."

"Don't try. Not now." He paused to watch Hazel escort a man to a window table; a blandly ordinary man in dark glasses. Out of the red Ford, he didn't attract even a glance from Isadora, but Conan assured himself that the man had Berg's full attention.

"No question and answer period tonight." He smiled and took her hand. "We're going to enjoy a civilized meal, and I'm going to enjoy the pleasure of your company. At least, until you have to go to work, then I'll enjoy the pleasure of your music."

Her laughter was colored with relief.

"Oh, Conan, now I really do believe you're half-Irish."

It was 2:30 in the morning when Conan turned off Highway 101 to the Shanaway road, and there was little traffic. He had no doubt the pair of headlights behind them belonged to Albert Hicks's blue Ford. The car had followed them all the way from the Surf House, a mile south of Holliday Beach.

He glanced at Isadora, curled in the seat beside him. There had been a lively and demanding crowd in the Tides Room tonight. As he geared down to turn onto the road up to the crest, she stirred and raised her head.

"You must be exhausted, Dore,"

"At least, I'll sleep—that's strange. There's a light in Jenny's studio."

He looked up at the cottage, in the process letting the car fall into a teeth-jarring chuck hole.

"Is that unusual?" he asked, concentrating on the road.

"She's usually in bed by the time I get home."

He turned at the crest road and parked in front of the house. When he helped Isadora out, she gave a rueful laugh and leaned wearily against the car.

"You know, I used to think that 'play Melancholy Baby' business was a *joke*."

"It's a great old song."

"Oh, Conan—please."

The porch light was on, but at this distance barely delineated the pale oval of her face. Briefly, he wished for more light, remembering that irrational terror.

"How are you, Dore?" he asked finally.

"I'm just tired. Don't worry about me."

"I won't. I'm convinced you have the will and determination of an Army mule."

"Is that good?"

"Yes." It was only a matter of leaning down a few inches; he crossed that space without thinking, feeling her arms moving around him as he kissed her.

But somewhere in the long passage of seconds, the thought came to him that not only had his objectivity gone to hell, Isadora Canfield was a client. She was also very young, and at this point in her life, very vulnerable.

She laughed softly. "Was that in the script, Conan?"

"No."

"I'm glad to hear that."

"Come on," he said, slipping his arm around her waist, "before I lose sight of my professional ethics entirely."

At the front door he stopped her before she unlocked it.

"Back to mundane matters. I still have a job to do."

"What does *that* mean?"

"Only that right now, I'm going to escort you inside in case Jenny's still awake."

She sobered, frowning. "But, why?"

"Nothing sinister. I want her to hear me confirm our plans for a picnic lunch on the beach tomorrow."

"Oh?"

"Didn't I tell you? Yes, we have a date. Meet me at the shop tomorrow at eleven."

"All right. Shall I bring fried chicken, or should it be a loaf of bread and a jug of wine?"

He laughed. "I'll take care of the gastronomic accessories. Or rather, Mrs. Early will."

The living room was dark as they went in, but a shaft of light appeared suddenly from Jenny's studio.

"Dore? Is that you?"

"Yes, Jen. Conan's with me."

The light disappeared as the door closed, but a moment later, a table lamp near the windows went on, and he saw Jenny standing there, her back to the light.

"Oh. Hello, Mr. Flagg."

"You're working late tonight, Miss Hanson."

She made no move to approach them, and the light was dim, yet he could see that her eyes were swollen and red. He wondered what made Jennifer Hanson weep in solitude.

"I—I like to work at night, sometimes," she said. "It's quiet then."

"I've always been convinced the Muses are creatures of the night." Then he smiled at Isadora, putting no restraint on the affection behind it. "I'll see you tomorrow about eleven, and be prepared for lunch seasoned with sand."

Her smile was a little uneasy in Jenny's presence. "There's no better seasoning. Sounds like fun."

"The best seasoning is good company." Then he nodded to Jenny. "Good night, Miss Hanson."

She still hadn't moved. "Good night."

When he reached the main Shanaway road, Conan stopped long enough to open the compartment between the seats and take out the radio mike. The response to his call was immediate. Carl Berg was on the hill above the cottage, a lookout he'd manned since nine o'clock.

"Conan, I had some action here early in the evening."

"I'd like a first-hand report, then." He turned onto the main road, keeping his speed down, frowning up at that rearview mirror; the only lights visible were street lights. "What happened to my escort?"

"He retired to the duplex. No lights in the house, but he's probably at the window with his infrared 'scope."

"See if he decides to tail me, then meet me—" He paused to shift up to third as he hit the open stretch by the golf course. "There's a drive-in a few blocks south of the shopping center. Dilly's. Meet me in back."

"Right. No sign of pursuit yet."

"I think Hicks has a one-track mind, but give him a few minutes."

Dilly's Drive-in was bleakly dark. Conan drove around behind it, startling a scavenging alley cat. He parked and got out to pace the asphalt, listening to the cold, rustling night sounds animating the darkness. It seemed a long time before Carl Berg's Thunderbird came thrumming around the rear wall of the restaurant. Berg turned off his motor and lights, restoring the silence and darkness.

"You're right about Hicks having a one-track mind," he

commented as he walked over to Conan. "He didn't budge from his blind."

Conan lit a cigarette and offered one to Berg. The flare of the lighter momentarily etched his aquiline features against the darkness.

"What about the action out at the cottage, Carl?"

"Well, it seems Miss Hanson had a little rendezvous about nine-thirty."

He nodded. "When she could be sure Dore was safely at work. Where was this rendezvous? The cottage?"

"No, she drove down to the shopping center. Whoever she was meeting was parked by the telephone booth near the supermarket."

"Did you see who it was?"

He shook his head. "That parking lot's big as a football field and just as open that time of night. I couldn't get anywhere near without being seen. I ditched my car and came around the supermarket on foot, but by that time the meet was over. I didn't even get a license number."

Conan shrugged, displaying an indifference he couldn't really feel.

"Can't win 'em all, Carl. What kind of car was it?"

"A sports car; dark color, either blue or black. It looked like a Lotus Elan."

"An Elan? Well, that didn't come from a rental agency. How long did the meeting last?"

"About ten minutes. Not long enough."

He frowned, remembering Jennifer Hanson's red, swollen eyes and Isadora's surprise that she was awake so late.

"It was long enough for something. What happened after the rendezvous?"

"Miss Hanson headed for home. By the time I got back to my car, I'd lost the Elan. All I know is he took 101 north. If I'd caught him at Skinner Junction, I'd at least know whether he was heading north or east."

"East, probably."

"Portland?"

"Salem. The road to Salem branches off about halfway to Portland. Jenny was at the cottage when you returned?"

"Yes. Conan, I'm sorry I didn't get a better look at that car or whoever was driving it."

"It wasn't worth the risk of someone seeing you, and the Elan gives us a good lead; it isn't a common car."

"Well, we might salvage something out of it. I'd better get back to Shanaway." Then he added with a short laugh, "The night's young yet."

CHAPTER 9

It was a crystalline day, the sky a flawless pool of blue shading from ultramarine at the zenith to cerulean at the horizon. A calm sea made a cadenced murmuring, a light wind moved Isadora's hair against her cheek.

For some time they walked together in silence. Conan was well aware of the red Ford waiting in the picnic area half a mile behind them, but that didn't detract from the perfection of the day, nor the profound sense of privacy.

Isadora stopped to pick up a white, sea-worn shell.

"Look at that," she said, "built without a conscious thought. How can it be so beautiful?"

He studied the delicate, perfect spiral, finding his pleasure quickened by hers.

"Where do you think we learn the canons of conscious beauty, Dore?"

She glanced up at him, but made no response except a gentle smile. Finally, he took her arm and guided her toward the jumble of drift near the bank.

"Come on, let's find a comfortable log."

As she seated herself on the silvered flank of a long-uprooted giant, he saw a shadow of anxiety in her eyes. He sat down facing her, taking time to light a cigarette.

At length, she turned and looked at him.

"You want to know about my father's death."

"If you feel like talking about it."

"I just don't understand why you want to know about it—what it could possibly have to do with those men."

"Dore, I don't enjoy opening old wounds, but it asks too much of coincidence that the tailing began so soon after his death. Unless something happened in the month before you moved to Shanaway."

She swallowed hard, eyes fixed on the shell.

"Nothing happened in that month. Nothing."

He nodded, recognizing in her flat tone a stone wall.

"Then I'm left with your father's death. I have to know about it if only to eliminate it as a factor."

"But I can't really tell you about it. I can't remember anything after I went into that . . . the library."

He paused, deciding on a more oblique approach.

"You're sure he had no prior history of heart disease?"

"I'm sure, but he'd been working awfully hard."

"What about the day of his death? Were you at home?"

"No, I live at the dorm during the school year."

"But you came home that night. Why?"

"Well, I certainly hadn't planned on it. The usual winter flu virus was making the rounds, and it finally got to me. I went to a concert with Ben that night."

"Ben?"

"Oh—Ben Meade. He's a fraternity brother of Jim's."

"Anything serious?"

"Well, not as far as I was concerned. I think—well, maybe Ben was a little serious."

"You put it in past tense. Does Ben?"

She looked up at him sharply, then shook her head.

"No. He writes to me and even calls occasionally. But he never pushes. I guess that's why I always enjoyed him."

"You have a problem with pushy young men?"

She smiled. "I'm a status symbol. The Senator's daughter. But Ben lives in an ivory tower; theoretical physics. Still, he's rather single-minded in some ways."

"You had a date with him for a concert," he said, prompting her, seeing her mouth tighten.

"Yes, but we had to leave in the middle. All of a sudden I was sick; nausea, chills, everything. Ben took me to the infirmary. I remember a doctor sticking a thermometer in my mouth and saying I had a fever of one hundred and three, then he told me to go home and call our family doctor. Ben drove me to the dorm to pick up a few of my things and took me home."

"Have you any idea what time it was when you got home?"

"No. I was so sick, I don't even remember the drive home, except—" She frowned, her hands rigidly tense on the shell. "I remember seeing the light in the library and thinking that—that Dad must be working late."

"Were there any other lights on in the house?"

"I'm not sure." Her voice faltered; she cleared her throat. "I know the porch light was off; I had a hard time finding my key. But then, no one was expecting me."

He felt a chill at that, but couldn't explain it.

"Ben took you inside the house?"

"Just into the foyer, then I told him to go on."

"And he left?"

"Yes."

Conan paused, watching her closely. "And after that?"

"I—I remember the light under the library door." She was trembling, every word a halting effort. "I thought I should tell Dad why I was home. I remember . . . going to the door. No, I just remember the *door*. Only the door, and after that—oh, God, I can't—Conan, there's *nothing*. Nothing but *nightmare*—" The shell snapped in her fingers.

She stared at it as if it had somehow betrayed her, and her defenses collapsed into a ruin of anguished weeping. He pulled her into his arms, offering no words of comfort, trusting neither words nor his voice. He wondered how long it had been since she'd allowed herself this necessary release. Grief couldn't be stoppered; it was too volatile.

But there was more than grief here. *Nightmare.* Why had she used that particular word? Finding her father's body would be a profound shock, but the victim of a heart attack wouldn't present the grisly aspect typical of some forms of death. Her experience might be described in strong terms, but nightmare sounded a jarring dissonance. There was fear behind it; fear that was wrong in the context of grief.

At length, she drew away from him and fumbled in her pocket for a handerchief, eyes averted.

"Conan, I'm sorry. I don't usually fall apart like this. You'd think by now—"

"By when? Do you put a time limit on grief?"

She shook her head distractedly.

"Oh, I must be a mess. I'm sorry."

He smiled at her. "Stop apologizing. I've seen you looking better, but the condition isn't permanent. Dore, there's only one thing that worries me. I can understand the grief, but you're afraid, and I must know why."

"I'm *not* afraid," she insisted. "Unless it's . . . those men. The surveillance."

"No. That's not the nightmare, the fear I'm talking about. It's connected with your father's death, isn't it?"

For a moment he thought she was going to lose control again, but she held on and finally looked at him intently.

"Conan, there's something I . . ." She stopped, and he found himself holding his breath; then she turned away. "Why would there be any *fear* connected with Dad's death?"

He let his breath out slowly. A good question, but that wasn't what she had started to say.

"Well, you've been under a great deal of strain."

She only nodded, pushing the sand over the broken shell with her foot.

"Dore, you said something last night about practicing in the afternoons. Is that a regular habit with you?"

She turned, relieved at the change of subject.

"Yes. I put in at least three hours every afternoon."

"What about Jenny? Does she stick around for these practice sessions?"

"No. Maybe the racket drives her away, or else she thinks I want privacy when I'm playing; she's such a private person about her own work. She usually goes down to the beach for an hour or so. Why do you ask?"

"Would you mind if Harry and I searched the cottage?"

"Well, no, but—"

"But, why? For one thing, I want to check your phone for bugs, and if you don't mind, I'd like to install a bug of my own."

"You're welcome to do anything you think necessary."

In Shanaway, at least, he thought, remembering her anxiety about the "third operative's" investigation.

"It's two-fifteen," he said. "About time for your practice session, don't you think?"

She gave a short laugh. "I'll take your word for that."

The house was empty. Isadora called Jenny's name and knocked on the studio door, but there was no answer. Conan found the note by the telephone. *I'm on the beach—Jen.*

Isadora frowned at it. "She must've gone out earlier than usual." Then she took a quick breath. "Well, I suppose I'd better get at the piano."

The door of the music studio opened off the south wall of the living room. It was flooded with sunlight, sparsely furnished with bookshelves, music cabinets, and a Steinway grand. Conan went to the west windows, noting the shadowy figure in the window of the duplex below, but there was no sign of Jenny on the road. When Isadora began a scale exercise, he walked over to her and leaned close to her ear.

"Keep playing. I'll be back."

She only nodded, the precise sequences never faltering.

He went out to his car and within a few seconds was in radio contact with Munson.

"Harry. Jenny's gone to the beach, but I have no idea when she'll be back. We'll have to watch for her. You have the equipment for the phone?"

"Yes, all I need for that is maybe two minutes."

"Good. Dore's practicing, which will give us some cover noise. I'll leave the front door open for you."

"I'm on my way."

Conan took a small, flat tool kit from the glove box and returned to the house. He went first to the telephone. There was no monitor in the mouthpiece; instead, he found a tiny mechanism under the jack cover. The design and brand were unfamiliar, but it was wired in and probably powerful enough for area as well as telephone monitoring.

He frowned as he replaced the cover, hoping the piano would at least confuse the sounds of the screwdriver. Then he saw a shadow at the door; Harry Munson entered silently.

Conan tore a page from the scratch pad on the telephone table and wrote a brief message: *Bug in phone jack—wired in. May be area monitor.*

Munson read it and nodded, then followed him into the music studio. Isadora turned, but Conan's whispered admonition to keep playing was superfluous; she didn't miss a note.

He leaned over her. "Dore, there's a bug in the phone, and it may be strong enough to pick up other sounds, so keep up the cover. The man with me is Harry Munson."

She smiled briefly at him, her fingers still flashing through the scales. Conan made a casual pass by the windows to check the road, then returned to Munson.

"Clear for now. You take this room."

While Munson deftly assaulted a bookcase, Conan went back to the living room and the telephone table. In the shallow drawer he found, predictably, a local directory with a list of names and numbers written in the inside cover.

Lambda Delta. Probably Jim Canfield's fraternity. *Ben*. That would be Ben Meade. He made a mental note to have Sean check out that "rather single-minded" suitor of Isadora's. *Bob Carleton* would be C. Robert Carleton, the family attorney. Then a final enigmatic notation: *Dr. K*.

He tore another sheet from the scratch pad and copied the numbers, then went to the windows. The road was still empty. Munson emerged from the music studio, read his gestured instructions, then disappeared into the south wing.

The scale progressions ceased, and Conan tensed, then relaxed as he heard the rushing arpeggios of the *Revolutionary Etude*. Isadora was doing her part, he thought wryly.

He opened the door of Jenny's studio.

The curtains were closed. That struck him as unusual, but they were thin enough to let some light in. Then he stopped dead, feeling a sudden, stomach-turning wrench.

He was looking at a scene of devastation.

Like the debris of an explosion, paint tubes, brushes, palette knives, broken bottles littered the floor among bleak, sullied drifts of dismembered sketch pads and torn drawings. On the easel was a large painting with a few color areas blocked in, but it had been viciously ripped, the canvas hanging from the stretcher bars in stiff, curling strips. Every canvas in the room, even those that hadn't yet been touched with paint, was slashed repeatedly.

He gazed numbly around, his pulse hard and fast.

A self-inflicted wound. There was no other explanation for it. Otherwise, Jennifer Hanson, who was afraid of intruders, who carefully locked the doors at night and kept a gun by her bed, would have sounded some sort of alarm.

Finally, he went to the easel and knelt to examine the broken remains of a bottle of linseed oil. It told him one thing: this havoc hadn't been wreaked in the last few hours; the oil was too viscid. And last night, Jenny had a rendezvous with someone driving a Lotus Elan, and her eyes had been red and swollen.

He remembered his purpose at length, and began sorting through the debris, pausing at ten-minute intervals to look for Jenny. At the third check, he turned and saw Munson at the door, looking around the room with a puzzled frown.

When Conan walked over to him, he whispered, "I want to show you something."

He followed Munson into the south wing and turned at the first door. A glance at the paint-daubed clothing on the bed told him this was Jenny's room. Munson went to the table by the bed and pointed into the drawer where a small .22 revolver lay.

Conan took the gun out and opened it. It was loaded, but he doubted it had been fired—or cleaned—for some time. He put it back and leaned close to Munson.

"Anything else?"

"No. I went over the other bedroom, too."

"Okay, take the kitchen."

They left the room together but parted in the living room. Munson waited for him to check the road again, then crossed to the north wing. Conan finished his search of the studio, but found nothing unusual—except the evidence of some terrifying self-destructive power unleashed here.

At length, he turned his attention to the living room. He was busy feeling behind the cushions of the couch, when Munson came around the corner from the kitchen, and something in his expression said, "Pay dirt."

It was on a low shelf in the pantry.

Conan knelt, noting the sprinkling of white grains on the floor as Munson removed the lid from a cannister marked SUGAR. It was half full; the top of a plastic sack sealed with a wire tie protruded from it.

"Did you take it out, Harry?"

"Just far enough to see what's in it. That's the way I found it. The sugar on the floor was what made me check."

He nodded. "You'd better go keep an eye on the road."

When he was gone, Conan gingerly pulled the sack out of the cannister. It held a syringe and a dozen rubber-capped 10 cc. multi-dose vials. They were labeled MORPHINE.

He stared at them for a long time, then closed his eyes, wondering at the palling weariness that overwhelmed him.

At least, he had one answer out of all this—what had happened to Jennifer Hanson; to the painter she'd once been.

Munson was bending over the telephone. He straightened when Conan emerged from the kitchen, then at his beckoning gesture, followed him outside into the patio.

"You hit the jackpot, Harry."

"You don't seem too happy about it."

He laughed bitterly. No, he thought, he felt sick.

"Did you see the studio?"

"Is that some new kind of painting? What happened in there?"

"Attempted suicide. Or maybe it was successful." Then seeing Munson's puzzled look, "Did you find anything else?"

"No, but I'll lay you odds there's more to find. Morphine. Somebody's past the joypopping stage."

"You have a tap on the phone?"

"Yes, and I'll set up a tape recorder in my car. It's around the turn on the crest road; close enough for good pickup. Any idea which of the young ladies is hooked?"

"Yes. Jenny."

"I suppose you've considered the possibility *both* of them might be users?"

Conan said tightly, "The symptoms of morphine addiction are fairly obvious."

"But the symptoms of a few other drugs I could name *aren't* so obvious." He had more to say on the subject, but restrained himself. "Will you be with Miss Canfield again tonight?"

"Yes. I'll probably send Carl out here before nine."

"Okay. I'd better get going before somebody shows up."

"All right. Thanks, Harry."

Munson crossed the road into the woods, but Conan was hardly aware of his departure. He stood motionless, listening to the music still emanating from the house.

CHAPTER 10

Isadora stared straight ahead as Conan turned off the Shanaway road onto Highway 101. He had the radio mike in his right hand.

"Harry, did you check your pickup on that bug?"

"Yes, all systems go. Your friend in the red Ford just left the duplex, by the way."

"Right on schedule. Jenny wasn't home from the beach when we left. If she isn't back soon, let me know."

"Don't worry about her. She's coming up the road now."

He frowned and looked at his watch. Nearly six. He wondered if Jenny had purposely delayed her return so long.

"All right, Harry. I'll talk to you later."

As he put the mike away, he was aware of Isadora's blue eyes fixed on him now, somber and full of questions.

"Conan, what about the search?"

"The type of monitor they're using can pick up conversations in the room, so keep that in mind. And it's wired in;

that takes time. It was probably installed before you and Jenny moved down."

"Or while Jenny was alone in the house."

He glanced at her, then shrugged.

"Possibly. Have you been in her studio today?"

"No, she was still asleep when I left this morning. I never go into her studio unless she's there. Why?"

"Because it looked like the wake of a hurricane; paint, brushes, paper, everything thrown all over the floor, and every canvas was cut to ribbons."

He turned and saw her look of uncomprehending shock.

"But who would . . ." A pause, then, "Not *Jenny*?"

"To your knowledge has she ever done anything like this before?"

"No. Oh, God, Conan, why would she do that?"

"I don't know. I want to talk to her, but it can't be at the cottage. Did you tell her about the Knight?"

"No, not yet."

"Perhaps you should. It might give me an opening gambit. Or a crack in the armor."

"All right." She sank into thoughtful silence as the blocks flicked past, finally shaking her head slowly. "Poor Jen. I don't understand her, Conan. I wish I did."

"Are you sure you can't tell me anything about the illness that brought her home from Chicago?"

"No. She was almost fully recovered by the time I saw her, and no one ever talked about it much."

"You were away when she first came home?"

"Yes, at boarding school." When he slowed as they passed the bookshop and signaled a right turn, she asked, "Where are we going? Your house?"

"Yes. I thought you might enjoy a change in cuisine." He sent her a quick smile. "How are you at cooking?"

"Me?" She laughed. "I'm great with a can opener."

"Who does the cooking at the cottage? Jenny?"

"Oh, no. Mostly, we just fend for ourselves."

He pulled up by the house and turned off the motor.

"Well, one reason for stopping here is that I have some phone calls to make. I also have a couple of beautiful T-bones in the refrigerator."

"Wonderful, but *you're* elected meat chef. Steaks make me nervous except for eating them. But I can put together a passable salad and a rather tasty garlic bread."

"Sounds fair enough, but wish me luck on the steaks."

She eyed him dubiously. "Luck? I thought you'd be a gourmet cook like most confirmed bachelors."

"The cooking talents of bachelors is another of those comfortable myths. If Mrs. Early didn't occasionally take pity on me, I'd be left to a fate worse than TV dinners."

She laughed at that, but after a moment, the sober question was back in her eyes.

"Conan, there was something more, wasn't there? I mean, you found something else at the cottage."

He hesitated. "I'd rather not discuss it yet."

"Why not?"

"Just . . . trust me."

"I do, but do you trust *me*?"

"You're my client, after all."

"Which doesn't answer my question."

"True. But if trust depended on every question being answered, should I trust *you*?"

She turned away abruptly, she had no answer to that. Conan reached out and touched her cheek.

"Come on, let's go inside. I'm getting hungry."

She nodded mutely, holding his hand against her cheek, then smiled at him.

"Okay. Lead me to your kitchen."

Conan closed the library door and went to the desk. There was music in the background, but not Isadora's. He'd shown her how to operate the tape system and left her to choose an accompaniment for her culinary efforts.

He smiled to himself. Ravel: the *Pavane pour une infante défunte*. And he was thinking of Isadora Canfield in a makeshift dish-towel apron, looking as out of place in the kitchen as a Bird of Paradise in a chicken coop.

Then he opened the compartment and took out the phone. The first call went to his answering service. There was only one message. He hurriedly dialed the number.

"Marion Hotel, may I help you?"

"Room two-seventeen, please."

He lit a cigarette, listening to the buzz of the extension until finally Sean Kelly came on the line.

"Sean, this is Conan Flagg. I just got your message."

"Oh, good timing. I was about to leave for supper."

"Sorry to delay that. How are you progressing?"

"Very well. That Steve Travers is a jewel. I tracked down your specific questions and picked up a lot of background info. I was lucky on that; made an inside contact." She paused briefly. "Conan, I don't trust extensions, and I'd like to see the situation down there first hand. It's only an hour's drive to Holliday Beach from here, isn't it?"

"Yes. Less than an hour if you push it."

"Well, this is what I called about, really. If it's okay with you, I'll drive down and report to you personally tomorrow morning. I'll have to be back by two, though. I have an iron in the fire that may lead to a ringside seat."

He laughed. "You'll have to come down just to explain that. Besides, after all Charlie Duncan said about you, I'm anxious to meet you."

"Well, just don't believe everything Charlie says."

"Don't worry. I'll meet you at the bookshop at ten; that'll give you plenty of time. Oh, here's something else for your list. See if you can get copies of both Isadora and Jim Canfield's transcripts from Willamette University."

"That might take a while. Okay, anything else?"

"Yes. Have you come across a Ben Meade among Dore's friends and associates?"

"Not personally, but he's been mentioned. Apparently, he has quite a thing for her."

"Apparently. See what you can dig up on him. Have you a list of the cars belonging to the family, etcetera?"

"Yes, right in my notebook . . . here it is."

"Have you a Lotus Elan on the list?"

Her short laugh didn't make sense at first.

"This is your lucky day, fellow Irishman. I have not one, but *two* Lotus Elans."

"Two Elans? Sean, that's ridiculous. There can't be more than half a dozen in the entire state."

"Truth is stranger than fiction, so they say."

"And far less reasonable. Who do they belong to?"

"Jim Canfield and C. Robert Carleton."

"What is this, some sort of one-upmanship?"

"I guess so, but from what I've heard, Carleton is one down on Jim in the sporty playboy role."

"All right." He tore off a sheet of scratch paper. "Give me the colors and license numbers."

"Jim's is dark blue; license CFM230. Carleton's is black, AAM938."

"Dark blue and black; hard to distinguish at night."

"Is someone trying to distinguish them?"

"I'll tell you about that later. Do you know if anyone would have access to them other than Jim and Carleton?"

"I don't know about Carleton, but I guess Jim's pretty free with his, which is odd for a sports car buff. Maybe he likes to impress the brothers with his largess."

"His fraternity brothers? He lets them drive his car?"

"I think so, but this is gossip from a waitress who works in a bar near the Lambda Delt house. She seemed to be very friendly with quite a few of the brothers."

He frowned, absently doodling the Greek letters lambda and delta.

"I wonder if Jim's ever shared his car with Ben Meade. By the way, who's the Canfield family doctor?"

"I have it right here. Johnson. Emil Johnson."

He studied the phone numbers from the directory at the cottage. That wouldn't be "Dr. K." But he didn't pursue the question; it might have no bearing on the case, and it could wait until Sean arrived for her personal report.

"All right, Sean, thanks. I'll see you in the morning, and I'm looking forward to it."

"So am I. Charlie's had a lot to say about you, too."

When she hung up, Conan took a long pull on his cigarette, then began dialing again. It was Steve Travers's home phone, and Travers himself answered.

"Steve, this is Conan."

"You know, I had a feeling it was when the phone rang. Who else always calls in the middle of the sports report?"

"Give me a schedule and I'll try again."

"Never mind. How're you coming on your current case?"

"That's what I'm calling about. I have a compliment to pass on to you."

"Softening me up? Who's it from?"

"Sean Kelly. She says you're a jewel."

"She's kind of a jewel herself. And good, as well as decorative. She's really been moving."

"I was a little surprised at the fast work, but she says it's all due to your fine cooperation."

"Sure, and that Irish charm. How come you didn't pick up any of that from your old man?"

"What do you mean? Just yesterday a very attractive young lady told me I was full of Irish charm."

"Sure that wasn't blarney? Oh, by the way, I have something on that first license you gave me. Rental, of course. It was hired out by a man named Roger Garner. Now, it so happens I've had some dealings with Garner. He works for a Salem outfit; the Worth Detective Agency."

"Sean was right; you're a jewel. What can you tell me about the agency?"

"Oh, they work divorce cases, mostly; nothing big. But here's something I picked off the grapevine, and considering the questions Sean's been asking, I thought you'd be interested. They do a lot of work for C. Robert Carleton."

Conan took a quick puff on his cigarette.

"I'm interested. Who runs the agency?"

"Guy named Everett Worth. He has six men working for him, none of them top grade, but as far as I know, the whole bunch is clean."

"I could've told you they aren't top grade."

"So, what else could you tell me about what's going on down there?"

He frowned, remembering the sugar cannister and the mutilated canvases in Jenny's studio. But he wasn't ready to discuss either with Travers yet.

"There isn't much to tell yet, Steve, so I'll leave you to your vicarious athletics. Thanks for helping Sean."

"It was my pleasure, and I mean that."

After he hung up, Conan put his cigarette out, forehead lined as he considered the fruits of the day's work. Some answers only breed more questions. He looked down at the list of phone numbers.

"Dr. K." A Salem exchange. On impulse, he reached for the phone again.

The answer was cool and mechanical.

"Dr. Kerr is out of the office. At the tone please state your name, phone number, and purpose of the call."

Dr. Kerr. That told him little more than "Dr. K."

He put the phone back in the compartment. Sean would probably have the answer to that particular enigma. Meanwhile, Isadora was at large in the kitchen, her pianist's hands at the mercy of assorted sharp instruments.

His smile at that thought faded abruptly.

It occurred to him how odd it was for a pianist to choose

cutting her wrists as a means of suicide; the need to protect her hands should be so well ingrained as to be virtually instinctive and impervious to conscious control.

But suicide defied instinctual imperatives.

CHAPTER 11

Beatrice Dobie smiled at him from behind the counter where she was checking out a rental book for a frail, white-haired woman leaning on a silver-headed cane.

"Good morning, Mr. Flagg."

"Good morning, Miss Dobie—Mrs. Hollis."

The woman turned and gave him a sprightly smile.

"Mornin', Mr. Flagg. You're lookin' chipper today."

"Not half so chipper as you. How are you?"

"Fit and full of vinegar. Had a bit of a cold last week, and all my relatives gathered 'round for the wake." Then she laughed gleefully. "But I fooled 'em again."

"Good for you. Just keep on fooling them."

Mrs. Hollis, at ninety-odd years, was a local institution, the widow of one Hiram Hollis who had, in partnership with another real estate speculator named Day, founded Holliday Beach, incidentally amassing a considerable fortune.

Conan left the office door open, poured a cup of coffee, and sat down at the desk, musing idly on the chagrin of Mrs. Hollis's relatives. But a glance at his watch diverted him from that. It was exactly ten o'clock. He looked through the mail, opened one letter and was engrossed in it when Miss Dobie came in. She filled her cup and sat down, favoring him with an arch smile.

"Well, I didn't expect to see *you* for another week."

"I said I'd be in and out, not totally out of it. By the way, I'm expecting Miss Kelly. She should be here any moment now."

"Uh-huh. I'll evacuate when she arrives, if that's what you're hinting around about."

He smiled at her. "You're a woman of rare sensibility, Miss Dobie. Where's Meg?"

"Oh . . . probably upstairs asleep; resting on her laurels. I found another trophy at the front door this morning. That makes eleven mice this year."

"You're keeping a body count?"

"That's for that snippy IRS man; the one who was complaining about deducting cat food for pest control. Anything in the mail I should take care of?"

He handed her the letter he'd been reading.

"You can answer this. A man in Malheur County; his great-grandfather left a journal which might give me a lead on that Lost Pueblo project." He looked at his watch again, then at the shop door, while Miss Dobie eyed him curiously.

"How goes the new case?"

"It goes, but I'm not sure where."

"Well . . . I suppose it's none of my business, but have you turned up anything exciting yet?"

He sent her a sharp look, then laughed.

"It *is* none of your business, but what do you mean by exciting? A body or two?"

She made an exaggerated shrug. "Of course."

Before he could respond to that, he was distracted by the bells on the shop door. The young woman coming in was smartly dressed, endowed with long, elegantly formed legs, a pert, creamy-skinned face, and short, curly red hair.

He smiled to himself. "That has to be Sean."

A glance at Miss Dobie impelled her to her feet. She evacuated as promised, venting a gusty sigh when Conan closed the office door.

Sean Kelly settled herself in Miss Dobie's chair while Conan eyed her beautifully tailored beige wool suit.

"A very becoming outfit, Sean. City of Paris?"

She looked up at him with a crooked smile.

"I. Magnin, and I know it isn't exactly beach clothes, but at two o'clock I'm playing the reporter from Back East, and I was afraid I wouldn't have time to change."

He laughed. "It's still becoming. Coffee?"

"Yes, thanks. Black."

He poured her coffee then sat down, watching her as she took a notebook and a manila envelope from her purse.

"The transcripts," she said, handing him the envelope.

His eyebrows went up. "Well, that was fast. Thanks."

"I asked Steve to put in a word for me. I figured that'd be the fastest line between two points."

He smiled at that and took the transcripts out of the envelope. Isadora's presented no surprises, except the electives in anthropology, nor did Jim Canfield's.

Jim's major was recorded as "Business Administration: Management." His choice of electives showed a marked tendency to the path of least resistance, although he'd devoted six hours to psychology courses, and judging by his grades, done well in them. But he apparently found chemistry too strenuous. He'd taken an incomplete in Chemistry I.

"I wonder what Jim intends to 'manage' when he graduates," he commented as he put the transcripts aside.

"His mother's share of the estate, I suppose." Sean had her notebook open on her lap, her piquant features intently businesslike. "Let me give you this from the top so I won't leave anything out."

"Fire away," he said, thinking that Sean Kelly could read stock market quotations and make them sound entrancing.

"The license numbers; Steve checked those for me."

"I called him last night. He told me about Garner and the Worth Agency. I assume Hicks is also on Worth's payroll."

"Yes, and that's all I have on them so far." She turned a page. "So, on to John Canfield's will. These are all round figures. I didn't think you were concerned about exact amounts or specific assets."

"No, but generally what form do these assets take?"

"Real estate, mostly. Valuable stuff, that Willamette Valley dirt. I wish I'd been smart enough to have some ancestors settle there. There are some stocks and bonds, too; blue chip. The estate totals about seven million. There are quite a few minor bequests to assorted distant relatives, foundations, charities, and the Republican Party. I have a list if you're interested."

"I'll check it later. Let's get to the *major* bequests."

She turned another page. "Those go to the immediate family. Catharine Canfield gets the tidy sum of one and a half million; her children are due for five hundred thousand each, but only at age twenty-five *or* on marrying."

"On marrying? Does that apply to Dore, too?"

"Miss Canfield? Yes, both stipulations."

"That's interesting. Jenny's already eligible for her inheritance, isn't she?"

"Yes, and I assume she has it; the will was probated with no hitches. Miss Canfield is the only other major beneficiary. She gets the remainder of the estate. That was the wording; no specific amount. Right now, that remainder totals about three and a half million."

He sighed. "That could buy a lot of piano lessons."

"And a lot of trouble."

"True. I understand the estate is controlled by the Ladd-Bush Bank and C. Robert Carleton."

"Yes, but there's a clause about Catharine having a say in the management of it. I heard some rumors—I met a very talkative young man from the Ladd-Bush Bank—to the effect that Carleton is trying to ease the bank out of the triumvirate, but the man in charge at the bank, Marvin Hendricks, is fighting it. And Bob Carleton is *not* held in high regard by the local legal fraternity. In fact, one lawyer's secretary said the word had gone out that Canfield was looking for a new man to handle his legal affairs."

"That sounds like a very sticky situation."

"Here's something stickier: my talkative friend at the bank says he thinks the Senator was considering changing his will a couple of weeks before he died."

"What brought him to that conclusion?"

"Well, this will was written right after he married Catharine, and he hadn't touched it since, but two weeks before he died, he took it out of his safe deposit box. It was found in his desk in the library after his death."

"Had it been changed?"

"No. If there were any notes or suggestions of changes they weren't found."

"Sticky, indeed." He paused, eyes narrowed. "By the way, you said something about an inside contact."

Sean smiled. "Ah, yes. The ineffable Maud McCarty, the Canfields' housekeeper for the last thirty years."

"How did you manage to get to her?"

"Well, I checked the household staff, of course. There are only two live-in, full-time employees; Maud and Alma Blackstone, the cook. Anyway, I found out Maud's a staunch Christian Scientist. Steve told me about a local printer who'll set up anything short of counterfeiting, and he isn't so sure about that. So, I am now a card-carrying staff writer for *The Christian Science Monitor*, and I'm doing an in-depth story on the late great Senator Canfield."

"And Maud fell for that?"

"Clear down to the sinker. And Maud's a doll; a congenital blabber. She keeps forgetting all this supposedly might get into print."

Conan shook his head. "Sean, you're amazing."

"Oh, you haven't heard the best part yet. I've been buttering Maud up for the kill. I'm meeting her this afternoon. That's why I have to be back in Salem by two."

He eyed her suspiciously. "Buttering her up for what?"

"Well, I think I have her persuaded that I can't write the real story of the Canfield family unless I get to know them personally *without* their knowing I'm a reporter."

"Sean, exactly what are you planning?"

She smiled enigmatically. "I'm getting to that. Now, Maud has a sister in Calamine-something-Falls."

"Klamath Falls."

"Yes, that's it. God, these names. Anyway, sister has a heart condition, so she'd make a great excuse for Maud to be away for awhile, and with Jenny gone, they'll need a temporary replacement; Maud's been tending Catharine. And it just so happens Maud knows somebody who's looking for a job as a domestic."

"Look, even if Maud goes along with that—"

"She will. The *Monitor* is willing to pay for her cooperation." She smiled innocently at him. "Aren't you?"

"That isn't the point. It's too risky, and what do you know about being a—a domestic?"

"Conan, back in my CIA days I worked for some of the finest families in Washington, New York, and London."

He couldn't muster a smile at that.

"Sean, there's a new factor now. Harry and I did a quick search of the Canfield cottage yesterday and turned up a cache of morphine."

She frowned thoughtfully. "Yes, that does put a new turn on things. Is the morphine all you found?"

"Yes."

"Who's on it?"

"Jenny. The drug angle *does* change the picture, and I don't like putting you in a potentially dangerous situation."

"Now, look, if you think because I'm a weak little woman I can't take care of myself, maybe I should give you a demonstration. If I can't lay you out flat on the floor in ten seconds, I'll turn in my license.''

He held up a hand in mock surrender.

''I believe you, and I'll pass on the demonstration, but I don't like sending someone else out on *my* limbs.''

''Well, Conan, that's very chivalrous of you, but I can't see you playing a domestic. It's me or nothing, so don't look a dark horse in the eye.''

''You have a point there. I think.''

''Then that settles it.''

He hesitated, then nodded reluctantly. ''All right.''

''Good. Now, shall we get back to the Canfields?''

''By all means. I need something to take my mind off your wild schemes.''

''You're an ulcer type, I can see that.'' She frowned at her notes. ''You understand, a lot of this is gossip, mostly from Maud, but some of it checks out. She doesn't care much for Catharine, so she's been quite informative there.''

''Does her antipathy extend to Catharine's children?''

''Well, not to Jim. She doesn't really approve of him but she keeps saying he's a good boy at heart. He must be a bundle of charm to get that from Moral Maud; he's Willamette U.'s star swinger. He's totaled out three cars and had so many traffic citations, he's supporting half the Salem police force. He even got picked up at a pot party once.''

Conan's head came up. ''He was arrested?''

''No. He was clean, and nobody wanted to step on the Senator's toes. He was released; no charges.''

He nodded and took a swallow of coffee.

''What did Maud have to say about Jenny?''

Sean's eyes turned heavenward. ''Nothing good. She thinks all artists are perverts to begin with, and I gather Jenny isn't exactly the friendly, outgoing type.''

''No. Did Maud know anything about her illness?''

''Well, Jenny was *very* sick, but it seems to be a deep, dark family secret. Maud let something slip, though, when she was ranting about the low morals of artists. She said it figured Jenny would—quote—get herself in trouble.''

''Pregnant, then?''

''Coming from Maud, that had to be it.''

''Dore saw Jenny soon after she came home. I can't believe she wouldn't notice something so obvious as pregnancy.''

''Maybe she isn't telling all she knows.''

''I doubt she'd cover for Jenny, and extramarital pregnancy isn't that big a thing these days.''

''Extra-marital pregnancy still isn't acceptable in some circles, Conan, especially not political circles.''

He nodded. ''Neither are abortions.''

''No. I think that's the answer, judging from Maud's attitude. But the illness means a botched-up job. You'd think she could find a decent doctor somewhere in Chicago.''

''If she had, she probably wouldn't have come home for help, and you can't expect good judgment of someone under that kind of stress. Jenny had the Senator's lady to consider, and God knows what personal considerations.'' He paused, adding absently, ''Septic poisoning. That could be extremely painful.'' He lapsed into silence, thinking of a room full of slashed canvases.

Then he roused himself, frowning. ''This is highly speculative, Sean. Let's get back to Catharine. Where does she fit into the Canfield family history?''

She smiled faintly as she turned another page.

''Right in the middle, and it dates back to John Canfield's college days at the University of Oregon. It seems he first met Catharine Clary—later Hanson—in his freshman year when she was waiting tables at a campus cafe.''

He raised an eyebrow. ''What happened?''

''Mm. Well, that's speculative, too, but I guess they had quite a romance on until the Canfield family shipped John off to Harvard. About six months later Catharine married George Hanson. A couple of years later, Canfield married

Anna Morrisson, and apparently it was a love match as well as a union of two wealthy families. But Catharine picked a real dud. She stuck it out for six years, then contacted Canfield again. The family lawyer—that was Carleton *senior*—acted as her counsel in instigating divorce proceedings against Hanson."

"What were the grounds?"

"Desertion. George did a lot of selling on the road and I guess he didn't spend much time at home. The last time Catharine saw him was in February before she filed for divorce in May. But George was actually out of the scene well before February. He got into a barroom brawl in Los Angeles and spent five months in the LA County jail—September twelfth to February twelfth. He came home to Catharine then, but she didn't want him, so he hopped a Liberian freighter, and that's the last he was heard from. Now, keep the dates of his stay in the LA County jail in mind, because Catharine was pregnant with Jim when she filed for divorce."

Conan reached for Jim's transcript. His date of birth was at the top: August fifth, twenty-two years ago.

"You said Catharine 'contacted' Canfield before the divorce. When, and what do you mean by contact?"

"I don't know when *or* what. Maud says Catharine came to him for legal aid on the divorce—period. But Maud *does* occasionally remember to keep the Senator's image polished."

He frowned and pushed the transcript aside.

"So, Hanson wasn't Jim's father, but that doesn't mean Canfield was. Look at the will. Five hundred thousand to both Jenny and Jim; equal shares, and rather small ones out of such a large estate. Canfield had adopted Jim; giving him a bigger cut wouldn't raise any eyebrows."

"True, and this is another speculative line."

"But interesting." He took time to light a cigarette, still frowning. "What happened to Catharine after the divorce?"

Sean referred to her notebook again.

"For the next five years, it was rough going for her. Her widowed mother helped tend the kids while she took night classes at a business school and worked days."

"She had no financial help from Canfield?"

"I don't think so. I checked the Social Security records, and she was working at everything from waiting tables to scrubbing floors, which doesn't sound like she was getting much help. In fact, it was another five years after she graduated from business school before Canfield put her on as his private secretary."

"You said Maud didn't care much for her. Why not?"

"Oh, Maud's practically sanctified Anna, in spite of her booze problem. Besides, Catharine's the ambitious type and probably a lot harder to please. But Maud gives her credit for aiding and abetting Canfield's political career, even after the accident. You know about that?"

"Yes."

"She's what you might call a determined woman. Her behavior after the accident is kind of interesting."

"How so?"

"The new Congressional session began two weeks afterward, but Maud says Canfield didn't want to leave; Catharine was still in the hospital and totally blind. But she nobly insisted he carry out his duties to his constituency, and he *did* leave. The next day, she checked out of the hospital."

Conan stared at her blankly. "She what?"

"She went home. The hospital was so much against it, she had to sign an affidavit absolving them of responsibility. Emil Johnson, the family doctor, took over from there."

"I can think of adjectives other than *determined*. How did she deal with the little problem of her blindness?"

"Very well, I guess. Of course, she could afford all the special help and equipment she needed; Braille typewriter, recording equipment, that sort of thing. She even taught herself Braille with Jenny's help."

"She taught herself—how did she manage that?"

"I told you she was determined." Sean paused, pursing her lips. "Actually, I think Jenny's been her eyes when it comes to reading and writing. Maud softens up a little on Jenny there; mother and daughter seem to be very close."

Conan sighed, then put Catharine's determination aside. "Sean, did any of your sources tell you Canfield was considering divorcing Catharine before the accident?"

Her eyebrows came up. "No. Maud gave the impression all wasn't roses with them, but nothing that drastic."

"That came from Isadora. What did you dig up on Canfield's death?"

"Quite a lot. I have Maud's testimony, of course, and Steve let me see all the police records."

"I'm particularly interested in it from Dore's point of view. She's had a memory lapse, and her reactions to his death are strange. It isn't just grief. Something happened that night that frightened her; terrified her, in fact."

Sean seemed peculiarly uncomfortable at that.

"Well, I'll give you what I have. According to the examining physician, death was due to cardiac arrest."

"That's a hell of a vague term."

"I know, but no one was curious enough to wonder about the exact cause of the arrest."

"So, no autopsy was done."

"No, and the body was cremated. That was the Senator's express wish."

"To whom did he express this wish?"

"His wife, his lawyer, and it was in his will."

"Oh. What about his medical history?"

"No record of prior attacks or any hint of heart trouble. You knew Isadora found his body?"

"Yes."

"There's no testimony from her on record. She was . . . in a state of shock. But she came home that night—"

"Yes, I know. I got her as far as the library door."

Sean glanced at him uneasily, then focused on her notes.

"Catharine said she was wakened at one-fifteen by—"

"How did she knew what time it was?"

"Braille watch."

"Oh, yes. Go on."

"She heard screams, and when she got no response from her husband on their intercom, she called Jenny. She also rang the servants' quarters. That's a separate building; an old coach house. Jenny went down to the library and found Isadora on the floor, hysterical, and John Canfield slumped over his desk. Catharine came downstairs, and when Jenny explained the situation, she called the police."

"Not a doctor?"

"Maud says Jenny took Isadora up to her bedroom, then the police, an ambulance, and Jim arrived more or less simultaneously. Catharine called Jim at his fraternity, and it isn't far from the house. Carleton showed up about then, too. Anyway, Jim went upstairs to take care of Isadora and sent Jenny down to help Catharine. A few minutes later, Jim came downstairs and asked one of the ambulance attendants to help him; Isadora was still hysterical."

"She was alone while he went for help?"

"Yes. The attendant went upstairs with him, and a little while later, Jim came back down—white as a sheet, according to Maud—and said Isadora had cut her wrists."

He asked tightly, "Do you know what she used?"

"A razor blade."

"Where did she get it?"

"Jenny testified that Isadora's overnight case was in her bathroom—that's where they found her—and a ladies' razor was on the floor with the blade removed."

"Single or double-edged?"

Sean had to check her notes. "Double-edged."

"Double-edged? All right, then what happened?"

"Another ambulance arrived, and two attendants went upstairs. About fifteen minutes later, they came down with Isadora." Sean glanced up at him. "She was on a stretcher, and from what Maud said, I assume heavily sedated."

"Where was she taken?"

"Morningdell Sanatorium."

"Morningdell?" It came with the solid sensation of a physical blow.

"Yes, it's a private men—"

"I know about Morningdell." One of the finest private hospitals in the country, catering to those who desired and could afford anonymity, specializing exclusively in one kind of illness: mental illness.

Then his hands came down hard on the arms of his chair.

"That's *it*, Sean. That *must* be it."

"That's what?"

"What she's been holding back; what she's been so afraid I'd find out. Damn." His breath came out in a weary sigh.

"Well, that's the answer to one of your questions—where Isadora was after her father's death."

"She was in Morningdell all that time? Over a month?"

"She was released February twenty-third and put on an out-patient status."

"What did you find out from the hospital?"

She gave a short, sarcastic laugh.

"Not a damned thing. Steve got the release date for me and the name of her psychiatrist. Dr. Milton Kerr."

Dr. K.

Conan reached for his cup, finding the coffee cold.

"What was the diagnosis?"

"*That* is a state secret. Morningdell protects its patients; that's partly what they pay for, and I guess they pay well. But Maud said she heard the family talking about it once, and she remembered the word, 'schizophrenia.' "

"Schizophrenia? What form?"

"Look, from Maud you're lucky to get the general idea. It came out something like 'skizzerfrizzled.' "

He nodded. "I'll have to talk to Dr. Kerr."

"Good luck. That place is like an armed fortress."

"Dore might provide a key to the gates for me." *If* she'd trust him, now that he knew her dark secret.

He looked out at the pristine sky, thinking of fear and its many masks, and the gaunt image of the Knight came inevitably to mind. And Jenny, who slashed at her soul's flesh in those torn canvases; a wordless cry for help. Isadora might be capable of answering that plea if she understood it; it might crack the armor of her own mistrust. Yet Jenny seemed to be purposely avoiding her, staying on the beach yesterday until they left the cottage, her bedroom door closed when Conan brought Isadora home last night, although the light in the window said she wasn't asleep. Somehow, he must find a way to talk to Jenny privately.

He frowned. That could wait; it was more important to talk to Isadora now. There were answers in her stay at Morningdell to more than her secretive attitude.

"Well, Sean, Charlie said you're damned good at digging up information. That was an understatement."

Her laugh was brief and constrained.

"Maybe *too* good? Conan, I'm sorry about Isadora."

"Sorry? Why?"

"Well, it sort of makes you wonder when you find out your client's been diagnosed as a schizo."

His eyes had a cool sheen even as he laughed.

"Yes, it makes you wonder. Harry's decided she's an addict, and the cottage is a den of drugged hedonism."

"*Is* she an addict?"

"Or is she insane? Makes you wonder. Was this her first mental crisis? Any prior history of mental illness?"

"None I could find."

He nodded. "Sean, we're still no closer to explaining the surveillance, and Dore's stay at Morningdell eliminates the one factor that made me doubt it was connected with John Canfield's death—that month-long gap before the tailing began. It wasn't necessary when she was in Morningdell. She wasn't going anywhere, and it'd be easy to keep track of any visitors she had."

"You don't think somebody's just worried about her trying suicide again?"

"No. Anyone seriously concerned about that would be wiser, and money ahead, to keep her in Morningdell rather than paying for full-time surveillance. Beside, Jenny was sent here to monitor Dore's emotional state." He hesitated. "Although, I think she's the one who needs monitoring."

Sean's brows were drawn in a perplexed line.

"How do you tie the surveillance to Canfield?"

"Not to him. His death."

"But, Conan—"

"Yes, I know. It was a heart attack, pure and simple, and I haven't any evidence to the contrary. Just a lot to wonder about. And a number of intriguing potential motives. A drug addict; a failing marriage to an ambitious woman—a relationship of long standing; an illegitimate son who may be Canfield's; a lawyer he may have intended to replace; and a will he may have intended to change."

"Don't forget a boyfriend who may have an interest in Isadora's future as an heiress."

Conan laughed. "Ah. Ben Meade. See what you can find out about his interest in Dore. Or perhaps I'll have a talk with him myself. Anyway, all this wondering isn't getting us anywhere. Anything else in that noteboook?"

"Sorry, but I've about blown my wad." Then after a glance at her watch: "About time, too. I'd like a fast tour of the local scene, then I'd better be on my way. I have to get back in time to put on my wig before I meet Maud."

"Your wig?"

"Red hair is a very conspicuous trait; I've found wigs quite useful. Maud knows me as a blonde."

Conan laughed at that. "You'd make a beautiful blonde, but you're a fantastic redhead."

"Well, the Irish is finally coming out."

"You inspire me, Sean." He reached for the phone. "I'll have Carl give you the tour. I want to talk to Dore. When you get back to Salem, see if you can find out where all the members of the family—and Carleton—were on the night of Canfield's murder."

"His *what*?"

He smiled crookedly. "Sorry. Habit, I guess. The night of his *death*. And if Maud goes along with that wild scheme of yours, just . . . be careful."

She sighed. "Conan, you worry too much."

"I hope you're right about that."

CHAPTER 12

Conan had just reached his front door and unlocked it when the silver Stingray roared to a stop a few yards away, and Isadora got out, looking morning crisp in a blue and white pantsuit. Class, he was thinking; wealth is a prerequisite, but never guarantees it.

"Dore, if you were any more prompt, I'd be late."

She laughed. "You called, sir, and I came. Posthaste."

"Incredibly posthaste. Come on in." He held the door for her. "Have you had breakfast?"

"Breakfast? It's nearly noon. But don't offer me lunch yet. I don't rise *that* early."

"Not with the hours you keep, I hope. Let's go out on the deck. It's a beautiful day."

She acquiesced with a willing smile and followed him through the living room to the glass door at the north end of the window wall. When she stepped out onto the deck, she paused to take a deep breath.

"It *is* beautiful. What happened to our April showers?"

He sat down on the bench lining the railing and looked out at the opalescent clouds fanning out from the horizon.

"They're coming; tomorrow or the next day. The barometer's dropping." He turned as she sat down beside him, then following the direction of her suddenly cold gaze, looked past her. Part of the beach access was visible.

"My escort has arrived," she noted.

"At least, he's dependable. I have a name for him, by the way."

"What is it? Fred Weird?"

"No, just plain Roger Garner. He and Hicks work for the Worth Detective Agency in Salem."

"Salem?" She frowned. "I wonder what that means."

"I don't know."

"And you *still* don't know who hired them?"

"Not yet."

"But, when—" She stopped, sighing. "I'm sorry. I don't mean to sound impatient."

"I know. Dore, you look awfully tired."

"I . . . I didn't sleep too well last night."

"Haven't you anything to take to help you sleep?"

"You mean sleeping pills? No. Dr. Johnson gave me some Seconal last year for a case of pre-concert nerves, but I don't like taking them. I suppose it's because of Mother. The bottle's still in my medicine cabinet at home."

He frowned at that, then called up a smile.

"I should give you the standard lecture on leaving dangerous drugs around, but I don't think I'll bother. Did you talk to Jenny this morning?"

"Oh, a few words, but we never really talk. Conan, I looked in her studio this morning while she was still asleep."

"What did you find?"

"Well, she'd cleaned it up; last night, probably, while I was at work. But I saw some stains on the floor, and all the canvases were gone. I think she burned them. There were a lot of ashes in the fireplace, and carpet tacks. She uses them to tack the canvas to the stretchers."

He had to smile at that. "You're quite a detective. Did she say anything to explain what happened?"

"No. She isn't even admitting anything happened, so I couldn't admit I knew about it. Oh, I managed to work in a casual reference to the Knight."

"What was her reaction?"

"Well, she seemed . . . upset. First she said she'd forgotten it, then she said she *wished* she could forget it. That seems an odd thing to say about one of her best works."

"I think it's to be taken with a grain of salt." He looked out at the gentle surf, letting the subject drop. He hadn't asked her here to talk about Jenny, but he hesitated now; there was no easy approach to what he had to say.

"Conan, what is it?"

He turned to face her. "I told you I had an operative working in Salem; Sean Kelly. She came down to report to me this morning."

He watched her turn away, her hands tightening on the railing.

"She came here to report? It must've been important."

"Look, I won't hedge with you. I know why you were so worried about her investigation. She told me about Morningdell."

A small muscle at the corner of her mouth tightened; in her eyes, fixed on the horizon, caged resentment flared.

"So. Now, you know. Your client is an escapee from a nut house. I guess that changes things, doesn't it?"

That cold challenge cut deep, but it was born of fear. He might have been annoyed that she underestimated him, except for an equivocal intimation of another kind of fear: fear that she *belonged* in a nut house.

He smiled at her. "An escapee? I was told you were *released* from Morningdell."

Her shoulders sagged. "Oh, Conan, I didn't want you to know."

"Why not?"

"At first it was only because I was afraid you wouldn't take me seriously about the surveillance."

"If it's a figment of your imagination, you have one hell of an imagination."

She smiled weakly, still not looking at him.

"There's more to it. When you're labeled *insane* it's worse than having some vile, contagious disease. I had a taste of it in Morningdell. Not that the insane aren't treated very well there; like prize specimens in a zoo, with great solicitude and even kindness. But not as human beings; not *equally* human beings. Conan, I was afraid it would change the way you felt about me, and I couldn't tolerate that; it's become too important to me."

He was at a loss for words, in the pendant silence, sharply aware of a fragility about her. Lucid as crystal, and as easily shattered.

Finally, he took her hands in his and for some time studied them as he might a finely constructed work of art.

"Look at these hands," he said quietly. "Bernini in the flesh, and yet they're probably capable of bending steel rods. More important, they're capable of bringing music out of a jumble of ivory and wire and doing it exceedingly well. A talent so unique isn't just a gift, it's an obligation. I know the scope of that covenant, Dore, and I have no choice but to honor it as you do."

She listened intently, and this oblique response seemed to satisfy her. She smiled, a smile reflected more in her eyes than the slight curve of her lips, then she leaned toward him, and he let his eyes close as he felt her mouth against his. It came to him with a dull shock that in some sense he was no less vulnerable than she.

When she looked up at him, her laughter was a welcome sound; it came so easily.

"Conan, you're a rare man."

He touched her hair, like silk under his hand.

"And you're a rare young woman; extraordinarily rare." Then he leaned back, reluctantly refocusing his thoughts while he lit a cigarette. "Dore, I have some questions. It seems I always do."

She sighed, then squared her shoulders.

"Well, that's your job, isn't it, asking questions?"

"My job is finding some answers. You talked about being labeled insane. What do *you* think?"

She turned away, uncertainty shadowing her eyes.

"I don't know. It never occurred to me before to question my sanity; not really. I think anyone suffering the normal slings and arrows of outrageous adolescence sometimes wonders, but I was actually a boringly well-adjusted child."

"What about after your mother's death?"

"It was bad, but there was no breakdown, or memory loss, or . . . unusual reactions."

"Unusual reactions? You mean like the other night at the Surf House?"

She nodded tensely. "Yes."

"Dore, it wasn't just the whiskey. You looked out at the beach and you saw something. What?"

Her eyelids fluttered closed and she shivered.

"Oh, I—I can't explain it. The colors all seemed to flicker somehow. I kept thinking, why don't they stay where they *belong*. And the lines of foam, they seemed to be writhing; alive, like . . . snakes." She pushed her hair back with a trembling hand. "The same sort of thing happened one day when I was practicing. The piece was a favorite of Dad's, but I wasn't really thinking about that. In the middle of it, my wrists seemed to . . . to stretch out and dwindle down to threads, but my hands were still playing."

"How long did it last?"

"Only a few seconds. They never last long."

"Any other?"

"Yes. Kelp. Those long strings of kelp that wash up on the beach. One day I stepped on one, and it seemed to wrap itself around my leg and crawl—" She stopped, her hand pressed to her mouth.

"All right, Dore. Were there others?"

"Not since I left Morningdell, and then only in the first week. Dr. Kerr put me on some sort of tranquilizer, and it seemed to help. I still have sessions with him every two weeks. I'm officially an out-patient."

"Have you discussed the surveillance with him?"

She sent him a oblique glance. "No."

"Why not?"

"Oh, he's very good, and I respect him; I even like him, but he tends to look at the world through neurosis-colored glasses. He'd consider it just another symptom."

Conan frowned; she didn't seem to realize the ramifications of that if she were right.

"Do you remember any of the 'unusual reactions' you had during the first week?"

"No. I mean, I couldn't describe them. There's nothing but . . . feelings." And obviously not pleasant ones.

"Any other symptoms since your release?"

"No. Just a few minor hallucinations. I guess I *am* insane, Conan. Most of the time I'm all right, but sane people don't have things like that going on in their heads."

"You'd be amazed at what 'sane' people have going on in their heads. Have you ever had any aural hallucinations?"

"What do you mean?"

"Sounds that aren't there; voices, for instance."

"No. You'd think I'd at least hear music."

"What does Dr. Kerr say about your sanity?"

"Not much; he's so damned cagey. I kept trying to pin him down, and he finally went out on a limb far enough to say I *might* be a *latent* schizoid." She paused, then, "Schizophrenia is the one they can't cure, isn't it?"

"I gather you've taken Psych I. Dore, it isn't that simple.

Schizophrenia has many forms; as many as each victim needs to satisfy the psychic demands made on him."

"You seem to have gone well past Psych I."

"Far enough to know better than to jump to conclusions." He took a puff on his cigarette, studying her. "What can you tell me about your stay in Morningdell?"

"Not much, really. At first, I thought I was in the university infirmary because of the flu. Of course, the virus didn't help matters any. My first clear memory was a week after Dad died, although I didn't remember he was dead. Jim was there. He came every day at first, and I'll always be grateful for that. I needed him desperately then."

"He told you about your father?"

"Yes. Just that he was dead. The details came out later in my sessions with Dr. Kerr. He seemed anxious to get at that lost week."

"And you?"

She frowned, and it was a moment before she answered.

"I'm not really sure I want to know about that week. I don't even like to think about it. That's when the hallucinations seem to—oh, Conan, I don't understand it. I mean, when Mother died, it was bad, but it wasn't anything like this. But maybe it's all just part of—of the symptoms."

He tapped the ash from his cigarette impatiently.

"Symptoms of insanity?"

She gave him a sharp look, then mustered a smile.

"Dr. Kerr had the same complaint. Self-diagnosis. Very dangerous, he says, but I can't stop wondering and looking for explanations."

"Well, it's hard to draw a line between 'know thyself' and self-diagnosis. Dore, I want to talk to Dr. Kerr."

"That's fine with me, but getting him to agree won't be so easy. I told you he's cagey."

"Yes, but a word from you would help, and I think I can line up a character reference that might impress him."

"From whom?"

"A man I studied with at Stanford a few years ago. I was a sort of assistant and guinea pig for some experiments he was conducting. Dr. Lawrence Decker."

She tilted her head to one side. "You know, I wouldn't be surprised to learn you had a degree in psychology."

"Sorry to disillusion you, but I can't claim a degree in anything. Will you talk to Dr. Kerr for me?"

"Of course, but I don't understand what this has to do with the surveillance." Then before he could protest, she added: "I do have faith, but I can't help wondering."

"And worrying? I have to look at all the angles, Dore. For instance, I've given some thought to what that 'label' of insanity does for you in a legal sense. You're an heiress, remember? Now, there's someone else I want to talk to, and I'll need a word from you again. Ben Meade."

"Ben? But—" She stopped herself before she asked *why*, and Conan laughed at that.

"Because he took you home the night your father died, and I assume his memory wasn't confused by flu."

She still had more *whys*, but she didn't voice them. He turned her face toward him, his hand against her cheek.

"Be patient, Isadora." Then he kissed her lightly. "By the way, do you have to work tonight?"

She gave him a slow smile.

"This is my night off, Conan."

He paused, then returned her smile.

"About time."

CHAPTER 13

The hectic hum of Salem's early morning traffic was audible in the distance, but here on the tree-shaded walks, the spacious lawns separating the venerable, red brick, college gothic buildings, was a purposeful hush.

Conan watched the students moving toward their rendezvous with teachers and classrooms as he moved toward a rendezvous of his own, taking a circuitous route that brought him finally to the Physics Building.

Near the entrance was a stone bench occupied by an angular young man totally absorbed in the book on his lap, lank blond hair falling forward over his forehead.

"Ben Meade?"

"Yes."

"I'm Conan Flagg."

Meade put his book aside, regarding Conan with a steady, speculative gaze as he sat down at the end of the bench.

"Description fits. Maybe Dore should've given me a password."

Conan laughed, although Meade didn't seem amused at his own attempt at humor.

"It isn't so Machiavellian as that. Miss Canfield explained my purpose here when she called you, didn't she?"

"She said you were private fuzz, and she hired you to 'find a lost week.' " His eyes, pale yellowish brown, had the vitreous gleam of amber. "She also said she trusts you."

Conan curbed his inclination to smile at the shading of jealous suspicion in that.

"Obviously, she trusts you, too. This is a very personal inquiry. She gave me specific instructions; none of her family or friends are to be told about it without her approval."

"Is that what you call a subtle hint? Dore told me to keep it to myself, and I will." His steady gaze faltered. "How . . . how is she?"

"She seems to be quite well."

"Did she say when she's coming back to school?"

"She hasn't discussed her plans with me." He paused, watching Meade's face. "She speaks very highly of you."

"Highly?" He laughed bitterly. "Look, I know what you mean. It won't be news to Dore that I'm in love with her, and it isn't news to me that it's one-sided. But I've got patience, if that's what it takes, and I'm not afraid of her money or her name." He hesitated, then: "Mr. Flagg, I have a class at eight. Dore said you wanted to ask me some questions."

Conan didn't respond for a moment. He was trying to assess the depth of purpose behind those quiet eyes. Isadora called him single-minded, and no doubt she judged him well.

"Ben, Miss Canfield's memory lapse begins the night of her father's death. What I'm trying to do now is reconstruct the events of that night as accurately as possible. How are your powers of recall?"

"I have nearly perfect recall," he said with a curiously egoless confidence.

"Good. I'm particularly interested in details. Sometimes a very trivial incident or image will bring back a memory."

He took a notebook from his breast pocket. His jottings would be superfluous; it was primarily a prop, useful because it was expected. "Miss Canfield said you took her to the infirmary when she became ill, then to her dormitory to pick up a few personal things."

Meade leaned forward, resting his elbows on his knees.

"Yes, then I drove her home."

"Let's start there. That's where her memory begins to fail. I understand the house is surrounded by a stone wall and there's a gate on the drive. Do you remember if it was open?"

"Yes. It's always left open."

"All right. Now, when you were approaching the house, do you remember seeing anything—a car, for instance—on the drive?"

"Not on the drive, but there was one parked outside the gate on the street."

"What kind of car? I mean, was there anything unusual about it?"

"Well, I guess I noticed it because I'm kind of a sports car nut; I have an old MGA. It was a Lotus Elan."

Conan made an indecipherable notation, disciplining his features against any real show of interest.

"What color was it?"

"I don't know; the light wasn't very good. It was a dark color, though. It looked like Jim's car, but I guess he was at the Lambda Delt house that night."

"Did you see anything else unusual, or maybe Miss Canfield commented on something she noticed?"

"I don't remember anything like that."

"Were there any lights on in the house?"

"Only the one in the library. It's a spooky old place, you know. I remember thinking how weird it looked with just the one light."

"The porch light wasn't on?"

"No. I guess they weren't expecting anybody at that time of night."

Isadora's words found an echo in that . . . *no one was expecting me.*

''What time was it when you arrived—approximately?''

''I can tell you exactly: 12:28.''

Conan stared blankly at him.

''Are you sure of that?''

His eyes narrowed. ''I'm sure. Dore said something about her dad working late, and I looked at my watch.''

Conan scrawled a few words in the notebook to give himself time to recover, then moved hurriedly to the next question.

''You took her into the house then?''

''Yes.''

''She says she's sure she had a suitcase with her. Did she?''

''Not exactly a suitcase. One of those small overnight cases. I carried it in for her and left it by the library door.'' His big hands knotted together. ''Then she told me to go on; said her father would look after her. That's one of those 'if only I'd known' things. Damn, I should've stayed with her.''

''But you couldn't have known, Ben, could you?''

Meade shot him a quick, searching look, but Conan only smiled vaguely and turned a fresh page.

''Now, perhaps you could describe the foyer for me as it was that night.''

He leaned back, frowning in concentration.

''Well, the only light was a table lamp upstairs on the landing. When you go into the foyer, there's a set of double doors on both sides. The ones on the left go into what you'd call a parlor, I guess; the ones on the right into the library. Then straight ahead, on the left, there's a door leading to the kitchen and dining room and the back of the house. All the doors were closed.''

''Could you see any of the upstairs rooms?''

''Yes. The Senator's and Mrs. Canfield's bedrooms are at the top of the stairs. I think . . . yes, both doors were open, but there weren't any lights.''

"Miss Canfield said you'd been in the house several times. Did you see anything—well, out of place; different?"

"No. Nothing ever gets changed around because of Mrs. Canfield. I mean, her being blind. I wish there *had* been something different; something to give me a warning."

"Do you remember any unusual sounds?"

He thought a moment, then shook his head.

"No, I didn't hear anything. Of course, I wasn't inside the house more than two minutes total."

"When you were leaving you heard nothing? No cries or screams?"

"You mean from Dore?" he asked hotly. "If I had, do you think I'd have just driven off?"

Conan put a hint of apology in his reply. "No, of course not. Well, that should cover it then, unless you can think of something I haven't asked about."

Meade loosed a sigh. "No. Everything was so . . . so normal. The only thing I was worried about was Dore. She was so sick, and it hit so damned fast. Maybe that's why she can't remember anything."

Conan didn't point out that amnesia wasn't generally associated with viral infections. He made a show of checking his notes, nodding approvingly.

"Perhaps some of this will serve to revive her memory. You went directly to the Lambda Delta house after you left her? I thought she might've tried to phone you or Jim when she found her father."

"Well, I didn't go straight to the house. I took a drive up the West Bank Road. Didn't get back till two."

Conan wondered why he volunteered that, especially the time of his return.

"Did you talk to Jim about the Senator's death or Miss Canfield?"

"No. Nothing beyond the usual word of sympathy. Jim and I aren't exactly buddies. He's out of my league. I mean, I can't afford to approach life as one big party."

He closed his notebook, choosing his words carefully.

"I understand Jim hasn't adjusted to wealth and prestige too well."

Meade laughed sarcastically. "Oh, he's adjusted fine. If John Canfield had known about some of the parties Jim threw at that beach house, he probably would've *un*adopted him fast."

Conan smiled at that. "Those parties were a mainstay of gossip in Shanaway. On the third telling, they made Hollywood's versions of Roman orgies sound tame."

Meade was relaxing now with the notebook out of sight.

"Well, the music was different. I went to one of his parties. It was supposed to be just some guys from the fraternity; a weekend surfing. But Jim brought a few cases of booze and some girls. I'm not against booze and girls, but I don't think any of those chicks had seen eighteen yet, and besides, somebody pulled out some pot and acid, and I don't have a Senator to bail me out if *I* get busted. Then when Jim started playing games with hypnosis, I'd about had it." He paused, laughing at the memory. "The funny part was, after he put on this big build-up, he couldn't get the girl under. She just sat there and giggled. Jim's big with games, you know."

"Yes, I got that impression. I'm not sure I'd find him entertaining."

Meade shrugged, turning predictably defensive.

"Oh, sometimes he's a real kick. Like he has this routine with imitations; the famous people bit, voices and the whole bag. He's damned good, too. I've seen a lot worse on TV. Jim's all right. I mean, if you ever need anything, he'll come through with no strings."

He nodded. "Miss Canfield said he's unusually free with his car, at least, which surprised me."

"Sure. Any of the guys want to impress a chick with the fancy wheels, he'll turn over the keys, except when *he's* doing the impressing, which is quite a lot."

"He has an Elan? That's a beautiful piece of machinery. Have you ever driven it?"

"Yes. But not because I needed it to line up any dates. I told you I dig sports cars." He frowned uneasily. "Look, Mr. Flagg, don't—well, I mean, I'd just as soon all this about Jim didn't get back to Dore."

"Don't worry. I'm well aware that she's a little biased when it comes to Jim."

"Well, he's all she's got to call family now, and like I said, he's all right. Maybe I just envy him."

"Envy him what?"

"Oh, the money, I guess." His eyes were cold slits, the amber light glinting. "Everything that goes with it."

Conan made no response except a polite smile, wondering if in Ben's mind "everything that goes with it" included Isadora Canfield. Then he looked at his watch and rose.

"Ben, you'll be late for class if I keep you longer."

Meade stood up and gathered his books.

"Look, if there's anything I can do for Dore . . ."

"You've already done a great deal for her in answering my questions. Thanks."

He hesitated, then with an uneasy shrug turned away.

"Tell her I miss her."

Conan didn't return directly to the parking lot where he left his car; he made a detour to the Student Union and a phone booth. The call went to Steve Travers.

"Conan, you're running up a hell of a phone bill calling me every other day."

"This one is cheap, Steve. I'm in Salem."

"Oh. Well, where're you calling from?"

"A phone booth."

"What's the matter? You don't want to be seen around low types like cops?"

Conan was watching the people moving in and out of the building closely, and he laughed at that.

"Exactly. I had a tail when I left Holliday Beach this morning, but I think I shook him."

"A tail? Okay, I suppose you have a license number for me to check."

"Yes, as a matter of fact. Tan Chevy, Oregon BLC381."

"Got it. Anything else on your mind?"

"How are your relations with the Salem city police?"

Travers laughed. "That depends on why you're asking. If they're good, I'm not sure I want to risk fouling them up with any of your bright ideas."

"Would you take that risk for Sean Kelly?"

"For Sean I'd lay my badge on the line. By God, Conan, if I wasn't a happily married man—"

"You'd still be courting Marcie Schultz. Right?"

"Probably. What's this about Sean?"

"She conned the Canfields' housekeeper into leaving town for a few days while she takes her place. She assures me she can take care of herself, but I'd feel better if I knew you could get the local police to her fast."

"Tell her to call me if she needs help; I'll see that she gets it. Now, what's going on with this Canfield thing?"

He hesitated, the muscles of his jaw tensing.

"I'm not sure, but there's a new factor in the equations. Drugs. That's why I'm a little worried about Sean."

"*Drugs*. Now, listen, what are you—I mean, if you've turned up anything—"

Conan let him splutter a few seconds, then cut in, "Steve, I can't tell you any more about it. Not now."

"What do you mean? You expect me just to *ignore* it?"

"I expect you to give me time to find out what's going on before you jump in with both flat feet. All you'd come up with now is one sad user, and if I'm reading this thing right, the drugs are just the tip of the iceberg."

"Okay, so what's at the bottom of the iceberg?"

"Murder."

"Oh, for God's sake—*whose* murder?"

"John Canfield's."

"Sure, anything you say. But just as a matter of curiosity, how do you turn a heart attack into a murder?"

"You must've missed the class on poisons at the police academy. However, I'm not too worried about that little detail now. Do you have the report on Canfield's death handy?"

"Just a minute, it's on my desk somewhere. I had it out for Sean. Oh—here. What do you want to know?"

"What time did Catharine say it was when she first heard Dore screaming?"

"Uh, let's see . . . here it is: 1:15 A.M."

"I just talked to Ben Meade. He's the young man who—"

"Yes, I know. Sean asked me about him."

"All right. Dore told me she started to go into the library to tell her father she was home as soon as Ben left the house. He says he left at 12:30."

Travers was silent for a while, then he asked guardedly, "This Meade, he'd swear to the time?"

"I didn't ask him, but I'm sure he would." Especially, Conan added to himself, if Ben thought it advisable to establish his departure from the house at that point. "Steve, if he's right, I want to know what happened in the forty-five minutes between 12:30 and 1:15."

"What does your client say about it?"

"Nothing. She remembers nothing after she started to go into the library until she woke up at Morningdell a week later."

"Well, where does that leave you?"

"Up a creek."

"And you want me to hand you a paddle?"

Conan managed a laugh. "I'm just asking you to give me a little elbow room, but have that paddle handy."

"Okay. But damn it, keep me up to date on this."

"I will. Steve, I have to go; I have an appointment."

"What kind of appointment?"

"A doctor's appointment."

"I hope it's a head doctor. I think you need one."

"As a matter of fact, it is."

CHAPTER 14

A fortress, even if it appeared to be nothing more formidable than an old Georgian mansion reincarnated in a more functional guise. Sean Kelly's description of Morningdell Sanatorium was apt, Conan thought, as he waited at the third check-point—Dr. Milton Kerr's reception room—where a blue-haired woman in a white uniform was speaking into the inter-office phone.

The first check-point was at the ornate iron gates where a uniformed guard made the first phone call, then directed him down a road lined with flowering plums in full vernal glory to the hospital, which was set in an expanse of lawn better tended than most golf courses.

The second check-point was in the large, sunlit lobby where another uniformed personage stopped him at the desk and made another phone call. He was then sent up a curving stairway to the second floor and this last check-point.

The receptionist hung up the phone, managing to do it without a sound, and motioned toward the door behind her.

"You may go in now. Dr. Kerr is expecting you."

He sighed. "I should hope so."

The room behind the door was spacious and decorous, with white enameled woodwork, Delft blue carpet and drapes, and well-stocked bookcases. Between the tall windows on the opposite wall, a massive mahogany desk presided with a cushioned armchair in attendance before it. The man behind the desk was in his forties, his bearing and appearance as refined and as calculatingly comfortable as his surroundings, his smile courteous and noncommittal.

"Mr. Flagg, won't you sit down?"

"Thank you, Doctor."

Milton Kerr waited until Conan was seated, then began: "I think it only fair to tell you I'm a little dubious about this interview, but you had a very persuasive advocate in Isadora." Then he added casually: "I called Lawrence Decker at Stanford, incidentally. He remembered you. In fact, he was—well, for Decker, quite complimentary."

Conan laughed. "Then he called me nothing more insulting than a damned dilettante?"

"Something like that." His smile warmed a little. "I've also had the privilege of studying under Decker, by the way." He paused, his thoughtful scrutiny subtly shaded with skepticism. "Isadora gave me no satisfactory reason as to why she was so anxious for me to see you."

"Perhaps because I'm the one who's anxious to see you."

Kerr coolly declined comment on that.

"May I ask the nature of your relationship with her?"

"It began as a client-consultant relationship, but obviously it's more personal at this point."

"A client-consultant relationship?"

"Yes. Among other things, I'm a licensed private investigator."

There was a spark of interest in his eyes at that.

"That's how you make your living?"

"Perhaps it's one of the ways I *justify* my living. Doctor,

Isadora said you diagnosed her as a latent schizoid. Is that true?"

He frowned slightly, taken off guard.

"It's true I told her she *may* be a latent schizoid, and perhaps I was in error to give her what I tried to make clear was a tentative diagnosis."

"But you *do* regard her as a latent schizoid?"

"Mr. Flagg, obviously Isadora has great faith in you, but that doesn't justify my discussing her case with you."

"Especially if my concern is simply idle curiosity?" He smiled as Kerr's eyebrow came up a sixteenth of an inch. "I assure you it's far more than that. Your diagnosis may be of crucial importance to her. Now, I'll assume you wouldn't lie to her in saying she *may* be a latent schizoid."

"Of course not," he replied, a little sharply.

"I'll also assume you were being conservative with her, and actually you consider her more than a *latent* schizoid."

"I cannot, unfortunately, prevent you from making assumptions. Mr. Flagg, you speak of Isadora as a client. Perhaps you could explain that."

Conan repressed a smile at that deft shift of subject.

"Explain it? I sell a service, just as you do. She hired me, which makes her a client."

"Hired you? May I ask why?"

"Isadora has great faith in you, too, Doctor, but that shouldn't justify my discussing her case with you." He blunted that barb with a slight smile. "But your position as her psychiatrist *does* justify it."

"If it's justified, then you might start by answering my question. Why did she hire you?" He was annoyed, but curious now, and perhaps a little uneasy.

"First, I should tell you how she approached me. It was rather unusual. She didn't call me, or come to my office, or make an appointment by mail. Instead, she slipped an anonymous message into my place of business. The gist of it was that she wanted to meet with me, alone, at *my* house, and insisted on entering by a back door."

The doctor was shocked enough to frown at that.

"Did she offer any explanation for this approach?"

"Yes. She said the secrecy was necessary to make sure no one found out she was seeing me privately."

Kerr hesitated, his tone cautiously constrained as he asked, "Was she concerned about someone in particular?"

Conan nodded, but didn't answer the question directly. "Doctor, consider a hypothetical case. Isadora Canfield comes to you in some similarly secretive manner and explains it by telling you she's being followed; that two men are constantly watching her, day and night."

Kerr learned forward. "She told you that?"

"This is a hypothetical case. She's talking to you."

"Oh, very well. Does she say who these men are?"

"She doesn't know. She thinks one of them lives at Shanaway, and says he drives a red Ford."

"Red?" A hint of regret, even defeat, etched his disciplined feature. "What else does she say about these men?"

"Very little, except she first noticed them soon after she moved to Shanaway. She's never spoken to them, and they've made no overtly threatening moves; they simply follow and watch her. Now, my question is this: If Dore came to you with this story, what would your reaction be?"

Kerr studied him for some time before he replied.

"I assume these 'hypothetical' statements were actually made to you, and your real question is what should *your* reaction be." He paused, but not for a response from Conan; he seemed to be trying to come to grips with a decision. "I'm . . . disappointed Isadora hasn't discussed this with me. I thought her condition a temporary one catalyzed by her father's death, but I'm at a great disadvantage, first because her initial symptoms were confused by physical illness and grief, and now because I'm getting this second hand."

"I'm only asking for a hypothetical reaction, Doctor."

"Then *hypothetically,*" he said with an edge of impatience, "I'd have to reconsider my decision to release her."

"You'd suggest she return to Morningdell?"

"Yes, I'd certainly consider that advisable."

"And if she didn't wish to return?"

"I'd be helpless, unless her family was willing to go through the legal procedures necessary to commit her."

Her family. The words had a hollow ring, as if he were hearing them through Isadora's ears. But when he spoke, he carefully restrained the impulse to irony.

"Wouldn't you consider investigating her story?"

"Investigating it?"

"Occam's Razor; dispose of the most obvious possibility first; in this case, the possibility that she's telling the simple truth."

Kerr stiffened. "The truth is seldom simple when you're dealing with unstable minds, and with Isadora you'll admit the instability has been amply demonstrated."

"Has it?" Then he shrugged. "I'll admit *something* has been demonstrated. Fortunately, *my* judgment wasn't clouded with preconceptions about her mental equilibrium."

"Clouded? Really, that's hardly appropriate—"

"Doctor, Isadora hired me to find out why she's being followed and by whom. Before questioning her sanity, I began *investigating* her story. That included hiring three operatives to assist me. I can assure you she is in fact under full-time surveillance by two men, one of whom drives a red Ford, any symbolism being purely coincidental. Their names are Albert Hicks and Roger Garner, and they're employed by the Worth Detective Agency in Salem. They've also bugged the phone at the Canfield beach house, and today someone went to the trouble of tailing *me* from Holliday Beach."

Milton Kerr's professional façade crumbled; he stared at Conan, open-mouthed, the color draining from his face.

"What are you saying? Do you mean—"

"I mean Dore *was* telling the simple truth. Forgive me for testing you, but perhaps now you can understand why I consider your diagnosis so crucial. If you'd been asked to testify in court on her mental competence, what would your expert opinion have been?"

Kerr sagged back into his chair.

"Well . . . on the basis of the data previously available to me I . . . suppose I'd have testified that her mental competence was at least in doubt." He paused, frowning. "But that data still hasn't been negated."

"No, it hasn't, but weren't you diagnosing the surveillance as paranoia? I'm only saying that the data on which you based your original diagnosis might also bear investigation. And please keep in mind that Dore is heir to an estate valued in the millions." Then he gave Kerr a slanted smile. "If you'd like to test *me*, I suggest you call Steve Travers at State Police headquarters."

Kerr was still pale, his expression distinctly anxious as he reached for the phone.

"Mr. Flagg, I'll take that suggestion."

Conan gave him the number, then left his chair to go to the bookshelves. This was only in part to give the doctor a semblance of privacy for his call. He was looking for a particular book, and knowing Kerr had studied with Lawrence Decker, he wasn't surprised to find it here. He opened it to the title page. *Experiments with Psychotomimetic Drugs.*

When at length he heard the click of the receiver, he returned to his chair and casually put the book on the desk.

"I have a copy of this myself; first edition and autographed. One of my most prized possessions."

Kerr only glanced at it, but his eyes narrowed speculatively. Then he leaned back, regarding Conan with the subdued sobriety of a man stripped of a cherished delusion.

"Mr. Travers bears you out entirely. It occurs to me, as I'm sure it has to you, that Isadora may be the victim of some sort of conspiracy. I'm well aware that an appalling number of people are committed to mental hospitals to serve someone else's purposes. But I can't act on a possibility.''

There was still a hint of skeptical challenge in that, but Conan was satisfied.

''I can't give you any concrete evidence at this point. I need more information; that's why I'm here.''

''I'll help if I can, of course, but I hope you understand I can't divulge privileged communications.''

''I doubt the information I need falls under that heading. I'm interested in events, primarily. I just want to know what happened while Isadora was here.''

'All right, Mr. Flagg. Just a moment.'' He reached for the intercom. ''Miss Dorn, bring me Isadora Canfield's file, please.''

Miss Dorn, the blue-haired receptionist, proved to be a woman of exemplary efficiency; she produced the file in less than two minutes. When she retired, Dr. Kerr opened the folder with a reluctant sigh.

''What in particular did you want to know?''

''I'm not sure in particular. Let's start with Dore's admission.''

''Very well.'' He frowned at the file. ''We sent an ambulance out in response to a call from Mrs. Canfield. Isadora was taken immediately to Emergency where Dr. Hayward treated her for a severe viral infection and her injuries; the cuts on her wrists, which were, fortunately, superficial.''

''Do you know if she said anything to Dr. Hayward?''

''Nothing coherent enough for him to understand; I questioned him. She was under heavy sedation when she arrived.''

''When did you first see her?''

''Early the next morning. She thought she was in the university infirmary and had no memory of her father's death. I deferred further questioning and put her on a no-visitors status because of her illness, but when her stepbrother arrived, I let him talk to her for a few minutes.''

"Was Catharine or Jenny with him?"

"No. In fact, they visited her only once, a few days later. Isadora asked that I not allow them to return."

He smiled at that. "Did she say why?"

"No, but she's obviously quite antagonistic toward her stepmother, which isn't unusual, and she's transferred some of this antagonism to Jenny."

"Did you talk to Jenny?"

"Yes, later I talked to all the family privately."

"What did you think of her?"

He considered the question, or perhaps Conan's motives for asking it.

"I think she has some very serious problems of her own, and frankly, I wish I could help her, but I can't until she's ready to reach out for help."

Conan nodded. "I understand Jim was quite faithful in his visits to Dore."

"Yes. I think that more than anything else helped her recover as well as she did from her father's death."

"Did Bob Carleton visit her at any time?"

"Carleton? Oh—the attorney. Only once. That is, he came here with the intention of seeing her. He had some legal papers which needed her signature."

"Legal papers? When she was in a mental hospital?"

"I questioned that myself. He said they were routine; without them the probation of the will would be delayed."

"Doctor, I know the will was probated with no delays."

"That doesn't surprise me. At any rate, Isadora refused to see him or accept his calls."

"I see. Did she have any more hysterical outbursts like the one that occurred the night her father died?"

Kerr turned a typewritten sheet in the folder.

"Yes. That first morning. Uncontrollable hysteria and hallucinations; a fairly typical schizoid attack. Unfortunately, I was occupied with another emergency at the time. Dr. Hayward gave her a Thorazine injection. She still had a high fever, so she may have had some delirium, although Jim said she was quite calm when he saw her earlier."

"Were there any other attacks?"

"Yes, the next day, in fact, while Jim was visiting her. He said she asked why her father didn't come see her. He tried to make excuses—I'd asked him not to tell her about his death—but apparently she guessed something was wrong."

"Were you present when this second attack occurred?"

He sighed. "No. At the time I was testifying at an HEW hearing. After that there were no more attacks, but no return of her memory. By the end of the week, I felt she'd recovered enough physically to be told about her father. I asked Jim to do it, but in my presence."

"How did she react to it?"

"Very strongly, of course, but she remained entirely rational. A week later I began analytic sessions with her. She was very cooperative, although the memory block on her father's death persisted."

"Isn't that memory block unusually strong?"

"Perhaps, but it's not an uncommon response to grief."

"Did you try to break it?"

"Yes, of course, but only with analytic techniques. Perhaps later I'll go to drugs or hypnosis, but she isn't ready for that yet."

Conan frowned. "That readiness might prove a costly luxury for her. Did she have any other visitors or calls?"

Kerr checked the file. "No. Of course, both Isadora and her family were reluctant to let anyone, even her friends, know she was in a mental hospital."

"I had a taste of that reluctance. Were there any unusual occurrences at all? Not necessarily anything that would go into your records; something you might remember."

He gave the question long and serious consideration.

"No. In fact, Isadora's history here was remarkably uneventful. She was an ideal patient, and there were no outside factors to cause any setbacks. When I learned about the beach cottage, and Jenny agreed to stay there with her, I was convinced full recovery was only a matter of time.'

He nodded absently. "Doctor, this might fall under the heading of privileged communication, but it's extremely important. Did she ever tell you anything at all about what happened when she found her father's body?"

"No. I could never get her past the conscious memory of the library door. I can't shed any light on what actually happened that night."

"I was afraid of that. I talked to Ben Meade, the young man who took her home that night. He left before she went into the library, so he couldn't shed much light, either, but he did give me one puzzling piece of information."

"Oh? What was it?"

"When he left her, she said she was going in immediately to talk to her father. That was at 12:30, according to Ben. But Mrs. Canfield said she first heard Dore screaming at 1:15. Can you suggest any explanation for that forty-five-minute time lapse?"

Kerr frowned. "Is Meade absolutely sure of the time?"

"Yes. He may be lying, but if not, I'd like to know what happened in that forty-five minutes."

The doctor fumbled for an answer, brows drawn, and there was little conviction in his response.

"Well, I suppose she may have fainted; finding him dead would be a tremendous shock. But to remain unconscious so long would be highly unusual."

"I'd probably be satisfied with that except for the surveillance—among other things. And her reactions to her father's death are strange. It's more than grief; it's fear."

"It *is* quite intense, but there could be many explanations for that. Guilt, for instance."

"The universal solvent? By the way, did she discuss her aversion for snakes with you?"

"At some length, and I consider it a true phobia."

"Did she mention any aural hallucinations?"

Kerr hesitated. "No, and that surprised me."

"Rather atypical, but I didn't find it surprising." He smiled slightly at Kerr's raised eyebrow. "I've taken enough of your time, Doctor. I have only one more question. Do you have any reason to think Isadora might take addictive or hallucinogenic drugs?"

He shook his head decisively. "No. I think it highly unlikely she ever has or ever will. Her emotional needs are quite different from those that usually lead to drug abuse."

Conan rose and took a business card from his breast pocket. Under his name he'd added the special line number.

"If you need to contact me, please use this number. And thank you for your help."

"You have my number." Then he added in a chastened tone, "I've been guilty of bad judgment, and I hope Isadora can forgive that. She's still my patient; I want to help her."

"Doctor, she may need all the help she can get."

The drive back from Salem was a scenic feast in any season, but with the heavy traffic, it seemed almost interminable. Friday, and the weekend exodus from the inland cities to the beaches was even worse than usual; it was also the beginning of spring vacation.

When Conan finally achieved the refuge of home, he indulged himself with a light bourbon and water, well iced, and retired to the library. He pulled the transparent inner drapes against the afternoon glare, looking up at the cloud-mottled sky. The forerunners, he thought, his gaze shifting down to the storm clouds gathering at the horizon.

He went to the desk, and it wasn't until he had the compartment open and the phone out that he realized he'd been purposely avoiding the Knight.

He looked at it now, thinking of its enigmatic creator. Can a soul cased in armor reach out for help?

The buzzing of the phone startled him; he picked up the receiver with a terse, "Hello."

"Well, you must've been right on top of the phone."

He smiled and relaxed as he reached for his glass.

"Almost, Sean. I tried to call you earlier; I was in Salem, but I couldn't track you down."

"I was probably out shopping. The toughest part of this assignment so far has been finding a decent maid's uniform. Look, I'm in a phone booth, so it's safe to talk."

"I hope no one's waiting for the phone. I had a very informative trip, and I'd better tell you about it."

"Nobody's beating on the door. Let me get my notebook."

He spent the next twenty minutes filling her in and answering questions. She was openly and gratifyingly amazed that he'd breached the walls of Morningdell.

"You've had a busy day," she said when he finished. "I haven't much to show in comparison, except I'm all set to begin my domestic duties at the Canfield house tomorrow."

"Any problems?"

"No. Maud got her 'emergency' call and set up the substitution with Catharine. I guess she could care less. Anyway, I report to Mrs. Blackstone at ten tomorrow morning."

"Not to Catharine?"

"She can't be bothered with lining out temporary help. Alma's supposed to show me the ropes. I'll be living in Maud's apartment in the servants' quarters."

"All right. Oh—I have a mission for you when you get settled. Check Dore's medicine cabinet for an old prescription of Seconal."

"Okay. Anything else?"

"Not at the moment. What are your plans, Sean?"

"Mainly just to keep my eyes and ears open, and plant a few bugs in strategic places. Just general snooping."

"Be careful. Please."

"Conan, taking unnecessary risks is a sign of slipshod technique. Incidentally, I checked the police records on Canfield's death again and got those alibis for you."

"Alibis? You sound like you're becoming a believer."

"I should doubt my boss's word? Anyway, Catharine was tucked in bed. Jim was at the Lambda Delt house; three brothers vouched for him. Bob Carleton was at home in bed. Alone, I assume. And Ben Meade was with your client."

Conan smiled; he hadn't asked her to check Ben's alibi.

"Yes, but my client doesn't know what happened after Ben supposedly left her."

"Neither does anybody else. By the way, I'll be answering the phone; that's one of Maud's duties. And I'll be using an alias. Sean Reilly."

"Not *O'*Reilly? Will you be a blonde?"

She laughed. "No, that wig gets tiresome full-time, and Maud will be off in Calamity Falls, or whatever."

"Klamath Falls. Sean, you may be seeing me tomorrow."

"You mean at the Canfield house?"

"Yes, I want to meet this so-called family. I haven't talked to Dore yet, but I'm planning an *un*planned jaunt to Salem. I want to be sure we aren't expected."

"Are you going to tell Miss Canfield about me?"

"Yes, but don't worry, she won't blow your cover for you."

"Okay, I'll be looking for you."

CHAPTER 15

Beyond the ivy-drenched stone walls, the roofs of the Canfield mansion loomed in awesome pitches of black slate studded with gables and chimneys, every ridge spiked with wrought iron. Against the dark slopes soared a magnificent, gleaming white turret, an outburst of Victorian whimsey as elaborate and airily ephemeral as a wedding cake.

Conan had the top down on the XK-E, so mesmerized only Isadora's warning gasp averted a collision with the gatepost as he turned off Mission Drive. They laughed together while the shaded drive led them to the porch and gracious train of steps he remembered from the snapshot in Isadora's billfold.

Then abruptly his focus of attention shifted as he stopped the car—directly behind a black Lotus Elan.

"Bob Carleton," Isadora said coldly.

Conan nodded, taking a glance at his watch: 12:25. "Yes, we're in luck."

"Since when is running into Bob a piece of luck?"

"Since now. I want to meet him, too."

As they climbed the steps to the front door, Isadora was tensely silent. She hadn't welcomed this trip, and the brave front she'd put up for him was slipping a little now.

"By the way," he said quietly, "we've been tailed since we left Holliday Beach. No, don't use your key." He pressed the door bell. "I want to be sure Sean knows we're here."

She only nodded, waiting silently until Sean, uniformed in black with a ruffled white cap perched winsomely atop her red hair, ushered them into the foyer. A grandfather clock ticked sedately, and the air smelled of wax and wood; a brown and ivory space with dark wainscoating and polished parquet floors. The double doors on each side were closed.

"May I take your wraps?" Sean asked. Isadora, who was wearing a light cardigan, shook her head absently, but Conan surrendered his jacket, recognizing a cue.

"Catharine and Carleton have been locked up in the library since I arrived," Sean told him, keeping her voice low. "I haven't seen either one of them yet."

"What about Mrs. Blackstone?"

"She went out for groceries about half an hour ago."

He frowned at the closed doors. "You'd better tell Catharine we're here. We'll wait in the parlor. Dore?"

"I'm coming." She looked back when Sean knocked at the library doors, but turned away quickly before they opened.

The parlor was a sunlit room full of Victorian bric-a-brac and plush upholstery. A couch and a few armchairs were grouped along the borders of a fine Aubusson. He heard voices from the library, but chose to ignore them, watching Isadora as she went to the windows overlooking the drive, tension evident in her every movement. When he put his hand on her shoulder, she mustered a smile, but it disappeared at the sound of the library door closing.

He turned, hearing a faint tapping that ceased as Catharine Canfield stopped in the doorway. Sean waited behind her, but it was Catharine who commanded his full attention.

And no doubt she was accustomed to command; her proud, regal posture defied her small stature. She was impeccably groomed, her light brown hair graying, but perfectly coiffed, and the frames of the dark glasses masking her eyes matched exactly the pale blue of her dress.

She turned her head to her right.

"Miss . . . Reilly, is it?"

"Yes, ma'am."

"Tell Mrs. Blackstone to bring coffee."

"Mrs. Blackstone went out for groceries, ma'am, but I can prepare a tray. She showed me where to find everything."

"Very well, then. Thank you."

As Sean hurried away, Catharine came into the room smiling, the white cane moving ahead of her in tapping arcs.

"Isadora?"

Conan was waiting for that; the inflections given a name were so often revealing. He was assured that Isadora's antagonism was reciprocated, but she would never be Catharine's equal in subtlety or control; her tone was too obviously tight and edgy.

"Yes, Catharine. I'm by the windows."

"What a delightful surprise." Her cane touched one of the chairs facing the center of the room, and she rested a hand on the back of it. "Jim will be so happy to see you."

Isadora seemed both to come alert and to relax.

"Is Jim coming today?"

She touched her watch. "He *should* be here now, but you know how he is. You have a guest with you?"

"Oh, yes, I'm sorry. Catharine, this is Conan Flagg. Conan, my stepmother, Catharine Canfield."

"Mrs. Canfield, I'm delighted to meet you."

Her head turned, homing in on the sound of this voice.

"It's always a pleasure to meet Isadora's friends. Please, make yourselves comfortable." She tapped her way around the chair and seated herself, smiling attentively as Conan sat down beside Isadora on the couch.

"Well, Isadora, you must give me a description of Mr. Flagg—if he'll forgive my curiosity."

She gave him a sidelong look. "Oh, I guess tall, dark, and handsome would do it. And a true native son."

"A . . . native son?"

"Conan's half Nez Percé, and not much of the Irish came through. At least, not on the *out*side."

Catharine's smile wavered. "Oh. How interesting."

Her constrained tone was ironically, if not bitterly familiar to him, nor did Isadora miss the hint of condescension.

"Oh, Catharine, you *must* remember the Flaggs."

"Well, I'm afraid—"

"Conan's father was *Henry* Flagg. You know, the Ten-Mile Ranch near Pendleton?"

One eyebrow arched up over the rim of her glasses.

"Oh, yes, of course. Henry Flagg was always one of John's staunchest supporters. It was such a tragedy he died so young." She paused for a respectful moment, then, "Oh, Isadora, you really should phone Jen. She called an hour ago wondering if you were here. She was quite concerned."

Her jaw set firmly. "Why should she be concerned?"

"Well, dear, she had no idea where you were."

Conan averted the threatened confrontation.

"Go ahead, Dore. We should've let her know we'd be gone so long."

She glanced at him, then rose. "All right. Excuse me, I'll use the hall phone."

When she was gone, he said, "I'm afraid this is my fault, Mrs. Canfield. We were just out for a short drive and decided on the spur of the moment to come to Salem for lunch." Then he added, "Of course, the truth is, I've always been fascinated with this house, and I couldn't resist the opportunity to see it from the inside."

She laughed politely. "Well, perhaps Isadora will give you a tour. Are you vacationing at the coast now?"

"No, I live in Holliday Beach." The small talk came easily; he steered the conversation to the bookshop, always a good subject for diversion, all the while listening to the distant murmur of Isadora's voice. And listening in a different sense to Catharine's. But her gracious restraint was as effective in hiding her feelings as the dark glasses.

Isadora returned in less than three minutes.

"Jen is duly reassured," she informed Catharine.

"Really, dear, she's only thinking of you."

"Of course. What's wrong with Bob?"

"He'll join us later. He had some papers to finish."

"More dazzling legal sleight of hand?"

She only smiled. "There have been a number of problems to work out with the estate."

Before Isadora could respond, Conan put in, "I'm afraid we've come at a bad time for you, Mrs. Canfield."

"Oh, not at all. We're delighted to have you, and anyway, Bob wanted to talk to you, Isadora, so actually your arrival is very opportune."

"I'm not sure I want to talk to *him.*"

Catharine's pause was eloquent. "I doubt Mr. Flagg is interested in estate legalities, but there are some matters pending you should discuss with Bob." Then she tilted her head to one side, listening. "Is that a car door?"

"It must be Jim!" Isadora hurried to the window, then a moment later turned, laughing, and ran out into the foyer.

Catharine smiled tolerantly. "Isadora's so fond of Jim. You must forgive her precipitous exit."

There was a burst of happy greetings and laughter outside, then Isadora came back, arm and arm with her stepbrother.

"The prodigal returns," she announced.

"With his ugly stepsister," Jim retorted, and Conan laughed almost in spite of himself, and undoubtedly Jim Canfield was as accustomed to that as his mother was to command. A handsome young man with deep-set blue eyes, whose dark brown hair had obviously been cut by a "stylist" and not a mere barber, who dressed well and—again obviously—expensively. But there was in his laughter an appealing air of ingenuousness only veneered with cynicism.

When Conan rose, Isadora went to him and took his arm.

"Conan, this is my ugly stepbrother, Jim Canfield. Jim, meet Conan Flagg, a . . . friend of mine."

Jim accepted his handshake with open curiosity.

"Welcome to Castle Canfield, Conan." Then he leaned down to kiss Catharine's cheek. "Mother, you look marvelous."

She laughed knowingly. "You're late, Jim, and don't try flattering me out of it."

"Now, would I stoop to flattery?"

"Of course you would."

"Well, I have more than flattery." He took a slim box from his breast pocket and put it in her hand. "For your collection, and that orange pantsuit I bought you."

"Oh, that pantsuit! From your description, I'm almost afraid to wear it." Her hands were busy opening the box as she spoke. "It might be too much for Salem."

"Salem could use a lift, and you look great in it."

"I trust your judgment implicitly. At least, in fashion." She had the box open and took out a pair of sunglasses with bright orange frames striped in white. "Ah, now the outfit will be complete. Are they orange?" Her fingers moved over the frames, assimilating their shape.

"Exactly the color of the suit, but there's a fine white stripe. You'll have to wear your white patent shoes."

She laughed delightedly. "Well, that will call for an *occasion.* Thank you, dear." Then she paused, turning toward Conan—or rather, where she'd last heard his voice, but he'd moved to sit on the arm of the couch beside Isadora.

"Mr. Flagg, perhaps I should explain."

"Explain?" he asked, more to let her hear his voice than as a question, and her head turned in his direction.

"This business with the sunglasses must seem a tasteless joke, but actually it's been my salvation. For a woman, part of the shock of being blind is the terrible blow to her vanity. Jim started me on this hobby, collecting sunglasses, and it's become a personal trademark; a salve for my vanity that makes my blindness easier to accept."

Conan smiled at Jim. "That shows rare understanding and imagination."

He laughed. "Not really. I just didn't want to be caught with a frumpy-looking mother."

"Oh, Jim!" She smiled fondly then handed him the box. "Would you put this on the table by the hall door, please?"

Jim was at the table when Sean appeared carrying a heavily laden silver tray. His initial surprise soon gave way to open admiration as his gaze strayed downward.

"Miss Reilly?" Catharine asked.

"Yes, ma'am. Where would you like the tray?"

"On the coffee table. Jim, is it cleared?"

He moved quickly to the table in front of the couch and pushed some magazines aside, then helped her with the tray.

"I'm not complaining, but what happened to Maudie?"

Catharine answered, "Maud's sister is ill again. Miss Reilly, this is my son Jim."

She nodded deferentially. "Pleased, sir."

"Sir, yet. What goes with Reilly?"

Sean's chin came up, " 'Miss' . . . *sir.*"

Catharine laughed. "Now, Jim, be a gentleman and don't give Miss Reilly the wrong impression."

He sighed and retired to one of the plush chairs.

"I wouldn't think of it, Mother."

"His bark is worse than his bite," Catharine assured Sean. "But be careful. He has a penchant for redheads."

Conan's eyes shot to Catharine, watching her as Sean cautiously placed a fragile cup in her hands.

"You take yours black, don't you, ma'am?"

"Yes. Mrs. Blackstone schooled you well in a short time. Oh—no pastries for me."

As Sean filled another cup, Jim quipped, "Dore's sugar and cream and everything nice."

Isadora laughed. "Jim, that doesn't even rhyme. Oh, thank you, Miss Reilly. Conan takes his black." She glanced at him, her smile fading at his preoccupied expression.

When everyone was served, Sean turned to Catharine.

"Will there be anything else, ma'am?"

"Yes, tell Mr. Carleton we'd like him to join us."

As Sean left the room Jim watched her with a private half smile, then rose to avail himself of the cookies.

"Hey, Sis, we have a bash on at the Lambda Delt house tonight. You and Conan are invited."

"Thanks, but I'll have to get back to the beach soon. After all, I'm a working girl now."

"And Heaven protects you—right, Conan?"

He turned at the click of the library doors, responding absently, "I wouldn't presume to doubt such a basic tenet of faith."

At first glance, he judged C. Robert Carleton to be in his fifties, but a closer look made him revise that estimate downward to the forties. His attire was almost formal; a dark suit with a vest and conservative tie. The collar of his starched white shirt looked a size too small and made his florid face seem bloated.

Jim hailed him nonchalantly. "Well, it's C. Bob, himself. How are you, counselor?"

Carleton eased himself into a velour chair.

"We've been waiting for you, Jim."

"Yes, that's what Mother said. Coffee, Bob?"

"No, thank you. Hello, Isadora." A pause as he smiled stiffly at Conan. "Well, I didn't realize we had a guest."

Her mouth tightened, then relaxed with a cool smile, and she leaned closer to Conan.

"Oh, Bob," she said sweetly. "I forgot you haven't met. Conan, this is C. Robert Carleton. Bob, Conan Flagg."

They rose to acknowledge the introduction with handshakes, and as Carleton resumed his chair, he said unctuously, "Flagg. Are you related to Henry Flagg of the Ten-Mile?"

"He was my father." Conan wondered what Carleton would do if he answered that rhetorical question with a denial.

"Well. A place like that must keep you busy."

"Not at all. I leave the intricacies of business to people better qualified to deal with them."

Jim laughed. "The only way to fly."

Carleton sent him a venomous glance, then cleared his throat and smiled ingratiatingly at Isadora.

"You're looking well, Isadora."

"I *am* well. At least, I haven't done any more carving on my wrists lately."

"Isadora!" This shocked outburst from Catharine.

"Don't worry about exposing the family scandal. Conan already knows about it."

"It isn't a question of scandal, dear. It was perfectly understandable . . . under the circumstances."

"Was it?" she demanded, suddenly angry. "Spare me your *understanding*, Catharine. I can't—"

"Dore, darling . . ." Conan pressed her shoulder gently. "Don't rake yourself over the coals of the past."

She stared tensely at Catharine, then finally, picking up his cue, relaxed and smiled at him.

"You're right, Conan. Let the past bury itself."

Carleton's sigh of relief was audible. He cleared his throat again and looked at his watch.

"Catharine, I have an appointment in half an hour."

"I'm afraid we've interrupted you." Conan put down his cup and rose. "Dore, perhaps we should be going."

She stood up, willing enough to take this cue, but Carleton

protested hastily, "Oh, no. I meant I'd just have time to talk to Isadora about some—uh, estate business."

She studied him coolly. "What business, Bob?"

"Well, I'm sure Mr. Flagg would find it quite boring."

"In other words, you don't want to discuss it in front of a witness?"

"Well, after all, it *is* family business."

"Family! Don't use that word with me."

"At least, it's *private* business," Conan put in quietly, and again she subsided. Carleton heaved himself to his feet, glancing covertly at him.

"I'll only take a few minutes, Isadora. Why don't we just go into the library and—"

"No!"

This objection wasn't for Carleton; she was rigid with fear.

"No," she repeated, "I won't go in that . . . that room."

It was Catharine who finally broke the long, taut silence that followed.

"Now, Bob, you should certainly understand her feelings about the library."

She started to retort to that, but the pressure of Conan's hand on her arm silenced her. He gave Catharine a brief smile, then turned to Carleton.

"I'm sure you can discuss the matter here as well as in the library. Would that be more agreeable, Dore?"

She nodded bleakly. "Yes."

"Then perhaps if Jim isn't needed in this discussion, he could show me around the house."

Catharine smiled with obvious relief.

"Yes, of course. Jim, would you mind?"

"Mind? I'm too hung over today for C. Bob's legal jazz anyway. Come on, Conan, I'll give you the fifty-cent tour." As he passed Isadora, he gently tapped her chin with his fist. "Hey, Sis, don't let that legal beagle get to you."

She laughed. "Don't worry."

* * *

Conan surveyed the library with no apparent interest; a warm room walled with bookshelves, dominated by the large deck facing the doors. There was a briefcase on it, but Carleton had left no loose papers exposed to casual view.

"This was the Senator's lair," Jim said. "You know, I think if he'd had a choice, this is where he'd have *wanted* to die."

Conan sent him a quick, speculative glance.

"There are worse places to die. Look, Jim, I'm really not that interested in the tour. It was just the only excuse I could think of at the moment."

"Well, that's a relief. Come on, then. I need something for this hellacious headache."

Conan followed him into the foyer, then through the door beyond the staircase into a wide, ivory-painted hall. They passed the dining room, then turned right into a large room whose walls were covered with blue watered silk.

"The *salon*," Jim announced as he crossed to the bar on the opposite wall. "Tranquilizer? Stick around here long enough and you'll need it."

He shrugged. "All right. Bourbon and water."

"Good. I'm not against drinking alone, but I never trust a man with no vices."

Conan laughed, his gaze wandering idly. The paintings were all originals, but there was nothing more contemporary than a Winslow Homer watercolor. The salon was obviously a room for entertainment. A few straight-backed chairs and Empire sofas lined the walls, but the only other furniture was a Steinway concert grand. He walked over to it.

"That's the inspiration for Dore's career," Jim said, playing bartender with a cavalier flourish. "That piano came around the Horn in eighteen-ought-something. Or maybe it came across on the Oregon Trail in a covered wagon. I get confused with all these historical monuments."

"I gather you're not too impressed with history."

He laughed at that. "Sure, I am. For instance, there's about half a million bucks worth of *historical* paintings on these walls. That chandelier—" He gestured upward with a bourbon bottle. "Baccarat. It probably came around the Horn, too; it's insured for ten thousand."

Conan didn't comment, waiting as Jim brought his drink.

"Here you are; something for the nerves. Come on out on the veranda."

The French doors opened onto a long porch overlooking the gardens. The air was sweet with narcissus and new-mown grass; a grove of patriarchal oaks cast a cooling shade.

"It's beautiful, Jim."

He took a deep breath. "It is, really. You can hardly hear the traffic back here." He gestured toward a pair of wrought-iron chairs. "Here, make yourself comfortable."

Conan seated himself and tasted his drink; it was loaded. For some time they talked about nothing more serious than the season, but eventually the subject shifted to Isadora, and Jim finally worked around to a casual probe.

"Well, now that you've met the happy group here, maybe you can understand Dore's problems a little better."

He hesitated purposely. "I doubt there's anything here she can't cope with."

"Oh, she can cope." He paused, watching Conan closely. "But when her dad died, that took more coping than she was up to, I guess."

"She seems to be recovering very well."

"Sure. She was brought up in the old stiff-upper-lip school. You can't always tell how bad she's been hurt."

Conan concentrated on his drink, smiling a little at Jim's oblique approach.

"I think you're underestimating her."

"Maybe. But you weren't around when the old man died. It hit her damned hard, and she isn't over it yet."

"And you're worried about her relationship with me?"

He laughed self-consciously. "Okay, I'll lay my cards out. I don't want to see her hurt. Any other time, I'd keep my nose out of her business, but right now I don't think she can take any extra strain."

"Well, Jim, if makes you feel any better, my intentions are entirely honorable."

Jim studied him intently a moment, then smiled.

"You know, I believe you mean that."

"Good, because I do mean it."

"You sound sort of serious."

"I am." He hesitated, then, "I hope you'll keep this to yourself, but it might reassure you to know that Isadora and I have discussed marriage."

There was a long silence, but Jim's only overt response was a slight narrowing of his eyes. Finally, he shrugged.

"Well, you aren't marrying her for her money if you're one of the Ten-Mile Flaggs, but isn't this a little fast?"

Conan laughed. "You sound like the father of the bride, but I appreciate that. You're very important to Dore; her only real family as far as she's concerned."

He shifted uncomfortably and tipped up his glass.

"She's in bad shape if I'm all she's got. The black sheep of the family. The *adopted* black sheep." There was an edge of pain in those words, but a moment later he put on his careless smile again. "Well, I've had my brother of the bride say, so I'll just shut up and wish you both luck from here out." He peered at his empty glass. "Refill?"

"No, thanks. I've just started on this one."

"Well, I'm having another. The day's young yet."

Conan waited until he heard the clink of ice from the salon, then took out a pen and scrawled a terse message on the inside of a match book. When Jim returned, it was safely secreted in his pants pocket.

"Dore tells me you're majoring in Business Management."

"Sure. There must be *something* around that needs managing. Of course, the Senator wanted me to study Law. That's with a capital L. At least, it always was with him."

Conan nodded sympathetically. "Living up to the ambitions of a man like John Canfield would be difficult."

"Oh, the old man meant well, and I wasn't exactly what he had in mind for a son and heir, but I'm smart enough to know I'd never make it at Harvard. Hell, I'm lucky I don't have to worry about the draft, or I'd be in boot camp."

"Well, that isn't as disastrous as it used to be. Uncle Sam's rather generous these days."

"With my luck, I'd end up in some damn hole getting shot at." He eyed Conan over the rim of his glass. "Did you ever try any of Uncle's generosity?"

"Yes, when I was younger and more idealistic."

"What branch were you in?"

"G-2. Army Intelligence."

"Intelligence? You mean the spy stuff?" He laughed appreciatively. "Man, a James Bond in our midst."

"Unfortunately, it wasn't that colorful."

"Don't disillusion me. Where were you stationed?"

"Berlin."

"Spy heaven, huh? Say, I read a book a while back about Smersh. *The Executioners*, I think."

"Yes, I've read it."

"Did you ever run into Smersh agents?"

He smiled distantly. "I don't know. They didn't wear name tags. At any rate, I got to see Berlin from both sides of the Wall." Then he glanced at his watch. "Any idea how long that legal discussion will last?"

Jim tipped up his glass. "God knows—and C. Bob."

"Dore doesn't seem to care much for him."

"No. Never did."

"What do you think of him?"

His eyes slid toward Conan. "Is this for publication, or do you want a straight answer?"

"Straight."

"Hell, I wouldn't trust him to mail a post card for me." Then he smiled slyly. "But he knows his business and all the angles, and don't worry about Dore; she can handle him."

"I don't doubt that." He turned at the sound of footsteps, his comment about speaking of angels dying on his lips when he saw Isadora, an angry flush coloring her cheeks.

He rose. "Are you ready to go, Dore?"

"Yes. Definitely."

Jim walked over to her. "Hey, Sis, how'd it go?"

"It didn't." Then she smiled and reached out for his hand. "Anyway, it was wonderful to see *you* again."

"Well, I'll take you over C. Bob anytime. Conan, bring her back again; brightens up the old homestead." He leaned forward and kissed her cheek. "I'll say good-bye here. No use *looking* for trouble. Bob can find me if he wants me."

"Good luck, and take care, Jim."

"You, too. You're my favorite step-sibling, you know."

Carleton had departed when Conan and Isadora reached the foyer, but Catharine was waiting, with Sean in attendance.

"Mr. Flagg, I'm sorry you and Isadora can't stay for dinner."

"Thank you, Mrs. Canfield. Perhaps some other time." He turned as Sean brought his jacket, but when she handed it to him, it slipped and fell to the floor.

"Oh—sorry," he said, leaning down to retrieve it.

"I'll get it, sir," she put in quickly, and they almost collided. When they straightened, a match book had unobtrusively passed from his hand to hers.

CHAPTER 16

Isadora tolerated his preoccupied silence only until he turned onto Mission Drive.

"Conan, what's wrong?"

"I was going to ask you the same thing." Then as the traffic stopped at a red light, he began searching through his jacket pockets. He wasn't surprised to find a slip of paper in one of them.

"Dore, tell me when the light changes."

Folded inside the paper was a gauze-wrapped ampule. He studied it curiously, then read the note. It was short and very sweet: *Jackpot! Couldn't identify this one. S.*

"The light's changed," Isadora said.

He pocketed the note and ampule, and moved slowly along with the traffic. A glance in the rearview mirror showed him a tan Chevy a few cars behind.

"The note was from Sean. She's going to call me later."

"What about?"

"I'm not sure, but I'll have to forego dinner with you

tonight unless she calls early. By the way, I've been casting a little bread on the waters.''

''What kind of bread?''

''I told Jim you and I are contemplating marriage.'' He sent her a wry smile. ''I thought you'd like to know.''

She laughed. ''Well, yes, and in this case, I think I'm entitled to ask why.''

''There's a condition to your inheritance other than your reaching age twenty-five which you neglected to tell me about. You're also eligible on marrying.''

''Oh, yes, I'd forgotten about that.'' Then seeing his skeptical expression, she added, ''Conan, I really did. Anyway, that doesn't explain the bread you've been casting.''

''Doesn't it? Your marriage would change things rather drastically with the estate. It could very well throw a first-class monkey wrench into someone's works.''

Her hair was blowing around her face; she reached into her purse for a scarf, frowning slightly as she tied it on.

''Whose works, Conan?''

''I don't know. I'm just trying to exert some pressure; I'm not sure yet what may break. What was Carleton so anxious to talk to you about?''

Her mouth tightened irritably. ''Oh, he was throwing a lot of legal jargon at me, but what it really boils down to, if I understood him, is that he and Catharine want to get rid of Marvin Hendricks and the bank.''

Conan nodded. ''What did you tell him?''

''First, to go to hell. Second, that I'm perfectly satisfied with Hendricks, and I intend to talk to him and make my sentiments quite clear—on paper, if necessary.''

''You've been casting some bread yourself.'' He changed lanes for the coast turn-off as they crossed the Willamette River bridge. ''What about your call to Jenny?''

''Well, I left before she woke up today, and since I always make up my bed in the morning, she wasn't even sure I'd been home last night. She called the Surf House and the bookshop and couldn't find me, so she got worried."

"Is that all?"

"No. She asked if anything had come up about the estate. When I told her Bob was there, she said, 'Be careful, Dore.' Just like that. Then she apologized for calling Catharine and hung up."

Conan was silent, concentrating on the traffic.

"Good advice," he said finally. "I wonder if it's the voice of experience."

When he turned into the parking area in front of the small, flat-roofed building, Conan was alone. The sign in the window read, DR. NICOLE HEIDEGER, PHYSICIAN AND SURGEON.

After he turned off the motor, he watched in the rearview mirror as the tan Chevrolet drove past. It had tailed them all the way from Salem. He considered contacting Harry Munson, but decided against it; he didn't want the man in the Chevy to see him using the radio. Time enough to call Harry when he got home.

Still, he was concerned about Jennifer Hanson. She was gone when he took Isadora home. On the beach. Again.

He checked his watch as he entered the empty waiting room. It was only four, but the gray, overcast sky made it seem later. Apparently, he was in luck; Nicky had no patients waiting. He crossed to the inner door and knocked.

"Yes?" Dr. Nicole Heideger looked up from behind a desk overwhelmed with papers and medical publications. "Conan—I'll be damned. Come on in."

The tiny office was crowded with bookshelves and filing cabinets. He went to the chair by the desk, feeling his usual claustrophobia in this apparently orderless lair, but it disappeared, as it always did, when Nicky smiled; a warm, easy smile born of Montana mountains. She had about her a typically Western air of capability, with her dark hair cut short, strong features showing an unconcerned lack of cosmetic adornment.

"Nicky, how are you?"

"That's *my* line. You look healthy enough. What's your problem?"

"I *am* healthy. I'm here for an expert opinion."

One eyebrow lifted. "You're on a case, then."

"An excellent diagnosis, Doctor."

"Okay, what've you got yourself into this time?"

"Well, it's a little complicated, and—"

"In other words, none of my business?" She shrugged. "All right. So, what kind of expert opinion do you want?"

He handed her the gauze-wrapped ampule.

"What is it, Nicky?"

She studied it a moment. "Offhand, I'd say amyl nitrate. Is this valuable, or can I break it?"

"Whatever you like. I just want to know what it is,"

"Okay." She pushed her chair back and went to the door behind her desk. "I'll take it into the lab."

When she returned a few minutes later, empty handed, she wrinkled her nose.

"Amyl nitrate. It's used for certain types of heart disease; a vasodilator. You have a client with heart trouble?"

"No, not my client."

"Somebody must have a problem to keep that around."

"Somebody *had* a problem, but he was never treated for heart disease, and back in my G-2 days I ran across another use for amyl nitrate." He frowned uneasily, then came to his feet. "Well, Nicky, as usual you've been very helpful."

"Is that all the expert opinion you need?"

"That's it, and thanks."

"That was easy. Okay, just take care of yourself."

He smiled back at her from the door. "I always do."

"Sure. That's why you're walking around as a living monument to some of my finest handiwork."

When he reached his car, the radio erupted with a dash of static and an inquiring repetition of his name. He surveyed the street as he reached for the mike. He couldn't see the Chevy, but that didn't mean its driver couldn't see him.

"This is Munson. Can you hear me, Conan?" The reception was bad, blurred with interference from the approaching storm.

"Yes, Harry, but the signal's weak. Where are you?"

He raised his voice. "About a block from your house."

"From *my* house?"

"I'm tailing Jennifer Hanson."

"How did she—okay, take it from the top."

"Well, right after you brought Isadora home, Jenny came back from the beach, then ten minutes later, she drove down to the supermarket. I followed her inside; she was after groceries, all right. Didn't talk to anybody, not even the cashier. She looked . . . well, kind of sick. Anyway, she took her groceries out to her car, then she went to that phone booth. She just stood there, like she was trying to make up her mind, then finally put her money in. The call lasted maybe three minutes."

Conan frowned, wondering why she used a pay phone instead of the one at the cottage.

"Did she use a phone book?"

"No, pulled the number out of her head. After the call, she headed for your house, but she couldn't seem to make up her mind about that, either. She got halfway home, then turned around and took off south. Anyway, she's sitting on your door step now."

Conan's jaw tightened. He'd wanted to talk to her; he should be pleased at this unexpected opportunity.

"Harry, what about Garner?"

"I guess he isn't interested in Jenny; he stayed home."

"All right, you'd better get back to Shanaway. I'll go see what's on Jenny's mind."

CHAPTER 17

Conan braked to a skidding stop behind the yellow VW. Jennifer Hanson was huddled on the porch step with her jacket collar turned up as if she were cold. Yet in spite of the threatening sky it was warm and windless; the taut stillness that presages a storm. The ocean had the dull sheen of molten lead given a yellow cast against the distant blue-gray curtains of squall lines. He thought of Harry Munson's outdoor blind and wondered if he'd brought plenty of raingear. The storm would break within the hour.

Jenny didn't move as he approached, only watching him with her round, quiet face nearly devoid of expression.

He asked, "Have you been waiting long, Jenny?"

"No." A hesitation, then, "I came to see the Knight."

"I've been wanting to show it to you." He unlocked the door and stood aside. "Come in."

She rose, but for a moment only stared into the house, then at length entered warily.

"It's in the library," he said. "This way."

She followed him silently down the hall to the library door, and when he stood aside for her, she again hesitated before going in. He watched her as her eyes moved around the room, finally stopping at the corner to her left.

For a long time she stared at the painting, and he almost expected her to weep. But she didn't, and he found something else in her face to make him wonder.

Her eyes. The dilation of the pupils was almost normal. And she was pale, a sheen of perspiration on her forehead. He was beginning to understand this pilgrimage.

"I like the setting," she said finally. "The niche."

"It isn't a painting to be exposed nakedly on a wall. It needs to be discovered."

Her glance was laced with skepticism.

"Tell me, Mr. Flagg, what does it—I mean, how do you interpret it?"

He didn't look at the painting, but she seemed to find it difficult to keep her eyes away from it.

"Fear," he said. "The mind protects itself against pain, but if it armors itself too well, it ceases to be human; it becomes trapped in its own armor."

She shivered and turned away, but couldn't seem to decide where to go or what to do. When he went to her and took her arm, she tensed in silent alarm.

"Jenny, come sit down."

She made no response, but offered no resistance as he guided her to the chair and side table by the windows. He pulled up another chair for himself and lit a cigarette, taking his time about it, studying her.

She seemed unaware of the growing silence or anything else except the Knight. He couldn't doubt it was her only conscious motive for coming here. It was evidence of past accomplishment and perhaps future potential. He wondered if it might also serve as a measure of the man who owned it.

"Is there anything about it you'd change, Jenny?"

Her eyes didn't leave the painting. "No. Nothing."

"That's the truest measure of a successful painting."

She looked at him now and even smiled tentatively.

''Yes, it is. The good ones have a life of their own. It must be like having children. You know they're yours, your own flesh and blood, but they grow up into separate, distinct beings. It's a kind of—of immortality.'' Then she averted her eyes, as if she were afraid she'd said too much.

''Which puts artists in a class with magicians and saints; admired, but also envied, and in a sense, feared.'' Then he smiled, his tone light now. ''I always find myself waxing ponderously philosophical when I talk about art.''

''Well, it's . . . a philosophical subject, but not many people seem to want to think about it that much.''

''There's very little that separates us from our animal cousins, Jenny. Cruelty is one thing, but so is art. I like to keep my personal balance weighed on the side of art. But I'm falling into philosophy again. Are you cold? I can turn up the thermostat.''

The question was prompted by a passing shiver. She shook her head, her mouth compressed and lined with white, and he felt a chill himself, as if it were contagious.

''No, I'm not cold,'' she murmured. ''I'm fine.''

A lie, and a poignantly unconvincing one. She was more than cold; she was ill and perhaps in pain. He cast about in his mind for words, because he understood now the heroic decision that brought her into the presence of the Knight; a decision born of the despair that drove her to slash the canvases in her studio. Yet it was a decision made in armored solitude. She had created that symbol of fear, recognizing a human constant within herself. So he searched for the words to reach past the armor without frightening her into total retreat.

But in the end, he said simply, ''Let me help you, Jenny,'' and winced at the blatancy of it even as he spoke.

She stared at him, poised to run, literally.

But she didn't run. She looked down at the floor, and he

could see the slight movements of her eyes tracing the geometric designs of a Navajo rug.

"Help me? Mr. Flagg, I don't know what you mean."

That annoyed him, and perhaps subtlety wasn't the best approach. At any rate, he'd already forfeited it.

"Jenny, you can tell me to mind my own business, but don't take me for a fool. The symptoms of morphine addiction are rather obvious." He paused, then, "So are the symptoms of withdrawal. You're going to need help."

One hand came up to her mouth, curled into a reflexive, impotent fist. Still, she didn't run; she sat trembling, locked in a paralysis of doubt and fear, until at length, her distracted gaze turned on the Knight.

"I don't need . . . any help."

He took a long drag on his cigarette, watching her.

"Then why are you here?"

"I—I just wanted to see the Knight."

"And there's no help in that?"

She seemed startled at first, then skeptical. For some time she was silent, reading his face, then she asked warily, "Why should you want to help me?"

"Not because of any altruistic or moralistic inclinations on my part, Jenny. Only because of the Knight."

"You don't know me just because you have that painting. You can't call yourself a friend; you owe me nothing."

"I don't call myself a friend, but I owe you something, and I know you." He smiled as her eyes narrowed. "An artist friend of mine once told me he's in the business of indecent exposure—of the soul. A painting is a failure if it doesn't expose something of the artist's soul, and I've lived with the Knight for six years."

Again, she looked at the painting as if seeking guidance of it, and after a long silence turned to him.

"How can you . . . what do you mean by help?"

He let his breath out slowly. The armor was cracking.

"It depends on what you'll accept, but I was thinking in

pragmatic terms primarily. For instance, you'll need a doctor. When did you have your last shot?''

The suggestion of a doctor alarmed her, but she was distracted by the question.

''Last night. I mean, early . . . early this morning.''

''Have you ever tried to quit before?''

''Yes.'' A dull, memory-weighted stone of a word. Then she went on with unexpected fervor: ''I'll make it this time, I *will*. Somehow, just to be out of that house, the Salem house, it made me *see*, really see so much for the first time since . . .'' Her mouth tensed into a determined line. ''I've burned my bridges, and I *will* make it this time.''

''I believe you, Jenny.'' But a seed of apprehension was burgeoning. ''What do you mean, you've burned your bridges?''

Her laughter was a careless, shattering sound.

''I've cut off my retreat. I dumped all my supplies and told my—my pusher I'd no longer need his . . . services.''

Conan stared at her, too stunned to control his reaction, wondering if that explained a certain phone call.

''You what?''

She laughed again. ''I told my pusher *finis*; to leave me alone this time or I'd—'' She stopped abruptly, but the implicit threat was all too clear.

''Jenny, who is he?'' He regretted the question before it was fully out. She stiffened, suspicious and defensive.

''If I wanted *that* kind of help, I'd go to the narks.''

''All right, but do you understand why I asked? That was a dangerous thing to do. Dealers in this business tend to regard ex-clients as a serious threat.''

She considered that, and it seemed to allay her fear of him, but there was no correlative fear for herself.

''Don't worry about that.''

His eyes narrowed. ''Why shouldn't I?''

''I—I mean, I can protect myself, and I . . . oh, I can't

worry about that *now*.'' Her teeth clenched on a jerking intake of breath, her folded arms pressing against her body.

He watched her until she seemed to recover a little, then he leaned forward to crush out his cigarette.

''Forgive me, Jenny, if my priorities fall out of order. The first priority is medical aid. I have an excellent doctor who's also a personal friend.''

''No, I—I can't go to a doctor.''

''But I know Nicky Heideger. Jenny, you can trust her.''

She shook her head. ''I don't want any doctors, and I don't want—I mean, no one must *know*. Please. *No one*.''

He felt the weight of dread, but again it was an emotional projection from her.

''You mean especially not Isadora?'' Then at her mute nod, ''Doesn't she know?''

''No one knows except . . . I don't want anyone to know, but especially not Dore.'' Then, as if recognizing his need for an explanation, she tried to laugh and added: ''It's bad enough to be a Cinderella whose fairy godmother never showed up, but on top of that, to live with a *real* princess . . .''

He wanted to reach out for her hand, but restrained the impulse. Instead, he laughed softly.

''Jenny, Isadora may be blessed with talent and good looks, but she's as human as you and I, and as much afraid.''

She was bewildered at that. ''Afraid? Dore?''

''You know what happened when her father died; you know she's susceptible to fear and pain. What makes you think she couldn't understand your being driven to morphine as she was apparently driven to suicide?''

Jenny turned away, confused and on the verge of tears.

''I don't *know*. Oh, please, you said you wanted to help me.''

''I do, but I don't understand what you expect of me.''

''I just . . . maybe if—if you could get Dore away from the cottage . . . if I could just have a few days *alone*.''

He felt a rush of heat in his face.

"Is that your idea of help? To leave you to quit cold alone? What kind of human being do you think I am?"

She shrank from his questions, her attempts to answer them dissolving into incoherence and finally silence. He was asking too much of her, he realized numbly; she was too ill to be rational. And he'd been less than rational himself. Jenny was reaching out for help, and he'd overlooked the most obvious alternative for her.

He said gently, "I won't leave you to fight this out alone. What I will do is take you to someone who can give you the kind of help you need, and if you're worried about Dore, he's also in a position to help her understand."

"Who—who do you mean?"

"Dr. Milton Kerr."

She seemed shocked. "Dore told you about him? But I can't believe she'd tell . . . anyone. She was so dead set against anyone finding out about—about that."

"As dead set as you are now?"

There was little logic in the comparison, yet it seemed to convince her. At least, she was ready to examine this alternative in the light of feasibility and even hope.

"I talked to Dr. Kerr once," she said.

"Did you like him?"

"I don't know. I trusted him; he had a good ear."

He smiled at that. "Jenny, let me take you to Morningdell. You can commit yourself voluntarily and be free to leave any time you want to."

The anxiety returned suddenly. "But if I do that everyone will know. They'll know why, and I don't want—"

"No one needs to know why you're there. Not exactly."

"Yes, I . . . I don't have to tell anyone *exactly* why." Then a perplexed frown. "But what about Dore? She shouldn't be alone; Dr. Kerr insisted on that, and she won't want to go back to Salem."

"She isn't quite alone here now, and I'll see that she has

someone to stay at the cottage with her. Miss Dobie, perhaps. Let me look after her. It's time for you to look after yourself."

The tears welled behind her lashes, and she closed her eyes to hold them back. After a while, she nodded slowly.

"I *could* talk to Dr. Kerr, and it's beautiful there. I mean, at Morningdell; so quiet. The oaks . . . there's courage in oaks, you know." She looked at the Knight once more, then as if she were finally satisfied, turned to him and smiled.

A beautiful young woman, he thought, when she smiled.

"Will you look after Dore, Mr. Flagg? And will you help her understand?"

"If she needs help. How much do you want her to know?"

The smile faded; she frowned uncertainly at her hands.

"Not . . . everything."

"Only that you felt yourself at an emotional crisis, that you simply recognized a need for professional help?"

She nodded. "Yes. Can you—would you talk to her?"

"No." Then at her stricken look he added, "I'll stay around to offer moral support, but you must talk to her. Please, Jenny, don't leave without talking to her."

"Would that bother her?"

"Yes. Believe me, it would bother her very much."

He wasn't sure she did believe him at first, but finally she seemed to accept it.

"All right, if you'll . . . be there when I talk to her."

"I will." He smiled as he came to his feet. "I'll call her now and have her come down here. Then I'll take you to Morningdell. We can call Dr. Kerr while—"

"*No.* Not . . . now."

He stopped, put off balance by her insistent one.

"Why not now, Jenny?"

"I'm not hedging. I made my decision before I came here." She looked up at him defiantly clamping her teeth against a shiver that would have set them chattering.

It came in waves, he thought; tides whose intervals would grow shorter in the hours to come.

"I don't doubt you, but you haven't answered my question. You're going to need a doctor, and soon."

"I've made it for—for two days on my own before, and I can't go tonight. I have to talk to—" She hesitated, but only briefly. "I mean, get my things packed. My painting equipment—will they let me paint at Morningdell?"

"I'm sure they will. How long will it take you to get packed?"

She paused, avoiding his eyes.

"Tomorrow morning. I'll go tomorrow morning."

"But *why*, Jenny? By then you'll be—"

"I'll be all right," she said doggedly. "Please, leave me some choices and some privacy. If you're afraid I'll back out, I'll call Dr. Kerr now. I know that doesn't guarantee anything, but it's the only commitment I can make. You'll have to take the rest on faith."

He sagged, chastised. But it was easier to take the rest on faith that put down the apprehension coming into focus in his mind. There was a reason for her procrastination. She'd almost slipped; almost said she had to talk to *someone.* The person she called from a pay phone?

But it was futile to argue with her, and dangerous. Her trust in him was too tenuous. She needed help, and if she didn't accept it from him, the consequences could be disastrous. It would have to be done on her terms. He could only assuage his anxiety with the thought that Harry Munson would be watching the cottage tonight.

He knew the answer to his question before he asked it.

"Will you talk to Dore now?"

"No." Her hands tightened in a double fist, the knuckles pressing white against the skin. "I thought if you'd be bringing her home from the Surf House tonight, maybe then we could—I could talk to her. I don't want to tell her before she goes to work; she might think she has to stay home with me.

That job's so important to her, and it's spring vacation. Max is counting on her."

His next question was as rhetorical as the last.

"Will you let me stay with you during the evening? Or Dr. Heideger? You shouldn't be alone."

"I don't *need* anyone; I don't *want* anyone! Don't you understand? Can't you just let me—" She covered her eyes with her hands, the words choked off.

A brief, dull flash lit the window, thunder rumbling in its wake. The timbers of the house creaked in the first gusts of wind.

"Jenny, the decision is yours, but make me a promise."

"What . . . promise?"

"I'm not going to the Surf House until later in the evening." There was still the matter of Sean's phone call, he reminded himself grimly. "Call me. If I'm not here, I'll be at the Surf House. Call me if you need help, or if you just need someone to talk to. Please, promise me that."

She came closer to actually weeping than she had yet, but the tears didn't fall. Instead, she gave him that smile that transformed her plain, colorless face.

"Dore said you were an extraordinarily kind man." Then she averted her eyes self-consciously. "It's a badly used word, kind, but she meant it in its best, truest sense. Yes, I'll call you if—if I need anyone. I promise you."

"Thank you."

She pulled herself shakily to her feet.

"I must get home. I told Dore I was just going out for groceries; she'll wonder if I'm gone too long. Mr. Flagg—" Her gaze was direct and clear. "Tomorrow morning. That's a promise, too. A promise to me."

CHAPTER 18

The first gusts of rain came as Conan accompanied Jenny to her car. He took shelter behind the redwood screen on the porch and watched her drive away, only aware that he was automatically searching the streets when he didn't find what he was unconsciously looking for: a tan Chevrolet.

His frown was equally unconscious as he wandered down the darkened hallway to the library and slumped into the chair behind the desk.

Jenny had reached out for help, and there was satisfaction in that. But few answers. He didn't know how her addiction was related to John Canfield's death or the surveillance, but he was convinced a relationship existed, and the vital link was the ''family,'' which in his mind included Bob Carleton. Tuesday night, Jenny had a clandestine meeting with someone driving a Lotus Elan. Her pusher? The secretive nature of the rendezvous suggested that, and the Elan pointed to the family. And Canfield's death, if it were in fact murder, had all the earmarks of a family affair.

But he had no proof Canfield didn't die of natural causes,

and despite the odds against the coincidence, the Elan might have belonged to someone other than Jim or Carleton. Or more likely, their cars could have been used by someone else.

Jenny had the answer to that and many other questions. Questions about her mother, for instance. But it was futile to look to her as a source of information. Not now.

He turned on the desk lamp. In the premature twilight, the gray sheets of rain curtaining the windows and its hammering beat produced a disquieting sense of isolation. He took the special line phone from the compartment, his uneasiness transmuted to vague annoyance as he recognized the voice that answered his call.

"Jamie, is your father home?"

"Ye-es," came the reply with an unprompted giggle.

"Ask him to come to the phone. Tell him it's Conan."

"Oh, hello, Conan. You didn't say it was you."

"Yes, well, it is. Now, tell Steve—"

"Y'know what, Conan?"

He sighed. "No, as a matter of fact, I don't."

"Daddy and me caught a great big fish today."

"That's marvelous, Jamie, now—"

"Mamma cooked it for lunch, on'y she wouldn't take the insides out. She said if Daddy caught it, he'd hafta take the insides out and peel it. Huh?" A muffled query was audible, then Jamie was hastily replaced by Steve Travers.

"Conan?"

"Yes, Steve. I've been hearing about your exploits as a fisherman."

He groaned. "One stunted, polluted steelhead, and for that I got up at five o'clock in the morning?"

"Try the fish market next time. It's cheaper."

"This was supposed to be an educational experience for Jamie. How're you coming on that Canfield case?"

"Glad you asked. I have a couple of new developments."

"Okay, but I hope you realize this is my day off."

"Sorry about that. I'll try not to ruin it."

"Sure. So, what are your developments? Any more drugs or anything like that you want to hint around about?"

"No, but I have a user who wants to quit, and I doubt her pusher's too happy about it. And to answer your next question, I won't tell you who the user is, and I don't know who the pusher is. I wasn't going to force that issue or I'd end up with nothing but a lot on my conscience."

"So, why tell me about it? To ease your conscience for holding back on a duly appointed officer of the law?"

"Maybe, but I was thinking that as a duly appointed, etcetera, you could find out if there'll be any state patrol cars cruising around here tonight."

"Oh, so that's it. Sure, there'll be patrols around, at least, on 101. Why?"

"Just nerves, I guess." He took a cigarette from the box on the desk. "But I'd like to have a state cop handy. Shanaway is unincorporated, so it falls under state or county jurisdiction, and Sheriff Wills isn't notably alert."

"Yes, I know. Okay, I'll check and make sure there'll be a patrol in the area. Now, I hope that's all you've got on your mind. There's a hockey game on TV tonight, and I'm damned if I'll miss *this* one short of murder."

Conan lit the cigarette, smiling to himself.

"Well, there *is* something else—speaking of murder."

Travers asked cautiously, "Speaking of whose murder?"

"John Canfield's."

"Not again. Okay, you have somebody I should arrest?"

"No, but I have something for you to think about. Catharine Canfield is *not* blind."

There was a tense silence, then a long, resigned sigh.

"All right, Conan. I suppose you have some reason for jumping feet first to that particular conclusion."

"You know Catharine left the hospital rather suddenly two weeks after the accident?"

"Sure, it was a little odd, maybe, but that doesn't mean she can see."

"Dore and I paid a visit to the old homestead today, and this was Sean's first day as up- and downstairs maid."

"Oh, yes. How's she doing as a domestic?"

"Beautifully, of course. Anyway, when we arrived, Sean told me she hadn't had a glimpse of Catharine; she'd been closeted in the library with Carleton. But she emerged to play hostess to Dore and me, then later, Jim arrived, and she made an offhand comment to Sean that her darling boy has a penchant for redheads. Steve, there was no way she could know Sean is a redhead unless she could *see* it."

Travers was still dubious. "Well, what about the regular housekeeper? Maybe she told her."

"No, she couldn't have because Sean has a penchant for wigs. Maud knew her as a *blonde*."

"What? Conan, are you sure?"

"Yes. There's no other explanation for it."

"But when she was in the hospital—I mean, maybe Emil Johnson would cover for her; he's what you call a society doctor, and he wouldn't spoil her game. But what about—"

"She did have head injuries; it may have been traumatic blindness, or even psychosomatic. I don't doubt she was blind immediately after the accident, but I'd stake my life on this: she recovered her sight within two weeks."

"But that means she's been playing blind for five years. That's—that's *nuts*."

"Here's something else for you to think about. Before the accident, Canfield was ready to divorce her, and for a woman like Catharine, that would be nothing less than a disaster. But afterward, he couldn't go through with it; he felt responsible for her blindness."

"Yes, that does make it interesting." A thoughtful pause, then, "But she didn't think she could get away with something like that indefinitely."

Conan frowned at the glowing tip of his cigarette.

"It was probably just a straw grasped in desperation to stop the divorce, then she was stuck with it. I'm sure Jenny must know about it; she's been playing nurse to her."

"What about her son? Or that lawyer?"

"Carleton?" His eyes narrowed. "I don't know. I'm not sure how close their relationship is."

"Well, if you put any stock in local gossip, it's plenty close. Marcie told me there's a rumor going around that the Widow Canfield plans to take on a new husband soon."

"A logical move. He probably knows, then. As for Jim . . ." He paused, thinking of the gift of the sunglasses. Jim had no way of knowing there would be unexpected guests at the house to impress with that gambit. Unless . . .

"What about Jim, Conan?"

"I can't say, and I'm only worried about whether John Canfield finally tumbled. He spent a lot of time in Washington, and I doubt he spent much time with Catharine even when he was home, but he was bound to catch on eventually, and if he did, she was threatened not only with divorce and possibly being cut out of the will—and maybe her children, too—but with public exposure of her ruse."

"Okay, so maybe Canfield caught on and Catharine got scared, but what'd she do? *Talk* him into a heart attack?"

"There are ways of inducing heart attacks, but I can't prove anything, and I'm not even convinced Catharine did the inducing. She isn't the only one who was threatened by him, or stood to gain by his death, and the whole thing is getting confused with the little problem of the drugs."

Travers gave a sardonic laugh.

"Well, I'll give *you* something to think about. Bob Carleton's been on the defense in a hell of a lot of drug cases in the last few years. The guys in Narcotics told me that. Maybe it's just the way the cases fall, but the word is he damned well knows his way around the business."

"Thanks. That's all I need to make the waters muddier."

"I thought you'd appreciate it. Hold on." There was a distant exchange of voices, then, "Anything else, Conan? Marcie's hollering about the pot roast getting cold."

He laughed, suddenly aware that he was hungry.

"I envy you the pot roast. Go to it, and give Marcie my love. Oh—enjoy your hockey game."

"Don't worry. I intend to."

Conan eyed the remains of a tuna salad sandwich, then pushed the plate aside and looked at his watch: 8:15.

He frowned at the open books on his desk. Seth's *The Executioners.* Decker's *Experiments with Psychotomimetic Drugs.* Serious study was beyond him now; they'd devolved into diversions; something to distract him from the slow passage of time.

He'd already consumed a quantity of the inching minutes in long conversations with Berg and Munson. The latter had been particularly protracted and frustrating. The storm made radio communication almost hopeless.

Munson assured him he'd come prepared with boots and a waterproof parka. His only complaint was the lack of visibility. For Conan, that was more than a complaint; it was a source of intense anxiety that made him decide to let Carl watch Isadora tonight. As soon as Sean called, he intended to join Munson in his damp vigil at the cottage.

The windows went white, then almost before the flash registered, they were black again; molten, like obsidian. He waited for the thunder, adding another stub to the overflowing ashtray, then rose to begin aimlessly prowling the room. At one end, the Knight brooded out of its shadowed niche; at the other, he faced the storm-washed windows. He was at the windows when the phone buzzed, but he reached the desk before the second buzz.

"Hello, Sean?"

"Sorry, Conan, this is Carl. I'm at the Surf House."

"Oh. What's going on down there?" He could hear a steady undercurrent of sound in the background.

"It's a madhouse; spring vacation. The place is packed and Max put on two part-time waitresses. But the reason I'm calling is Hicks hasn't shown up, and it's twenty after."

He frowned uneasily. "See if you can smell out any replacements. What about Dore?"

Berg's slight hesitation brought him to full alert.

"Well, she's here, and she seems okay."

"What's wrong, Carl?"

"I don't know. Maybe she isn't feeling good, or it's just nerves. There's nothing tangible."

"There must be something tangible or you wouldn't be worried."

"I mean she hasn't pulled a faint or gone into hysterics. Conan, she just isn't quite with it tonight. If I didn't know better, I'd say this was a kid with a good case of stage fright."

"Stage fright? Dore?"

"That's what I mean. It doesn't figure."

Conan looked at his watch, feeling a crawling chill.

"How does she look?"

"Gorgeous, as usual. Maybe a little flushed and—well, just shaky, I guess; nervous."

"Has she had anything to eat or drink since she arrived?"

"She got here early, and when I came in—that was about ten to eight—she was having a cup of coffee. Since then she's been working. Look, maybe it's just my tin ear."

"Carl, you have a fine ear for anomalies if not for music, so keep listening and call me if there's any change."

Conan made yet another turn down the length of the library and found himself again facing the Knight. He trust his hands into his pockets, crossed to the desk and glared at the silent telephone and radio, then checked his watch again and moved on to the windows: 8:38. The rain was coming in pounding torrents.

This time it was a static-blurred voice from the radio that sent him rushing back to the desk.

"Harry?"

"Yes, Conan. I've got some action up here." His voice was strained against the static.

"What kind of action?"

"About three minutes ago a car drove up to the cottage and pulled over at the south side. I couldn't see anything but the headlights. This damn rain is worse than fog, and there aren't any lights except in the house."

He sank slowly into his chair. "Which lights are on?"

"Uh—that must be Jenny's bedroom, but the shades are down. The living-room light was on. I can't see it now, but I could when the front door opened."

"What was that about the front door?" He was manipulating dials but with no apparent effect on the reception.

"Whoever was driving that car went in by the front door, and either he had a key or it was unlocked."

"It was a man?"

"I think so, but I just had a fast look while the door was open."

"All right, get down to the cottage and try to find out what's going on. And get a good look at that car—Harry?" The radio erupted with a fusillade of static that dissolved into a grating whine. "Harry, can you hear me?"

". . . coming in now. That lightning's getting too damned close for comfort. What did you say about the car?"

"Try to get a look at it and—" He jumped at the buzz of the telephone and reached for the receiver. "Sean?"

"Yes, I'm—"

"Thank God. Hold on a second. Harry, I'll call you back. Get down to the cottage, but be careful."

"I'm on my way, if I just don't break a leg crawling through this damned jungle."

"Conan, what's going on down there?"

A good question, he thought bleakly as he turned his attention to the phone and Sean.

"I haven't time to explain now. Where are you?"

"In a phone booth a block from the Canfield house on Mission. I went out the back gate and around by the alley."

"You're off duty?"

"Yes. Catharine said she was going to bed early and sent Alma and me on our way at 7:40, but I got stuck with Alma. She could talk your left foot off."

"Was Catharine alone when you were dismissed?"

"Yes. Conan, thanks for slipping me the warning. I've been watching her, and I think you're right. She's no more blind than I am."

"I'm afraid not. Tell me about this 'jackpot.' "

"Well, I found a regular cache of drugs; uppers, downers, grass, H, morphine, and something that may be LSD. I didn't sample it."

"That was smart. The ampule was with the drugs?"

"Yes, four or five of them. I couldn't figure it out. I didn't think you'd *swallow* something like that."

"No, the idea is to break and inhale it. Where did you find this cache?"

"In Jenny's studio. It's in a Chinese lacquer box in a drawer full of tubes of paint."

"In Jenny's studio? Are you sure?"

"What do you mean, am I sure?"

"I was just surprised, but it doesn't mean anything."

"It doesn't?" She gave a short laugh. "I was kind of impressed with that pile of loot."

"I mean, where it was found. And as far as I know, Jenny wasn't on anything but morphine."

"Oh. Anyway, there was something else in the box I couldn't figure out. A black metal cylinder—"

"A what?" He sat up, pulse quickening with both surprise and a kind of hope. "Sean, what did it look like?"

"Well, like an Arpège perfume spray; one of those aerosol things. Maybe five inches long and an inch in diameter."

He nodded to himself, eyes narrowed.

"All right. Look, don't fool around with it. I mean, don't get any bright ideas like trying to see what's in it."

She hesitated. "Sure, Conan, but—"

"Just don't touch it. What else have you turned up?"

"Isn't that enough for one day? Oh, I checked your client's medicine cabinet and found that bottle of Seconal. Also, I got taps on all the phones and checked—damn!"

His hand tightened on the phone. "What's wrong?"

"Oh, I just caught a glimpse of a Lotus leaving the Canfield house." A long pause, then a disgusted sigh. "He went the other way; I lost him in the traffic."

"Could you tell what color it was?"

"Black, I think, but I can't be sure with these street lights. I just had one quick look at him."

"Him? Could you—"

"No, I couldn't see the driver. I was just assuming it was Jim or Carleton. Whoever it was must've arrived after Catharine got rid of Alma and me."

His mouth tightened with annoyance; it could be important to know who had been visiting Catharine now.

"All right, Sean, I'll have to sign off now. Just keep up the good work, and be careful."

"Sounds like I should give *you* that advice."

8:47. Conan looked at his watch as he reached for the radio mike, finding it necessary to shout against the static.

"Harry, can you hear me?"

"Just barely. I've got bad news, Conan. I lost the car. By the time I felt my way down the hill, the visit was over. I heard the motor rev up and ducked out of sight. He took off hell bent."

Conan squeezed his eyes shut and missed the white flash, but heard Munson's startled exclamation against the static punctuated roll of thunder.

"Damn, I should get hazard pay for this."

"Harry, could you tell anything at all about the car?"

"From the set of the lights and the sound of the motor, I'd say it was a sports car."

"Well, that narrows the field to nearly everyone involved in this case."

"I'm sorry, Conan. You want me to go check on Jenny?"

"Can you see anything through the windows?"

A brief pause, then, "I don't think so. The shades are down on all the ones I can see."

"Try to find a crack in the shades, but don't go in. Jenny has that gun, and in her condition she might take a shot at a stranger breaking in on her. I'll try to call her, then I'm coming out. I'll be there in five minutes."

He didn't wait for a reply, but switched the radio off and reached for the phone. His hands were shaking. He thought fleetingly of Isadora, but there wasn't time to call Berg.

After the first two rings, each succeeding burr sounded a chilling alarm in his mind that was nearly paralyzing. But after the sixth ring, that mental alarm sent him across the room to the door in a headlong rush.

CHAPTER 19

"*Conan, this is a mayday!*"

The gears protested at his off-timed shift into first while he fumbled for the mike, wrenching the wheel around with his left hand to pull the car out of a shrieking skid.

"Carl? What's wrong"

"It's Isadora. She's headed for the cottage, and the state she's in, I don't know if she'll make it."

He hit the accelerator, the rain crashing against the windshield, blurring the line of lights marking the highway.

"What happened, Carl?"

"She got a phone call, said something to Max about Jenny, then took off for her car at a dead run. I didn't have time to call you. I'm right behind her—south of the bookshop. Where are you?"

"My car. Day street and the highway inter—good God!"

A swerving blur of headlights spun around the curve to the south, and Conan, froze, watching the car skid broadside, nearly colliding with another approaching from the north, then weaving back into the far lane. It passed him in an arching spray; a silver Stingray. He geared down, waiting in frenzied impatience for a break in the traffic.

"Carl, she just passed. Damn, she'll kill herself—"

"I tried to stop her; followed her out to the parking lot, but she didn't even recognize me."

"How did she *look*? Could you see her eyes?"

"Not enough light, then she got away from me and—"

"Never mind." He dropped the mike to take advantage of a narrow opening, careened onto the highway, then even before he had the car fully under control, he was reaching for the mike again.

"Carl, go to my house. I don't care how you get in. Call Nicky Heideger. Tell her it's an emergency and to bring some Thorazine. Leave the front door open for her, then come out to the cottage."

"Okay, but what—" Berg's question was cut off. Conan didn't have a hand to spare for the mike. The XK-E lunged ahead, in full cry, swerving from lane to lane, slipping through knots of cars with hair-breadth tolerances, the windshield wipers beating furiously. The red warning of the one traffic light he ignored, his speed never dropping under 50. When he reached the Shanaway road, the speedometer hit 80 in the open stretch by the golf course.

He kept anticipating the scream of sirens, half expecting to come upon Isadora cornered by a patrol car, or worse, crushed in a rack of crumpled steel. Yet somehow, incredibly, she escaped both fates, and he never managed to close the distance between them. When he roared up the rutted, muddy road to the cottage, the Stingray was already there, nosed in at a rakish angle, its headlight making shining paths in the rain. He skidded to a jerking halt and ran toward the open door of the cottage. Harry Munson emerged from the trees, shouting, a flapping apparition in his rain parks. Conan didn't pause; he was hardly aware of him.

But inside the house, he came to an abrupt stop.

Two things registered in that first split second: The white-draped figure sprawled on the floor, and Isadora Canfield kneeling beside it, one hand over her mouth muffling an anguished scream, the other hand raised, holding a gun that was aimed directly at him.

"No! Not again! Not again!"

"Dore, what—" Then he dropped to the floor, ears ringing with a shattering crack, something burning across his left forearm. He came up prepared to contend with another shot, but she was staring at him with dazed recognition.

"Conan? Oh, my God, Conan . . ." She began trembling uncontrollably, the gun fell from her nerveless hand, and he had to move fast to catch her before she hit the floor in a dead faint.

As he knelt, supporting her limp body, he became fully aware of the still figure on the floor.

Jennifer Hanson, shrouded in a voluminous nightgown, the left side of her face smeared with blood, her eyes half open, but unseeing.

Those eyes would never see again.

"Conan?"

He felt a hand on his shoulder, and at the insistent repetition of his name, turned his head. Harry Munson was bending over him.

"Conan, are you all right?"

He was too sick to answer. Only the helpless weight of Isadora in his arms finally brought his fragmented mental processes into some semblance of order. He rose, lifting her, his voice strangely flat even in his own ears.

"Harry, check the bug on that phone."

He carried her to the couch and moved some pillows under her head. Her pulse, like her breathing, was fast and erratic. She was clothed in a thin chiffon dress and soaked to the skin. A weak moan escaped her, but she didn't open her eyes. He left her to find the linen closet in the hall, then returned with a blanket to cover her.

"The bug in the jack is gone," Munson said, tossing off his raingear as he approached the couch. "But ours is still there. What happened to—"

"Stay with her, Harry." He went to the phone, using his handkerchief when he picked up the receiver. Munson frowned uneasily at the red-stained sleeve of his jacket, then knelt beside Isadora, his features drawn and perplexed.

"Conan?"

He began dialing. "Yes?"

"Did she—did she kill Jenny?"

He turned, looking down at Isadora, and she seemed as ravaged as the victim of some awesome natural disaster.

"Is that what you think?"

"I'm asking you."

"No."

"But—"

"Excuse me. Steve? This is Conan."

Travers began with an impatient, "Now, look—"

"I'm sorry about your hockey game, but I have a murder for you."

"A what? Are you putting me on?"

"I wish I were. The Canfield cottage at Shanaway. Jennifer Hanson."

"Oh, no . . ."

"Steve, I also have a—a nervous breakdown on my hands. I'm leaving Harry Munson here, but I'm giving him instructions to talk to no one but you or someone you trust."

"I'll be down," he responded tersely. "I'll send a patrol car out now, but tell Munson to sit tight until I get there. And I'll contact the county sheriff."

"Thanks. I'll talk to you later." He replaced the receiver carefully. "Steve's coming himself, Harry. He's sending a patrol car now, but you're to answer no questions until he arrives. How is she?"

He pressed his hand to her forehead with surprising solicitude.

"Coming around, but she's not with us yet."

Conan nodded, turning to look down at Jenny's body. Finally, he knelt beside her, fighting back an overwhelming urge to weep or be sick, but managing with a concentrated effort to study that silent flesh with some detachment.

The bullet had entered an inch above the left eye. He lifted her head; it hadn't emerged. The blood was beginning to congeal, even to dry at the edges. The nightgown was immaculately white, no stains or tears. A blue slipper covered one foot, but the other was naked.

Then he frowned at the hand lying near her head. Bloodstains under the fingernails. No. Too red; too blue a red. Alizarin crimson. Paint.

He used his handkerchief again when he examined the gun; Jenny's gun. Two bullets were missing. At length, he rose and returned to the couch. Isadora's cheek was wet with rain, but still hot to his touch. There was a flicker of movement behind her closed lids, but she didn't respond to her name. He straightened and crossed to the studio, finding a sterile irony in the newly stretched canvases propped against the walls; canvases that would never know Jennifer Hanson's brush on their pristine surfaces.

But the canvas on the easel was no longer pristine. The biting odor of turpentine was heavy in the air and the paint on the palette was fresh.

The canvas was a horizontal, about two feet wide and four long. He studied it, wondering what he expected of Jenny's last painting. A sign, perhaps, or a masterwork?

But it was neither; it was only a beginning. Two simple, abstract forms outlined in broad strokes of red against a mottled background of yellows ranging from earthy ochre to steely zinc yellow. The red lines formed two equilateral triangles, side by side, their twin apexes pointing upward. But as if to avoid a stultifying symmetry, the slashing horizontal line that might have made a base for both triangles extended only far enough to enclose the one on the right; the other was incomplete, the bottom side open.

He turned away, oppressed with a sense of urgency that impelled him back into the living room and made him tense at the sound of a car. But it was too early for the patrol car.

"That must be Carl." He leaned over Isadora, speaking her name. Her head moved back and forth fitfully, but she wasn't fully conscious yet.

Munson said, "Maybe I should find some brandy or—"

"No. No alcohol and don't try to shock her awake." A car door slammed. "Have Carl fill you in on what happened at the Surf House. I want to check Jenny's bedroom."

The light was on in Jenny's room, the bed covers thrown back, the pillows propped up for reading; a paperback lay on its open pages on the floor. Ben Shahn's *The Shape of Content*. He heard the front door close, a subdued dialogue; Berg and Munson. There was no gun in the drawer under the bedside table; only three vials of morphine and a syringe.

He stared at them, anger threatening the bonds of his control, then turned his attention to the door, attracted by the slipper lying near it. Its mate was on Jenny's body. He noted the black rubber sole, but only after he saw the dark, horizontal streak just above the doorknob.

When he heard Isadora's voice, overtones of hysteria in it against the counterpoint of Munson's soothing tones, he hurried back to the living room. She was sitting up, clinging to the back of the couch, oblivious to Munson, her face pressed into the cushions, muffling her ragged sobs.

"Conan?" Carl Berg, standing near the front door.

"Did you get hold of Nicky Heideger?"

"Yes, she'll be waiting at your house." He looked down at Jenny's body, then at Isadora. "Damn, I should've stopped her somehow. I never thought she'd do anything like this."

"Think again, Carl." Conan sat down beside Isadora and pulled the blanket up around her shoulders. At that, she drew back eyes wide, so dilated almost no blue showed.

"Dore, look at me," he said softly. "You know me."

"Conan?" She collapsed into his arms, the sobbing renewed. "Oh, God help me, I'm going out of my mind—*Conan!*"

"You'll be all right, Dore. Trust me, just trust me." He looked up at Munson. "Did you monitor any calls from this phone at—Carl, when did Dore get that call?"

"8:50."

"I don't know," Munson said. "I set up the tape recorder in the car, and haven't had a chance to check it yet."

"Check it as soon as you can." It was becoming impossible to keep his voice level against Isadora's agonized weeping. "Carl, go back to the Surf House; I want to know who served her that cup of coffee. And try to get a line on Hicks and Garner."

Berg glanced at Isadora. "Can you handle her?"

"Yes. Call me later. I'll be at home."

"Okay, and good luck."

At the slamming of the door, Isadora began trembling violently, the sobbing edged with panic. He held her tighter, his cheek pressed against her rain-wet hair.

"Harry, I have to get her out of here."

"What do I tell Travers?"

"Everything."

He hesitated. "Even where Miss Canfield is?"

Conan said coldly, "She isn't a fugitive. Dore, come on, I'll take you—" But she was suddenly rigid in his arms, terror-stricken. He heard the approaching wail of a siren.

"White . . . oh, too white . . . it hurts, oh . . . it—"

The words dissolved into short, gasping screams; she jerked away from him, the blanket slipped in his hands, and she was free, swaying to her feet, running blindly toward the windows.

Conan lunged, caught her, and almost lost her again.

Then abruptly, her cries ceased and she sagged against him.

"Oh, help me . . ."

CHAPTER 20

Building the fire was an esthetic experience; it occupied his mind and muscles and created an atmosphere of warm calm. Like the music on the stereo system. Debussy *Sirènes*. Green and crystal blue music for Isadora; for the part of her mind that listened even in tranquilized sleep.

He put the poker in its rack and looked up to the balcony and the open door of the guest room where Nicky Heideger tended her patient. He could only see the softly lighted walls and ceiling. All quiet now; the whole house warm and quiet. Yet an hour ago, it had echoed with screams.

Those screams were meaningful, however irrational.

Isadora wept during the interminable drive from the cottage, struggling against the seat belts, assaulted by hallucinations, terrified by every shadow and light, yet she'd still been capable of responding to his voice and touch. Only when Nicky took out the syringe for the Thorazine injection did the hysteria slip entirely out of control.

Then it had taken all his strength and Nicky's combined to hold her long enough for the injection. She fought with the desperate ferocity of mortal fear, the screams tearing her throat. Later, he saw the bruises on her arms and realized he had caused them, and the words kept echoing in his mind.

Not again . . . not again . . .

The same words she'd spoken when she looked up from Jenny's body and saw him; when she fired the gun at him.

Under the sleeve of his robe, a strip of cloth was wrapped around his forearm as a temporary bandage. A minor wound, only a graze; he could ignore the pain.

Not again . . .

Who had she been seeing when she pulled the trigger?

He looked for his watch, but he'd forgotten to put it back on. Once the Thorazine took effect and he'd carried Isadora up to the guest room, Nicky ordered him to get out of his soaked clothes and take a hot shower. He'd accepted her warnings of potential pneumonia knowing full well her real purpose was simply to rid herself of a distraction.

The storm had settled down to a steady, pelting rain. There was still some wind; it came in gusts that shimmered the reflections of warm fire in the windows. He looked out past the reflections into the blackness, thinking of death.

He understood more about John Canfield's death because of Jennifer Hanson's, but there was no comfort in that. He'd been forced to go into the library twice; both Berg and Munson had called with reports. Otherwise, he doubted he'd have ventured into that room to face the Knight.

"The least you could do is offer me a cup of coffee."

He turned, smiling at Nicky Heideger as she came down the stairs. She was carrying her medical case.

"I put a fresh pot on. Is there something else I could at least offer?"

"Coffee will do for now."

When he returned from the kitchen, she was sitting on the end of the couch that faced the fireplace, her medical case open on the side table. She tasted her coffee, then motioned him to the chair at right angles to the couch.

"Sit down. I'll take care of that arm."

He complied and rested his arm on the table, watching a vertical crease appear between her brows as she pushed his sleeve back and removed the cloth.

"How'd you do this?"

"I must've caught it on a nail."

"In that case, I'd better give you a tetanus shot."

"That's just pique. Nicky, how is she?"

"She's all right now, but that was a bad one; as bad as I've ever seen. Who is she?"

"A client."

She shrugged and began swabbing the long, red cut with antiseptic, only smiling at his quick intake of breath.

"Smarts a little? Well, my mother used to tell me, if it doesn't hurt, it doesn't help."

"Modern medicine marching on," he commented sourly, watching her deft, practiced movements. "Nicky, if you're worried about your legal position, my client is of age."

She didn't look up. "Who's worried? By the way, *Doctor* Flagg, thanks for prescribing the Thorazine."

"She's had it before. This isn't her first attack."

"*Attack?* What are you talking about?"

"A schizoid attack. That's how it was diagnosed on the previous occasions. Of course, her doctor didn't see her while the attacks were in progress, and her symptoms were confused by physical illness and grief."

Nicky methodically applied an antibiotic salve.

"Who's her doctor, or is that confidential, too?"

"Milton Kerr. Morningdell. I'll take her to him tomorrow unless someone stops me."

"Why would anybody—" Then she sighed and unwrapped a pair of gauze pads. "Well, it's a good idea to get her to Morningdell. Here, hold these."

He held the pads over the wound while she unfurled a length of gauze and began looping it around his arm.

"All right," she said when she had the pads anchored.

"Anyway, I hope you don't mind another guest for the night."

He frowned, watching the perfectly aligned, overlapping loops fall into place.

"Of course, I don't mind, but why—"

"Not to chaperone you," she said with a sidelong smile. "She'll probably be all right, but these things are funny, you know. I doubt you can handle another 'attack' alone."

"Nicky, didn't anyone tell you doctors don't stay all night at their patient's side anymore?"

"You think I'm doing this out of the kindness of my heart? Where do I send my bill, anyway?"

"To me. I'll put it on my expense account under miscellaneous. And you can have my room for the night."

"Thanks, but there's a couch in the guest—" She frowned, distracted by the door bell. "Who the hell's that?"

"Probably Steve Travers."

"Just keep that arm right there." She was already on her feet and on her way. "I'll let him in."

He relaxed and waited. His back was to the hall, but he didn't turn, listening to the friendly exchange at the front door, then the hall closet opening, Steve's comments on the weather as he hung up his coat, their voices drawing nearer, Steve asking, "All right, where's Miss Canfield?"

"I don't know a Miss Canfield," Nicky said as she returned to the couch and Conan's bandage.

Travers stopped behind the couch; a lean, spare, slack-shouldered man with brownish hair the color of desert flats, eyes the gray-green of sagebrush.

"Hello, Steve."

He nodded, looking down at Conan's arm.

"I guess she didn't hit anything vital."

"It was a rusty nail," Nicky put in.

Conan laughed. "Did I say it was rusty?"

"Does it matter what you said? How does it feel?"

He pulled his sleeve down over the finished bandage.

"Like hell."

"Take some aspirin. I mean, is the bandage too tight?"

"My hand hasn't turned purple yet. Just throw the debris in the fire, Nicky." As she cleaned up her makeshift surgery, he turned to Travers, who was waiting, but not patiently; his eyes had their old, long-distance squint.

"Steve, she's upstairs in the guest room."

"I want to talk to her."

"You'll have to ask Nicky about that."

He frowned irritably. "The run-around stops here, Nick. I want to see Miss Canfield. That's an official request."

"Well, you can certainly *see* her." The she added, "But you aren't going to *talk* to her."

"Now, look," he began hotly, but she only laughed.

"Steve, I'm simply stating a fact. That girl isn't talking to anyone for at least eight hours."

He nodded, apparently satisfied. "How is she?"

"Heavily sedated right now. She was in bad shape."

"That's what Munson said. Well, I'd better *see* her, anyway. I have to call Mrs. Canfield back."

Conan looked up. "You've already talked to her?"

"Yes."

"How did she take it? I mean, about Jenny?"

"I don't know. Quiet. I've heard it before; all cool and business as usual, and you wonder when they're going to fall apart." He paused, briefly withdrawn. "She seemed relieved you were looking after Isadora, but she wanted me to call back after I checked on her."

"Nicky, perhaps you should talk to her." Then at her nod, "One favor, though. Isadora is suffering from shock; nothing more."

She raised an eyebrow. "Really? Well, I guess it's just a question of semantics. Some on, Steve. It's time I checked my patient, anyway."

* * *

Travers's call seemed to take a long time. Nicky went into the library with him, emerging a few minutes later to assure Conan that Catharine Canfield was assured. Then she went upstairs; the guestroom door was closed now.

He busied himself with choosing more music for the stereo, and when Travers finally came out of the library, he was again working at the fire.

"What did she say, Steve?"

"Not much." He went to the bar and casually helped himself. "I'm supposed to tell you she's sure you'll 'protect Isadora from any unpleasantness.' Jim and Carleton were on hand; I had to talk to them, too."

"Did they have anything interesting to offer?"

"No, but I wasn't pushing it. Mostly, Carleton was making lawyer noises, so I gave him the story—with a few deletions. Like the fact Berg and Munson were on the job."

"Good. I hope you can keep a lid on that."

"I'm working on it." He had two glasses when he left the bar, one of which he presented to Conan. "Here, you look like you could use it."

"Thanks." He took the glass, cold in his hand warmed by the fire, and watched Travers as he slouched down on the couch. "*Can* you keep a lid on it?"

"Well, I passed the word that Berg and Munson will be surprise witnesses. That usually makes a pretty good lid. Anybody working for me knows some heads will roll if it leaks out. I can't put much pressure on Sheriff Wills, but he seemed impressed. Anyway, Carleton and Jim are coming down in the morning to take care of the arrangements for Jenny."

"You'll have someone at the cottage if they—"

"It's officially sealed. They'll have an escort, and if they take anything out, it'll be duly recorded."

"Did Carleton say when they plan to arrive?"

"About nine. I had a hard time talking him out of coming tonight. All I need is Carleton underfoot." He frowned down at his drink. ''You know, your client's in one hell of a mess. Sheriff Wills calls it an open-and-shut case.''

''No doubt. Is he making any trouble?''

''No. He's delighted to dump it in the state's lap. He expressed his opinion, then went home to bed. By the way, the sheriff's office had a call from a 'neighbor' at Shanaway; said he heard a shot from the Canfield cottage.''

''Sure. Harry was closer than any neighbors, and he couldn't hear a shot in that storm. When was the call made?''

''8:55. No name or address, of course.''

''Any calls to the state police?''

''No. I checked.''

''An open-and-shut case. Well, Sheriff Wills has demonstrated why he was called.''

''Maybe, but right now it looks like an open-and-shut case from the state's point of view, too. Your client *was* found by the body with the murder weapon in her hand, and on top of that, she took a pot shot at the first person to walk in, which happened to be you—her fiancé, no less.''

His eyes narrowed. ''Fiancé? Where'd you get that?''

''Catharine Canfield.''

''Oh.'' He smiled and sipped at his bourbon. ''That's interesting. Don't worry about it; it's only a ploy.''

Travers laughed. ''I already figured that out. You may have slipped once, but you're too confirmed a bachelor to slip twice.''

''Maybe Isadora is too confirmed a spinster. Does the state intend to simply ignore a few rather pertinent facts?''

''Like what, Conan? Can you think of any facts a good prosecutor couldn't dispose of without any trouble?''

''I won't bother with the surveillance; that'll be explained as concern for Dore's mental stability. Except it's interesting that Garner and Hicks and tan Chevy have apparently left town. Carl couldn't find any of them.''

''I know; I talked to Carl. Oh, I forgot to tell you, I got a name on the tan Chevy. Everett Worth, himself.''

"Well, he's no more subtle than his employees. Is your prosecutor going to ignore Jenny's unknown visitor?"

"No, but he's out as a suspect. I mean, for murder. Pushing drugs, yes. But that stash in the bedroom says he went away happy. The point is, he went away *before* Jenny called Isadora at the Surf House. That's according to *your* operatives. Munson said the car left the cottage at 8:45; Carl said Jenny called Isadora at 8:50."

"Munson also said *no* calls were made from the cottage at 8:50. He phoned me tonight after he checked the tapes."

"I know. So, maybe he had a mechanical failure."

"Oh, for God's sake, Steve—"

"He *recorded* no call, but Max Heinz *took* a call."

"And Max would recognize Jenny's voice?"

"Maybe not, but supposedly your client would. Max said she used Jenny's name during the conversation, and afterward she told him, 'Jenny's in trouble.' "

Conan's shoulders sagged. "You think she was capable of recognizing Jenny's voice in her mental state?"

"I don't know, but I can guess what a jury would say."

"All right, but what about the coagulation of the blood? Steve, it was already beginning to dry at—at the edges. Now, I wasn't more than a minute behind Dore when she reached the cottage. It couldn't have reached that state of coagulation in one minute."

"But who saw the wound *at that time*? Munson just had a glance at the body, then he was busy with Isadora. He didn't get a close look until after you left. By then it was too late for the state of coagulation to mean anything."

"And *my* testimony wouldn't mean anything?"

"Oh, Conan, you know any prosecutor worth his salt would tear you apart if you got on the stand. You aren't exactly an unbiased witness when it comes to Isadora Canfield."

"All right, but just answer me this: What possible motive would she have to kill Jenny?"

Travers's laugh was devoid of humor.

"Motive? Look, nobody's going for murder *one*. Not when your client has a history of mental illness."

Conan said angrily, "My client spent a month in a private hospital recovering from the shock of her father's death. That doesn't make a history of mental illness."

"You want to add the scars on her wrists and try that on a jury?"

He didn't respond immediately; instead, he went back to his chair and took a swallow of his drink. It tasted flat.

"So, the prosecutor will ask for mandatory institutionalization to lock away this insane menace to society."

"Probably," Travers said dully.

"That should please John Canfield's killer. It's exactly what he wanted from the beginning. If she ever recovers her memory her testimony will be inadmissible; no one will even listen to her. And you can be sure she'll never see her inheritance, nor anything beyond the gates of Morningdell for the rest of her life. She'd be better off with a murder one conviction; at least she'd have the hope of appeal or parole. But constitutional rights don't exist for anyone *accused* of mental illness." He stopped, cradling his head in his hands, his mind and memory full of music.

"Steve, have you ever heard her play?"

"No. I understand she's pretty good."

"She's more than good. Something so rare, so vital, you can't name it; you can only feel it." And weep for it, he added privately. "I wonder if they have a concert grand at Morningdell."

There was a short silence, then Travers said quietly, "I haven't called the case closed yet. Have you?"

Conan looked up at him, bridling at the question until he realized that was exactly his purpose.

"Is that what you call a rhetorical question?"

"It better be. But if you're interested in keeping the case open, we've got some figuring to do."

Conan's laugh was simply an expression of relief.

"All right, Steve. Where do we start?"

"With the facts; we'll get to the theories later. I want to know everything *you* know; every piece of information you've collected since Isadora Canfield first came to you."

He nodded. "I hope you have plenty of time."

"Not that much, probably, but I'll take it."

When Conan finally finished his account, Travers's glass was empty and his own was down to a watery mix barely colored with bourbon. But Travers showed no sign of impatience during the long recital, listening and questioning, outwardly so relaxed he seemed on the verge of torpor, except for the intent, horizon-spanning squint.

Now, he peered at his glass and rose. "Refill?"

"No. Help yourself."

Conan rose to replenish the fire, noting when Steve returned that the drink he'd mixed was both pale and short.

"Okay, Conan, let's talk about John Canfield."

"His murder?"

"I guess so. Bring on your theories. I'm braced."

He watched the fire a moment, then satisfied with his efforts, returned to his chair.

"I've only one basic theory, Steve; that Isadora witnessed her father's murder."

"How'd you arrive at that?"

He laughed. "Logically, of course; a gut feeling that something didn't ring true with that very convenient heart attack. The surveillance made me wonder why someone was so worried about Dore. I couldn't accept concern for her mental state as the reason for that, unless it was concern for her amnesia; for the possibility she might *recover* from it. The memory blackout begins right before she discovered her father's body, which made me wonder if that was all she discovered. Besides, the amnesia, and her attitude toward his death—in fact, everything about this so-called mental breakdown—smells. Steve, a lot more went on that night than showed up in the police reports. And, yes I *do* have some tangible evidence. Ben Meade gave it to me."

"That forty-five minute time lapse?"

"Yes, and her overnight case. Ben said he left it by the library door, but when she supposedly cut her wrists, it was upstairs in her bathroom; that's where the razor blade came from. So, how did it get upstairs? Would Dore make a trip upstairs with it before going in to talk to her father? Or when Jenny found her in screaming hysterics, would she pick it up when she took her to her room? Or when Jim arrived, would he even notice it, much less bother to take it with him when he went up to help Jenny with Dore?"

Travers slouched a little deeper into the couch.

"Not likely. You think somebody took it upstairs during that forty-five minutes? Why?"

"So the razor blade would be handy."

"By the way, what do you mean by her *supposedly* cutting her wrists? Was that a figment of somebody's imagination?"

Conan took time to light another cigarette, frowning at the dry, hot taste of it.

"They were cut. With a double-edged blade. Now, I defy anyone, particularly in a highly emotional state, to use a double-edged blade to cut *anything* without ending up with sliced fingers. Look at Dore's hands. Pianists are nearly manic about taking care of their hands, and hers are devoid of scars—except for her wrists."

"Well, I'll take your word for the state of her hands."

He managed a smile, but lost it as he went on.

"Take Sean's word for this: Dore had a bottle of Seconal handy in her medicine cabinet, so why would she choose a razor blade instead? That suicide attempt was just icing on the cake of her insanity. Someone cut her wrists *for* her, and thank God it was only for effect; no real damage was done. Steve, I don't know what Dore saw when she went into the library, but it was enough to make her a threat to someone. At the very least she saw Canfield's killer. And the way he handled her was very ingenious, considering what an unexpected shock her arrival must have been. He couldn't just kill her, too. Designing another 'natural' death on the spur of the moment would be rather difficult, and an unnatural one would draw undue attention to Canfield's. What he did was establish that history of mental illness you were talking about. It almost has a legalistic twist."

Travers looked at him intently. "Carleton?"

"I don't know. There was an Elan outside the gate, and Jim is alibied by three of his brothers at Lambda Delta."

He nodded. "Let's get back to the way the killer theoretically handled Isadora."

"The same way he handled her tonight. What did Nicky tell you about this 'attack' of Dore's?"

Travers eyed him skeptically. "She said it looked like a classic bad trip. Now, I notice you seem to think Jenny was the only user in this case, so how do you explain that?"

Conan said flatly, "Isadora isn't a user."

"Then Nick's off her nut?"

"No. The term implies *voluntary* use of drugs."

"Is that how she was 'handled'? Some kind of drug?"

"Yes. Specifically LSD. The night of her father's death, I think she was also given a particularly bad set; something so terrifying, she's locked it away in amnesia—along with whatever she saw in the library. That's what was going on during that forty-five minutes."

"But don't you think they could tell the difference between a bad trip and a schizoid attack at Morningdell?"

"She was already sedated when she arrived at Morningdell, and she was physically ill. No one there saw the symptoms like Nicky did tonight. And remember, when LSD was first discovered, it was called a 'psychotomimetic' because it mimicked psychotic states, particularly schizophrenia. Steve, they weren't looking for LSD symptoms. They had no reason to suspect it when she was admitted, and later Dr. Kerr diagnosed her as an unlikely candidate for drug abuse.

But I've seen one recurrence myself, and there were others; the sensory disfunction, distorted body perception, the absence of aural hallucinations—it's all there."

"But the amnesia isn't normal with LSD."

"No, it's just a normal means of dealing with something intolerable, and it was probably encouraged with the initial set."

Travers brooded over his glass, then, "That metal cylinder Sean found—she said it looked like a perfume spray—you didn't explain why you think it's a murder weapon."

"The amyl nitrate. It's something I encountered back in my G-2 days; a favorite technique of Smersh. Prussic or hydrocyanic acid fired in the form of a vapor into the victim's face. Death is almost instantaneous, and any pathologist will read it as simple heart failure."

"What about the amyl nitrate?"

"Protection for the assassin in case he gets a whiff of the vapor. Hydrocyanic acid is a vaso-constrictor; it constricts the vessels of the heart. Amyl nitrate is a vaso-dilator. An antidote of sorts."

"Then you think that cylinder had hydrocyanic acid in it? That's how Canfield was killed?"

"Yes. That's what caused 'cardiac arrest' in a perfectly healthy man with no history of heart disease."

"But that cylinder and the drug stash was in Jenny's room. How do you figure that?"

"It doesn't mean she had anything to do with Canfield's murder; she wouldn't keep the evidence so handy. But if anyone ever decided to investigate it, as an addict she was an ideal scapegoat, and she was already set up for the role."

"What about your theories on Jenny's death? You think she knew something about Canfield's murder? Maybe she was killed to shut her up."

"Yes, but not necessarily about the murder. Just the fact she could name her supplier would be motive enough. That wasn't a problem when she was safely hooked, but *un*hooked she was definitely a threat, and I had the impression she made that quite clear when she called her pusher."

"And yet you think she agreed to see him tonight? That doesn't make sense."

He took a long breath, aware of the aching of his arm.

"I know, but I'm sure she considered herself in no danger. Of course, I doubt she actually intended to betray him."

Travers frowned. "I guess he didn't get that message."

"He was under a great deal of pressure, and I made it worse hinting around about marrying Dore. When you bring in the Canfield name, you're dealing with money and power on a large scale. A conviction for drug peddling wouldn't be just an inconvenient interruption in business for someone with ambitions in that sphere; it would be a total disaster."

"Yes, *if* the pusher's the one with the big ambitions; if he killed Canfield."

Conan put out his cigarette and started to light another, then tossed the package aside irritably.

"He is, Steve. Otherwise, you wouldn't have an open-and-shut case against Isadora."

"What do you mean?"

"Look, if he simply wanted to get rid of Jenny, why not make it an 'accidental' OD, or even suicide? Either one would be far more reasonable and entail far less risk."

Travers nodded as he tipped up his glass.

"Okay, so why did he bring Isadora in on it?"

"Because he considered her as much a threat as Jenny. He disposed of Jenny by killing her, and with the same stone, disposed of Dore by framing her for it, and in the process reinforcing that history of mental illness. Dore wasn't a threat to Jenny's *pusher*; she didn't even know she was addicted. She's only a threat to her father's killer."

"But what about that phone call Jenny made to Isadora?"

"That's part of the frame. Jenny didn't make that call. She was already dead when her visitor in the sports car left the cottage, five minutes before the call was made. And I'm sure she was killed in her bedroom, by the way."

"Because of the slipper and the mark on the door?"

"Yes, and the unmade bed, the open book on the floor, and because she kept her gun in the drawer by the bed. I think she was carried into the living room after she was shot; her foot hit the door and knocked the slipper off."

"Okay, but why was the body moved?"

"So Isadora would all but stumble over it when she came in; so the gun would be handy and in all probability she'd pick it up, which she obligingly did."

"And fired it at you."

"Again, obligingly. But she wasn't firing at me; only at a memory."

Travers smiled crookedly. "She just happened to hit you. All right, let's get back to the phone call."

"After the killer left the cottage, he stopped at a convenient phone booth and called the Surf House, imitating Jenny's voice. It didn't have to be too good an imitation; Max had never talked to Jenny, and Dore was already embarked on her bad trip by then."

"Then he went on home and let nature take its course?"

"After calling the county sheriff's office. But he was ignorant of two vital facts. One was our county gendarmes' lack of alacrity; he probably expected Sheriff Wills to walk in on that tableau. The other was Munson and Berg."

"And you." He finished off his drink and put the glass on the side table. "Well, for gut logic it makes some sense. But how'd your killer get a dose of LSD to Isadora tonight? By phone?"

Conan shrugged. "The timing, if nothing else, points to the coffee she had when she arrived at the Surf House."

"I wondered why Carl was so interested in the part-time help down there."

"He gave me their names. I suppose you have them?"

"I've already called in and run them through the computers." He took out a notebook and thumbed through it. "Let's see—here. One's a local woman, clean as new snow, but the other you'll be interested in. Mildred Weaver, known as 'Milly.' At the present time, she's out on parole."

"What was she sent up for?"

"Prostitution and possession of narcotics. And one guess who her defense counsel was."

He smiled coldly. "C. Robert Carleton."

"Himself. That's all I've got on her now."

"Steve, there's another line to follow up, and you can put more heft behind it than I can."

"The Worth Detective Agency?"

"Yes." Then he frowned. "Although, I doubt whoever hired Worth would be fool enough to tell him too much."

"It might help to know who did the hiring." He paused, watching Conan. "Wouldn't it?"

He was scowling at the patterns in the Lilihan.

"I don't know. It seems . . . I mean, Canfield's murder was so perfectly executed there isn't a shred of real proof it *was* a murder. It seems a bit careless to leave such obvious trails through Milly Weaver or Everett Worth."

"Let's see where those trails lead before you start talking about carelessness. Do your theories include the name of this perfect executer? You keep using a masculine pronoun."

"Mainly because our language has no really functional neuter pronoun, and of course, Harry was relatively sure Jenny's visitor was male. No, I don't have a name in my theories, Steve, but I was thinking about something Dr. Kerr said; that Isadora might be the victim of some sort of conspiracy. It was just a figure of speech, but maybe a conspiracy is exactly what we're dealing with."

"And who's included in it?"

"In Canfield's death, logically the people who were threatened by him or stood to gain by his death: his wife, his lawyer, possibly Jenny, and Jim."

"Jim? I don't see how he was threatened by Canfield, and his share of the estate wasn't that impressive."

"That's relative, and don't you think he'd be interested in his mother's share? Of course, he's neatly alibied."

"But Carleton doesn't have an alibi."

"Neither does Catharine, and it's unlikely someone could come into the house, commit a murder, and subdue and drug an unexpected witness, without her being aware of it. Her bedroom is just above the foyer, and Ben said the door was open when he took Isadora in."

"I'd better have a talk with Meade." He paused, pursing his lips. "You said he was serious about Isadora—maybe you're looking in the wrong direction. Maybe he's running an illicit pharmacy on the side, and Jenny was one of his customers. Like you said, she was no threat while she was hooked, but what if Canfield found out? That'd shoot down Ben's hopes of marrying an heiress. So, the Senator had a handy heart attack. Then Jenny decided to get unhooked—"

"—and she got a handy bullet in her head. That did occur to me. Ben drives a sports car, incidentally."

Travers sighed. "Beautiful."

"But there are some flaws in the theory. Canfield's murder took careful planning and special equipment. Heart failure and schizoid attacks can be induced or imitated, but not viral infections. Ben couldn't *plan* on Dore's illness, and without it, he wouldn't have had the opportunity to kill Canfield. Not that night, at least. But the real flaw is Jenny's murder. He'd be a damned fool to involve his potential bride in such a way that she could lose control of her inheritance *before* he managed to marry her."

"So, we're left with Carleton and the Canfields."

"Maybe." He rose to tend the fire, although it needed no help from him at the moment. "But there are some flaws in that theory, too. What bothers me is Catharine. I can accept her involvement in a conspiracy to kill Canfield, but not Jenny. Her own daughter, Steve, who played nurse to her all these years, who must've known about the blindness gambit, but never betrayed her."

"How do you know she never betrayed her?"

He put the poker aside and stared into the flames.

"I can't believe Jenny would go on living in the same house with her if she had. She wasn't a game player."

"And how can you be so sure of that?"

He closed his eyes, but only briefly. He wasn't ready to face the image that waited there in memory.

"I have a painting of hers."

Travers's short silence and raised eyebrow were eloquent.

"The nice thing about being a professional dilettante is you can have fun playing around with theories and psychic analyses. Now, I'm just a plain, ordinary professional, and I have to deal with common *facts*."

Conan laughed and turned to face him.

"Then we'd better get more facts to deal with, and we won't collect any, common or rare, standing here talking."

"We? *I'm* the one who has to go out in the rain and collect facts tonight."

"And this is your day off. However, I think I've been out in the rain and collected enough facts for one night. Steve, we'd better make some plans."

"I was afraid of that. Plans for what?"

"Protecting Isadora, for one thing. If the killer isn't satisfied that he's silenced her, she's in danger, and not just physical danger. She's already had several good doses of LSD. Too much of it can cause true psychosis."

"I know. I've seen a few—well, never mind. But I hope you haven't forgotten she's still the most obvious suspect for Jenny's murder, and I'll be getting pressure from the brass to do something about it."

"I'm counting on your doing something, but even your most brazen brass will probably admit that someone suffering a nervous breakdown, to use the tried and untrue euphemism, is in no condition to be put in the Taft County jail."

"They'll probably admit it for a while, anyway."

"I want her in Morningdell, Steve. That's the only place she'll be safe, and Dr. Kerr is the only hope for recovering that lost memory."

He considered this for a moment, then nodded.

"Okay, I can probably get away with holding her as a material witness under Kerr's recognizance and with a police guard. For a few days, at least."

"She must have the guard, full-time and live-in."

"I can take care of that. What about Kerr?"

"I'll call him tonight. I doubt he'll offer any objections. And I want her out of town and in Morningdell *before* Carleton and Jim arrive tomorrow morning."

Travers gave him a sardonic smile.

"I'll have somebody on your doorstep with all the proper papers at eight. That's A.M."

"You get somebody here, and Dore and I will be ready."

"You're going to Salem with her?"

"That's where the action is—or will be."

Travers pulled himself to his feet, stifling a yawn.

"Sure, but meanwhile, I still have some more action here before I can go home."

Conan followed him to the hall closet, waiting while he shrugged on his coat.

"Steve, thanks for handing me the paddle."

He laughed. "It'll probably just put us both up the same creek. Call me tomorrow. I'll be at the office."

"On Sunday?"

"Listen, when this hits the papers, there won't be any more days of rest in my department."

CHAPTER 21

In spite of a flamboyantly blooming plum tree near the window, the view was depressing. Centered in a flawless expanse of lawn, a flagpole supported two limp banners; the blue Oregon state flag surmounted by the Stars and Stripes. Beyond that, a swath of asphalt and the flash of moving cars, then another stretch of lawn and another flag pole with the same banners. But that pole topped the corner turret on the concrete, slab-shaped walls of the Oregon State Penitentiary.

Conan stared at those walls, wondering how they could contain life in any form, then turned away, taking a quick look at his watch.

Steve Travers was on the phone, feet propped on his desk, the antique swivel chair tilted at a perilous angle. In the comfortably cluttered effluvium of his working existence, that relic of a chair seemed more appropriate than the other regulation, anodized appointments of the office.

Conan caught himself looking at his watch again, and turned to the window with a frown of annoyance. It was becoming a nervous habit, checking the time every few minutes.

Monday, and with the afternoon shadows crossing the lawns, another day was slipping away. His memory of the day before, beginning with the early morning drive in the wake of the police car that took Isadora to Morningdell, was a blur of frustrations exacerbated by closed offices, short staffs, and clamoring reporters.

The only hopeful note was the fact that Isadora had wakened with no apparent aftereffects from her ordeal by drugs, entirely rational and stubbornly defiant of public opinion or fate. Outwardly so, at least. Dr. Kerr had given up most of his Sunday to work with her, but in a private conversation with Conan this morning, he reported the amnesia still firmly entrenched. Even her memory of Jenny's death was vague and fragmented.

Conan turned at the protesting squeal wrung from Travers's chair when he leaned forward to hang up the phone without bothering to shift his feet from the desk.

"Donlevy's sending Milly Weaver over. She finally saw the light when the situation was spelled out for her."

"It's about time," Conan responded irritably.

"Well, the wheels grind slow, but we usually get there eventually."

"Unfortunately, the wheels of journalism grind rather quickly if not exceedingly fine. Did you see this morning's paper?"

"You're only the tenth person to ask me that. Have you seen the *evening* paper yet?"

"I refused to read it out of consideration for my digestive processes. I just got around to lunch an hour ago."

"Well, my digestive processes are shot to hell, and so are a few very highly placed processes. The governor called me this morning."

"A personal call? You should be flattered, Steve."

"That kind of flattery I could do without. I've got a mortgage and a family to think about. Conan, I can't hold off on an arrest much longer."

"Dore's arrest, you mean."

"Who else? No—forget I asked that. Have you been out to Morningdell today?"

He nodded and left the window to settle in the chair in front of Steve's desk.

"Dr. Kerr canceled most of his regular appointments for the next few days to work with Dore, and he's using everything in his psychiatric arsenal."

"He goes along with the LSD theory?"

"Yes, especially after talking to Nicky. But he wasn't very encouraging about breaking the memory block."

Travers frowned sourly. "Great. How is she?"

"Like the Rock of Gibraltar." He paused, looking out at the cloudy sky, patched with fragile blue. "But she's shaking inside. Anyway, Kerr's holding the line on his no visitors edict in spite of the complaints from the Canfields and Carleton. Oh, by the way, Dore said you have excellent taste in guards, especially Sergeant Michaels."

Travers smiled at that. "Ruby's got a string of stories from her NYPD days that'll last a good two weeks, non-stop."

Conan reached into his jacket for his cigarettes, noting that the package was almost empty. His consumption of cigarettes had skyrocketed in the last two days.

"What about the search of the Canfield house?"

He grimaced. "I got the papers and a team out there this morning, but the stash was gone. They came up with a big fat zero."

"Damn. Well, scratch one potential murder weapon."

"And the drugs? You heard from Sean lately?"

"This morning. She says the house is under siege by the press. Jim's been playing Horatio at the Bridge. Catharine's in a state of shock; Dr. Johnson was called in yesterday. Carleton's been in and out, in Sean's words, looking like a sick toad. I have Carl and Harry keeping an eye on Carleton and Jim, incidentally."

"Yes, and the state appreciates that, but just to ease your mind, I've got some guys watching the house, too."

"Glad to hear that. Have you gathered any alibis by now?"

Travers ignored his mildy accusing tone, swung his feet down, reached unerringly into one of the haphazard piles on his desk, and pulled out a manila folder.

"Right here. Let's see . . . Catharine dismissed the servants at 7:40 and went to bed. Bob Carleton left his office at six, ate at the Marion, got home at 7:30, and spent the evening working on briefs. Alone."

Conan sent out an impatient puff of smoke.

"Don't tell me Jim spent the evening studying."

"On the first Saturday of spring vacation? He and a fraternity brother went bar-hopping. When Catharine phoned the Lambda Delta house after she got the news about Jenny, they had to send somebody out to find him."

"It checks out?"

"Well, Jim and his buddy were definitely seen Saturday night in the bars they mentioned, but it was hard for anybody to pin down exact times. It was a busy night."

"Who's his buddy?"

"Kid named Chet Hinkle. Willamette's star halfback."

Conan's eyes narrowed. "Wasn't he one of the brothers who alibied Jim for the night of Canfield's death?"

"Right. Which may mean they're good friends."

"Apparently. What else do you have in that file?"

"Quite a lot for a couple of days' work, considering one was Sunday." He turned a few sheets. "Oh, speaking of Milly Weaver, which we weren't but will be, I have a statement from Max Heinz. Saturday afternoon about five, he got a call from somebody who said he was on the Parole Board. The guy gave him a long, sad story about Milly and asked him to give her a job, so Max said he'd put her on for the holiday. Then half an hour later, Milly's parole officer called asking if he'd *offered* her the job. Max thought it was a little odd, but to quote him, that's the government for you; the right hand never knows what the left hand is up to."

Conan smiled at that. "I suppose he remembered nothing pertinent about the first caller?" Then at Travers's negative head shake, "Do you have any of the lab reports yet?"

"Yes." He turned more pages. "The ME's report. Cause of death, bullet wound; time, about 9 P.M. No marks or bruises except a contusion on the back of the head."

"Was there any morphine in the body?"

"No, and those bottles hadn't been touched."

Conan wondered why there seemed to be some satisfaction in that; it wasn't unexpected.

"Any fingerprints on the bottles?"

"No. In fact, the fingerprint boys didn't turn up a damned thing. Nothing on the gun except Isadora's, and the rest of the house was a bust. No surprises from ballistics, either. The bullet that killed her came from her own gun."

"What about tire impressions?"

"With the rain, that road was just a big mudslide. They couldn't get anything worth—" He frowned at the buzz of the intercom and leaned forward to flick it on. "Yes?"

"Miss Weaver is here, sir."

His frown changed to a smile. "Send her in."

Milly Weaver eyed the chair Conan had vacated, then looked up to the window where he was standing and scrutinized him suspiciously. Her blond hair suggested brass, a little tarnished, but her eyes were polished steel. Conan wondered how old she was. Under night lights, she would probably look twenty; now she looked forty, and he doubted she was more than thirty.

Travers said pleasantly, "Have a seat, Milly."

She complied, crossing her legs in a posture of belligerent ease, took a cigarette from her purse, accepted a light, then informed him through a stream of smoke, "Listen, you got me up on a bummer."

Travers nodded agreeably. "Milly, you have a right to legal counsel, you know, before you answer any questions."

She made a succinct, unladylike comment, then, "*Legal* counsel. That's how I got into this mess. That damned shyster—" She stopped, rolling her cigarette between her fingers, steely eyes fixed on Conan. "Who's he?"

Travers laughed. "Not a shyster. Now, tell me what happened. How did you get into this mess?"

"I already told Donlevy."

"Well, you know how it is; we have to have everything in triplicate around here. I understand you've had a hard time finding a job lately."

"You're damn right. Then that—" She launched into a colorful description.

"You mean Carleton?" Travers asked finally.

"Yeah. He calls me up Saturday—"

"About what time was that?"

She shrugged. "Maybe five. Yeah, it was about five. I remember thinkin' he wasn't givin' me much time. I was supposed to be at the Surf House by seven."

"You're sure it was Carleton?"

"It was him. I mean, he said right off who he was, and then he has that kind of greasy voice. Likes to throw the big words around, too, y'know, like he's so damn eriodite."

"What did he say?"

She took a drag on her cigarette that pulled her rouged cheeks in.

"Well, he says he's got a line on a job for me; the Surf House, cocktailing. And listen, I was down and out broke, and I made up my mind I wouldn't go back to the street; there's nothin' in that when you get a few years on."

"So you accepted the job."

"Sure. I called Tomlin first; my parole officer. He checked

it out and said fine, good luck, and all that. Of course, that damn lawyer never did nobody any free favors."

"What did he expect in return?"

"Well, he gave me this big line, y'know, about how he has this client playin' at the Surf House."

"That was Isadora Canfield?"

"Yeah. Well, that kinda made me back off. I mean, everybody knows who *she* is. But he says there's some guy, a 'fortune hunter,' he says, and with her still shook from her old man kickin' off—well, anyway, he says she was gonna elope that night, and he had to stop her, y'know. Said it'd be a 'tragic and irredeemable mistake.' "

"And you were to help him stop her?"

"Yeah. He told me—well, I was supposed to slip her a mickey. He said he just wanted to make sure she didn't do any travelin' that night. Listen, you gotta believe me, I didn't know there was nothin' in that sugar could hurt her."

"Sugar?" Travers leaned forward. "What about sugar?"

"Well, he says she always uses sugar in her coffee, and I was supposed to look out for a chance to bring her a cup of coffee, like at her breaks, and switch the sugar packets."

"He gave you a packet to switch?"

"Sure." She made an attempt at a shrug. "I mean, he didn't *hand* it to me. He said it'd be in my mailbox along with . . . a little somethin' extra."

"Money?"

"Fifty bucks. Fifty lousy bucks."

"Did you see him leave it?"

"No. I live in this apartment house; the mailboxes are downstairs. All I know is there's this envelope in my box when I left for the beach. I gave it to Donlevy. He took the money, too."

"It'll be entered as evidence," he assured her, but she didn't seem convinced. "What were you supposed to do after you slipped her the sugar packet?"

"Call him. He gave me a number with an extension. I

can't remember the number, but it was extension seventeen, and I know it was the Surf House Motel, because when I dialed the number, somebody answers with that."

Travers looked over at Conan, who nodded.

"Room seventeen is where Hicks was staying. Carl said he left without checking out. You can be damned sure he left before Milly's friend settled in."

Travers turned to Milly. "All right, so you succeeded in getting the sugar to Miss Canfield?"

"Right. She came a little early and asked for a cup of coffee. Max was busy, so . . . well, I switched the sugar."

"And then called Carleton?"

"Yeah, from that phone booth in the hall."

"You're sure it was Carleton you talked to?"

She hesitated. "Well, sure. Sounded like him."

"What did he say?"

"He just wanted to know if there was any hitches, then he says I should forget the whole thing." She made a sour grimace. "I sure as hell wish I could forget it, damn him. If he figured I'd keep shut for a lousy fifty bucks—"

"Did you talk to him again?"

"No. Hell, I didn't find out till yesterday what happened. I mean, I never thought she'd go out and *murder* somebody."

Travers said tightly, "Milly, I appreciate your cooperation, and when the time comes I'll see that the judge hears about it. Sergeant Donlevy said you'd posted bail."

"Yeah." She rose and crushed out her cigarette. "He said I could go home when you're through with me."

"I'm through. But keep in touch."

Travers positioned his feet on top of the desk again.

"Charming young lady."

Conan was scowling out the window. "Lovely. Steve, don't you have enough pull to get an office on the other side of the building? You could have a view of Mount Hood."

Travers laughed. "I kind of like the view. Keeps my job in perspective. What do you think?"

"Of the perspective? Not much. As for Milly, I don't think she's lying, which doesn't mean she's telling the truth."

"Don't start getting philosophical on me. At least, now we have some proof Isadora was drugged."

"That doesn't prove she didn't kill Jenny, but it might sow some reasonable doubt." He wandered back to the chair and sank into it. "What else is in that pile of paper?"

Travers reached for the manila folder.

"Kind of an interesting statement from Everett Worth. Here it is. It was Bob Carleton who hired him. Beginning February twenty-fourth, he was to maintain full-time surveillance on Isadora. Carleton wanted to know where she went, who she talked to, and he was particularly interested in anything out of her usual routine. Worth said there was nothing along that line until you came into the picture. Carleton wanted a full dossier on you."

"Was anything said about her emotional problems?"

"Nothing. No reason was given for the surveillance. Anyway, Worth had a call from Carleton Saturday afternoon."

"He's sure it was Carleton?"

"Well, he signed this statement. Carleton called at 5:15, radio-telephone hook-up, to tell Worth he wanted him and his operatives off the case immediately. He got a little abusive; enough to get Worth good and steamed, so he and Garner and Hicks pulled up stakes and left town. But here's the really interesting part. Carleton gave specific orders for Hicks *not* to check out of his room at the Surf House. He said for him to leave the door unlocked, and he'd take care of the bill himself—which he neglected to do."

"He'd be a fool to show his face in the motel office. But Worth didn't actually talk to Carleton except by phone?"

"No. He says most of his business with Carleton is by phone. Anyway, that's the last he heard from him." He paused, eying Conan. "You don't seem very excited about all this. Wasn't Carleton your candidate for the bad guy?"

He shrugged. "All this business by phone makes me nervous. What else do you have?"

"Well, here's a statement from Ben Meade. Maybe you should check it in case there's anything he forgot to tell you." He put the report back in the file when Conan made no move to take it. "Okay, then I had a nice little chat with Marvin Hendricks from the Ladd-Bush Bank."

This roused his interest. "What did he say?"

"You can read it, but the real kicker concerns the will. He says he was at the Canfield house for a financial skull session with the Senator a week before he died, and he talked about changing his will. He didn't go into detail, but Catharine was definitely out entirely. Unfortunately, Hendricks is the discreet type; Canfield didn't volunteer an explanation, so he didn't ask. Anyway, there were some notes, dated and in Canfield's handwriting. Hendricks saw him put them in his desk drawer with the will. But after he died, only the will was found in that drawer."

"And all three principals were at the house at one time or another the night of his death."

"Right. Anyway, Hendricks had something else to add. Canfield told him he had his doubts about the way Carleton was using his power of attorney in connection with some trust funds, so he was holding off on the will changes until he found himself a new lawyer."

Conan frowned, then after a moment rose and wandered to the window.

"He really set himself up, didn't he? Take your pick of motives. And suspects. Any one of three, or any combination of two, or all three in conspiracy." Then he turned. "Carl told me Jim and Carleton took quite a few things from the cottage yesterday."

"I have the list here, if that's what you're after." He leafed through the folder and pulled out a sheet. Conan took it on his way back to the chair.

Most of the items were personal belongings, clothing and jewelry, both Jenny's and Isadora's. Only one entry caught his attention.

" 'One painting, oil on canvas.' Was that the painting on the easel in the studio?"

"Yes. The rest were just blank canvases, and I don't think that one was finished."

"No, I saw it."

"I talked to Sergeant Drew; he was at the cottage when Carleton and Jim were there. He said they got a little hot because there weren't any other paintings, as if we'd confiscated them. They looked through some of the sketchbooks, but that one painting is all they took from the studio."

"Whose idea was it, Jim's or Carleton's?"

"I asked Drew, and he kept an eye on them the whole time, but he couldn't hear everything they said. He really didn't know whose idea it was."

"Carl wasn't in a position to see the front drive at the Canfield house yesterday. Did any of your men see these things unloaded?"

"Well, as it happened, Dick Sims was there asking some questions. He's with the Salem PD, but he's helping on this. In fact, he gave Jim and Carleton a hand with the stuff. He said they put everything up in Jenny's studio, and he mentioned the painting. He belongs to Norman Rockwell school of art appreciation, and he had some comments on it."

Conan was silent, focusing on a memory; Jennifer Hanson's last painting, an unremarkable and unfinished effort in no way typical of her best work. Did someone want to remember her by that? But what other reason . . .

His pulse rate went up. A paradox that the first inkling of an answer elicited sensations so much like fear.

"Steve, may I use your phone?" He didn't wait for his shrug of permission, but rose and reached across the desk for the phone, in his haste misdialing so that he had to start anew. The voice that answered was clipped and formal, but still familiar.

"The Canfield residence."

"Sean, this is Conan. Can you talk?"

A brief pause, then, "Yes, for a couple of minutes."

"I'll make it fast. Were you around yesterday when Jim and Carleton brought the things from the cottage?"

"Well, not exactly. I mean, I was here, but I was stuck back in the kitchen with Alma."

"Then you didn't see any of it?"

"Not then, but I got a chance to check it this morning."

"Good. Did you see a painting, a large oil about four feet long, unfinished, in reds and yellows?"

"No, there weren't any paintings, any color."

"Could it be anywhere else in the house?"

"Not that I know of. It sounds like it'd be a little hard to hide, and nothing's sacred to a housekeeper."

"Check around, but don't be too surprised if you don't find it. Who was at the house last night?"

"Well, Catharine, of course; she's hardly left her room. Carleton was here yesterday evening and didn't leave until after us servants were dismissed. Jim wasn't here for supper, but he spent the night. I had his bed to make up as proof of that."

"So, all three of them had access to that painting last night. All right, Sean. Thanks."

"Sure. Did Steve tell you about the search?"

"Yes, I'm at his office."

"Oh, well, give him my love."

He laughed. "I'll make that regards. He might take you seriously. You'd better get off the phone now."

"Okay. I'll call this evening with a status report."

"I'll be at the hotel. Take care, Sean."

When he hung up, he stood frowning into space, so preoccupied he didn't even hear Travers at first.

"Sorry. What'd you say, Steve?"

He sighed. "I gather Sean didn't find the painting."

"No, and Carleton and Jim were both at the house last night, as well as Catharine."

"How come you're so hung up with that painting?"

"I'm just wondering why someone else was so hung up that it's disappeared. Let me have a piece of paper and a pencil." He leaned over the desk as Travers obligingly provided them, and sketched out the general proportions of the canvas. "It was shaped about like this, wasn't it?"

"Yes. Maybe a little longer."

"Okay." He made an adjustment in the lines. "Now, there were two triangles, side by side, outlined in red. Like this, right?" He hesitated, eyes narrowed. "Red and yellow; danger and caution. Interesting."

"Sure, but what do two triangles mean?"

"I don't know, Steve. There weren't any other shapes, were there? The background was kind of nebulous."

"I don't think so. I gave the thing a long look. I guess I was hoping she left some sort of message, as if she had time for that. Hey, maybe it's an M."

"For Mother?" He tossed the pencil down, regarding his crude artistic endeavor with a jaundiced eye.

"Why not? Or maybe those things stand for mountains."

"Stand for? What school of art appreciation do *you* belong to?"

"Grandma Moses. Wait a minute." He peered intently at the drawing. "You've got it wrong. There wasn't a bottom line on this triangle; the one on the left."

Conan reached for the pencil, almost laughing as he scrubbed out the erroneous line with the eraser.

"Damn, you're right. It was like this; more like an inverted V and a triangle." Then he stopped and stared at the paper, and again Travers had to repeat himself.

"That rings a bell for you?"

"What? I . . . yes. Maybe."

"What do you mean, maybe?"

"Just that."

"So, you think *maybe* Jenny did leave a message? Look, that guy in the sports car was only in the cottage ten minutes total, and besides, she was shot in her bedroom. There was no way she could've painted out any messages."

"I know. The painting was probably done earlier in the evening, and it was only a diversion; something to keep her mind off the chills and cramps. But I can guess what was foremost in her thoughts. It's a kind of doodle, really. I'm sure it never occurred to her she was pointing a finger at her killer. She didn't think she was in any danger."

"Then how come you're so excited about it?"

"Because someone *did* see a pointing finger in it. That's why it disappeared."

"Where does the finger point, Conan?"

He paused, studying the drawing, while Travers waited tensely.

"Steve, let me muddle this over awhile." Another pause. "Where does Milly's and Worth's testimony point? Rather consistently in one direction, wouldn't you say?"

He shrugged. "Well, I was sort of impressed with the consistency, and Carleton doesn't have an alibi."

"No, but don't forget Sean saw a Lotus Elan leave the Canfield house at 8:40 Saturday night."

"Don't confuse the issue with facts, and Sean didn't get a very good look at that car. Besides, Catharine says she was alone all evening. Have you considered the fact that *she* doesn't have an alibi either? She dismissed the servants at 7:40, and if she drove like hell, it's possible she could've made it to Shanaway by 8:35."

"Yes, I've considered that." He looked down at the sketch again, then put it in his breast pocket. "Take your pick. Steve, the only viable strategy for dealing with a conspiracy is divide and conquer."

He groaned. "Conan, don't—"

"I'm not getting philosophical on you. That's a very pragmatic observation, and here's another. You won't pin down this killer with proper police procedures. It's the old shell game, and this hand is faster than the procedural eye."

"So, what do we do?"

"Change the game, perhaps, and run a bluff."

Travers's face screwed up in a dubious frown.

"I think I'm going to regret this, but tell me more."

"First, *we* name the game and deal the cards. Then we sweeten the pot and make sure our mark has a good hand."

"He already has a good hand."

"But we hold the high cards."

"Really. I hadn't noticed that."

"If knowledge is power, then Jenny gave us the ace." He glanced at his watch and crossed to the door. "Steve, I'll have to play the hand, but I'll need your help."

"Sure, if you've got the hand to play, and if your mark doesn't have an ace up his sleeve."

"That I can't guarantee. Thanks."

"Wait a minute. What the hell's your hurry?"

"I have some muddling to do. I'll call you later."

Travers loosed a resigned sigh as the door closed.

"Sure, Conan. Later."

CHAPTER 22

It was like looking through a freshly washed lens, this April morning; the sky a burning blue, every blossom on the plums and cherries a distinct entity. Conan followed Travers's sedan past the police barricade at the gate of the Canfield mansion, wondering at the compulsion, even in a practicing skeptic, to read affinities in human experiences and casual meteorological phenomena.

Yesterday, Tuesday, it had rained; a misty, windless, gray rain. Jennifer Hanson had been buried in that rain, and it had seemed fitting. More fitting than this celebrant blaze of sunlight.

Travers parked his car and got out to wait for him, squinting up at the phantasmagoric turret with the dubious eye of a man born to simple clapboard homesteads.

"Doesn't look like anybody's home."

Conan glanced up at the house. "Well, we know Sean's home. Come on, we may as well get this over with."

Travers nodded, his forehead lined with a foreboding frown as they climbed the steps.

"Conan, you know, sometimes I wonder how you talk me into these things. I'm not even sure this is ethical, much less legal."

"Cold feet, Steve?"

"You're damned right."

"Mine aren't so warm, either. I just hope you can keep Carleton out of the way long enough."

"We've got enough to keep him occupied until tomorrow, anyway." He glowered at the front door. "How do you get into this place?"

"You ring the bell," Conan said, reaching for it. After a short wait, the door opened, seemingly of its own volition, but Sean Kelly was the motive power behind it.

"Good morning. Oh, it's Mr. Flagg."

He recognized her formal address as a warning and responded with equal formality, "Yes, Miss Reilly, and this is Steve Travers of the State Police. We'd like to talk to Mrs. Canfield."

"Well, I'll see if—"

"It's all right, Miss Reilly." The voice came out of the shadows behind her. "Ask them in."

Sean stepped aside to let them pass, and in the dim light, Conan saw Catharine Canfield coming down the stairs, one hand sliding along the banister, the other holding the white cane that felt out each step as she descended.

At Jenny's funeral she'd worn a black veil. Now, her dress was still black, but there was no veil to hide the ravages of grief; only the dark glasses, rimmed in black. And it came as a surprise that her hair hadn't changed; that it wasn't entirely white.

At the foot of the stairs she stopped, putting on a polite, emotionless smile as if she were waiting for an opening move. Conan made it.

"Mrs. Canfield, I'm sorry to intrude on you now. The gentleman with me is Steve Travers of the—"

"Oh, yes. You were the one who called me when . . . Saturday night."

"Yes, ma'am. I'm afraid that wasn't the best kind of introduction."

"You were very considerate and most thoughtful. Mr. Flagg, how is Isadora? I'm so upset that Dr. Kerr won't at least let Jim see her; we're all so worried about her."

"I'm sure Dr. Kerr has her best interests in mind. Mrs. Canfield, Steve would like to talk to you privately. He asked me to come along since I've been involved in the case and might even be regarded as a friend of the family."

Her smile barely faltered. "Of course. We'll go into the library." The cane preceded her to the double doors and into the room, and she asked casually, "Is it too dark?"

Conan closed the doors, finding it difficult not to stare at her; she played her role so well, even now.

"No," he answered. "The drapes have been pulled."

The tall windows on the right wall flooded the room with light, warming the varnished wood, glinting on gold-embossed book covers, glowing in the ruby patterns of the Kerman. Yet the desk in the center of the room seemed to absorb light; it had the monolithic stance of a monument.

Catharine avoided both the windows and the desk. She went to one of the armchairs facing a small fireplace framed with exquisite Belgian tiles.

"Will you sit down, gentlemen?"

Travers took the chair facing her, waiting until Conan drew up another before he began, displaying a reticence that seemed entirely natural.

"Mrs. Canfield, I wish I didn't have to bring up the subject of your daughter's death again, but I'm afraid I must. You see, we've made an arrest."

Her polite smile faded. "An arrest? Not . . . Isadora?"

"No, ma'am. Miss Canfield has been cleared. There's no question at all of her innocence now."

"Well, I'm . . . gratified, if that's the case." But it was obvious she didn't believe it.

"The way we read the situation now," Travers went on, "someone tried to take advantage of her—well, her illness; tried to make it look like she killed Jenny in some sort of mental lapse."

"Take advantage—perhaps you should explain that."

"Yes, ma'am. Well first, I talked to Dr. Heideger, and as I told you, she's a fine doctor. She said Isadora showed all the symptoms of a 'bad trip' Saturday night. A real classic."

"I—I don't understand."

"She'd been drugged. LSD."

It was frustrating, trying to read the responses behind the glasses, but her pallor betrayed her now.

"*Drugged?* That's impossible."

"I'm afraid not," Travers said levelly. "Someone knew LSD trips are a lot like schizoid attacks. I guess they thought that with Isadora's history, this would be passed off as just another attack, and it would've been except for Dr. Heideger. She didn't know anything about Isadora's problems; she just went on the obvious physical symptoms."

Catharine asked tightly, "What does Dr. Kerr say about that?"

Conan answered the question, watching her head come around toward him.

"He's in complete agreement. He talked to Dr. Heideger at some length."

"Fortunately, we have more than medical opinions," Travers said, and her head turned toward him. "We found the person who gave her the drug."

She listened, motionless and rapt, as he told her about Milly Weaver. But he didn't once refer to Carleton by name, forcing her when he concluded to ask, "Who was it? Who told this Weaver woman to give Isadora that drug?"

"The man who was Milly's defense counsel. C. Robert

Carleton.'' He paused at her audible gasp of surprise. ''I'm sorry, Mrs. Canfield. I know this is a shock for you.''

''Bob?'' She shook her head distractedly. ''No, he couldn't—I just can't believe that. Not *Bob*.''

''I'm afraid there's no doubt about his involvement in this. Did you know he had Isadora under surveillance since the twenty-fourth of February?''

Her reply was slow in coming.

''Of course, I didn't know. Why would he do that?''

''He says he was just worried about her making another suicide attempt, which is odd, because Dr. Kerr says he made it clear *he* considered that risk negligible. Yet Carleton was worried enough to pay for full-time surveillance, including bugging the phone at the cottage. But he says you and Jim agreed to it. Is that true?''

Her tone was cool. ''I said I didn't know about it.''

He nodded. ''That's what I thought. Anyway, the interesting thing about the tailing is that it was called off Saturday afternoon. Nobody wanted any witnesses around the cottage. Everett Worth—he runs the agency Carleton hired for the job—said it was Carleton who called him and told him to get off the case.'' He hesitated, looking at her almost apologetically. ''Another thing, Jenny supposedly called Isadora at the Surf House, you know.''

''Yes, I was told about that.''

''Well, Jenny didn't make the call. No calls were made from the cottage at that time.''

''How can you be sure of that?''

''The phone was bugged.''

''Oh. Yes, the—the surveillance.''

He didn't correct her misapprehension.

''We don't have a record of the call Isadora got, of course, and her memory of it is pretty fuzzy, but whoever made it knew she'd be in no condition to recognize an imitation of Jenny's voice. Only the man who had her drugged would know that.''

She frowned. "What about that Weaver woman? She certainly knew Isadora was drugged."

"Yes, ma'am, but at the time Isadora took that call, Milly was waiting for Max to set up an order for her."

"But, *why*?" She turned away, her hand clenching on the white cane. "I could understand Isadora killing her. Not purposely, or even knowingly, but I saw her after . . . after John died. But *Bob*—why would *he* kill Jenny?"

"We can't say for sure, but I'm afraid it has something to do with her addiction."

"No." She was suddenly stiff with offended dignity. "I will not believe that drivel about Jenny. Someone put that—that drug in her bedroom. She was my daughter. Don't you think I'd know if she were an . . . addict?"

Travers sighed, looking helplessly to Conan to answer the question.

"No, Mrs. Canfield, you wouldn't know. Even if you knew what symptoms to look for, you're at more of a disadvantage than most parents; you couldn't *see* them."

She took that broadside with no apparent effect.

"Then you think it's true?"

"I know it's true. I talked to her Saturday afternoon. She was trying to quit and was already in the first stages of withdrawal."

The pretense finally failed briefly, and he felt her *looking* at him from behind the dark glasses.

"Jen . . . told you she was . . ."

"Yes. She needed help."

"But why would she go to you for help?"

He paused, then shrugged. "She really didn't come to me for help, but she was willing to accept it when I offered it. We had something in common."

"You mean Isadora?"

"No. A painting. Mrs. Canfield, Jenny told me she had called her pusher, the person who supplied her morphine, and told him she was quitting, and I had the impression she threatened him with something—exposure, probably—if he didn't leave her alone. I also had the impression she intended to talk to him that night, but she considered herself in no danger. That suggests it was someone she trusted, or at least, knew well."

"And you think Bob is—was her . . . pusher?"

Travers answered, "We have no proof of that yet, but we know Jenny had a visitor that night. We found a witness who saw a sports car drive up to the cottage at 8:35 and leave about ten minutes later."

"A sports car? Do you . . . know who it was?"

"No. It was a stormy night; the witness didn't even get a license number, but he was sure it was a sports car."

She nodded vaguely, and for some time was silent; she seemed numbed, hardly aware that she wasn't alone.

Finally, she asked, "Where is Bob now?"

"At Salem police headquarters," Travers replied. "He has legal counsel, of course, but he wants to talk to you. In fact, he's been quite insistent about it."

Her head came up slowly. "Why to me?"

"He says you can clear him. That's the main reason I'm here." He paused, but she didn't question him, nor comment, nor even move. "When we first asked Carleton where he was Saturday night, he said he was at home from 7:30 until you called about Jenny. That was around ten, wasn't it?"

Her head moved in a tense affirmative nod, and Travers went on, "Well, now he's changed his story. He claims he was here talking to you from eight until 8:40. If that's true, he couldn't possibly have killed Jenny, and somebody else is trying to frame him for it." He paused again, waiting for a response, and when she still made none, he asked flatly, "Mrs. Canfield, was he here?"

A silence gathered; a silence she seemed to weave around her. Conan waited, caught in the web of sun-moted stillness until finally she lifted her chin, and in that small movement was the firm resolve of a decision made.

"No." There wasn't the slightest shade of doubt in the word. "No, he wasn't here. Does he really expect me to give him an alibi when he killed my daughter?"

Now, it was she who waited for a response, and when there was none, asked calmly, "Was there anything else you wanted to know, Mr. Travers?"

He cleared his throat. "Uh . . . no, not now. You *will* made a statement if we need it?"

"Of course." She rose, and both men politely followed suit and accompanied her to the door. The cane moved ahead of her, silenced by the rug, the studied smile was still intact.

"I'm sorry to be the bearer of bad news again," Travers said. "I mean, about Mr. Carleton. I know you considered him a friend."

"I was apparently wrong about Bob," she said tautly, then added, "One never really knows people. Not even those who seem . . . closest." For a moment, she was silent and withdrawn, but when Conan opened the door for her, she roused herself and preceded them into the foyer.

Travers looked at his watch. "Mrs. Canfield, I'll show myself out. Thanks for your help. Conan?"

"Go ahead, Steve. I'll be right behind you."

He waited until Travers had departed. Catharine stood at the foot of the stairs, one hand on the newel post; the polite smile was getting a little ragged around the edges.

"Mrs. Canfield, I know this is a shock for you, about Mr. Carleton, but I think you'll understand it's a great relief to me." Her expression didn't change; she seemed to need an explanation. "It means Isadora is safe."

At that, she tensed. "What?"

"Well, I mean free from any suspicion."

"Oh. Yes, of course, and I'm so relieved for her sake."

"I called Dr. Kerr as soon as Steve told me about Carleton's arrest. Since she's free of any legal restraint now, Dr.

Kerr said there's no reason for her to stay at Morningdell. He thinks she should come home."

"Home?" The word seemed foreign to her, and the smile collapsed. "You mean, here?"

He hesitated. "Why, yes. Dr. Kerr will continue to treat her, of course, but on an out-patient basis."

She made an attempt at recovering her smile.

"Well, that's good news, indeed. I mean, that he thinks she's well enough to come home. Did he say when?"

"Today. Or rather, this evening. He's scheduled one more session with her this afternoon."

"Today?" Another word that seemed foreign.

"Yes. Actually, I think Dore's the one who's pushing for the release; she'll be very happy to leave Morningdell. And she's looking forward to seeing Jim."

Catharine still managed to hold on to her smile, but her response was absent and distracted.

"Jim had an exam today. He . . . he couldn't miss it, but he'll be home this evening."

"Good. I'll tell Dore. Oh—" He paused, frowning. "There's something else, and I realize it's a terrible imposition, but Dr. Kerr suggested that—well, for the first few days, I should stay with Dore here at the house. I wouldn't ask you to put up a self-invited guest at a time like this, but he thought it was important."

She needed a little time to absorb that, but she didn't seem suspicious; only vaguely surprised.

"Yes, I know Isadora feels very strongly . . . I mean, she has . . . great faith in you. I can understand . . ." Then she seemed to remember herself and put on her courteous smile again.

"Mr. Flagg, don't be concerned about imposing. I'd be delighted to have you, and I'm so pleased about Isadora. When can we expect you? For dinner, perhaps?"

"Yes, I think so. I'll call if there's any delay."

"Thank you. And now, if you'll excuse me, I'm . . . tired."

She didn't wait for his murmured assent, nor his good-byes, but turned and began climbing the stairs slowly, as if every step were an overwhelming effort.

CHAPTER 23

The evening was less than stultifying only because Catharine suggested they retire to the salon after dinner so Isadora could play for them, and because Jim Canfield acted the role of host with deft grace, keeping the vein of conversation light, adroitly filling any dangerous vacuums. He also had the good sense to be quiet once they were comfortably settled around the piano, leaving his chair only between pieces to refill glasses or pour more sherry.

Isadora asked for the sherry, but neglected hers for the piano. Conan neglected his, too, but purposely. He noted that Jim showed some restraint with his scotch, but Catharine showed a surprising lack of restraint with hers.

But there was no restrain in Isadora's playing. The tense uncertainty, the undertone of anxiety and even hostility that marked her every word and gesture since her homecoming, disappeared when she began playing. She laughed with Jim over his references to her "stodgy" choices, and played Haydn for him; acquiesced gracefully to Catharine's request for the *Moonlight Sonata*; performed the Debussy *Feux d'artifice* for Conan brilliantly, apologizing afterward that she was out of practice.

Finally, at eleven, she ended the concert with the Liszt *Rhapsodie espagnole*. Her good spirits stayed with her as they adjourned from the salon and walked together down the hall to the foyer.

"Isadora, thank you so much for playing for us," Catharine said, pausing when she reached the stairs. "I've missed your music so much."

"Thank you." A hint of constraint entered her tone. "I've missed the old Steinway, too."

"It's missed *you*. Oh, dear—" this at the slight lisp in her S's. She pressed a hand to her cheek. "I'm afraid the music, or something, has gone to my head. Jim?"

He was only a pace away, ready to take her arm.

"If you're gong to accuse me of loading the drinks, I plead not guilty."

At that she turned away, trying to laugh.

"Well, you'll still have to help your old mother up to her room. Oh, Mr. Flagg, you must think me a terrible hostess. If you need anything . . ."

"I'm sure I won't, and you've been a charming hostess."

Jim put in, "If you do need anything, just ask me. Come on, Mother, you're tired, and whatever went to your head, maybe it'll get you a good night's sleep."

"Yes, that would—oh, good night, everyone. Please excuse me."

Isadora smiled stiffly. "Good night, Catharine. You, too, Jim."

"Night, Sis. You get a good night's sleep, too."

"I told you Dr. Kerr gave me some enormous pills."

"Well, get an enormous night's sleep. Knock on my door if you need anything, Conan."

"Thanks, Jim." He looked down at Isadora, seeing the

equivocal hostility doing battle with pity in her eyes as she watched Catharine make her way up the stairs, leaning on Jim's arm. Finally, they disappeared into her bedroom, and Isadora turned away.

"You know, you almost have to feel sorry for her." Before he could think of a suitable response, her eyes narrowed coldly and she added, "But she always was a great actress."

He hesitated, put off balance, not by her antagonism, but because he'd told her nothing about Catharine's ruse. But perhaps she had nothing specific in mind with that comment.

He asked. "What do you mean?"

"What?" Then she laughed. "Oh, I'm just being bitchy again. Don't mind me." She was staring at the library doors, closed as they always seemed to be, and her smile faded. When at length she took a few hesitant steps toward them, Conan tensed with the beginnings of both fear and hope.

"It's silly to be afraid of a room," she said, still staring at the doors. "Dr. Kerr keeps coming back to it, as if all the answers were behind these doors."

"Are they?" He almost regretted the question because it distracted her. But only briefly; she glanced at him, then fixed her gaze on the doors again and slowly closed the remaining distance.

"I don't know. Perhaps my sanity is there."

He walked over beside her, but didn't approach too closely; he only wanted to be sure he could see her face.

"There are answers in there, Dore, but it isn't a question of your sanity. Dr. Kerr explained that to you."

"Yes. It helps to understand why, but still, I have to . . ." Her right hand moved out as if of its own volition, hung in space, and finally rested on the doorknob. She stared at it, the color draining from her face. "I wonder if . . . if I have the courage."

He waited, seeing the pulse beat in her throat, feeling its quickening echoed in his own. If she intended to try to overcome the fear instilled in a mock madness, Dr. Kerr should be here. But he wouldn't discourage her; to advise caution would only reinforce the fear.

She began to tremble, her eyes suddenly wide, haunted with an unknown terror. He'd seen it before.

"There's something . . . I remember . . . something . . ."

He kept his voice low, nearly toneless. "Words, Dore, put it into words. As it comes, whatever you see or feel."

"The lamp . . ." Her lisp barely moved. "The lamp on the desk. That was the only light. I—I can see it. Remember it. I can *remember* . . ."

Another long silence. Still, she was remembering, and even if it were only the lamp on the desk, it was a beginning; a breakthrough.

"The lamp, Dore." He spoke softly, trying to make her aware only of the words, not of him. "The lamp on the desk, the light shining on something. On what?"

She seemed paralyzed, incapable even of blinking her eyes, but finally the words came, each one a separate effort.

"Shining . . . yes, something shining. His—his hair; silver hair. His head down on the desk. He's only fallen asleep . . . working so late . . . only asleep. But his—his hand . . ." Her face contorted, as if she were in pain, eyes narrowed, focused on something in memory, but still fixed on her hand and the doorknob; her breath came in shallow, whispering gasps.

"His arm . . . stretched out across the desk. Reaching out for . . . for help. Reaching out, and—" A choking sound in her throat, and her eyes were wide again, dark with that familiar horror. "Something in his hand . . . wrapped around his arm . . . something *moving*!"

"What, Dore?" He tried to keep his voice low, but the tension was cracking in it. "What is it?"

"They're all over the room!" He hadn't distracted her; she was still remembering, and still terrified. And something more. Revulsion. She was sick with it. "They don't move, they . . . *writhe*. All over the floor and the desk and . . . oh, God, in—in his hand. His *hand*!"

"What? Dore, what are you seeing?"

She shuddered, her head fell back, mouth open as if she were drowning, pulling for air.

"Snakes!" It came out with a hissing sound, and the very word seemed as repulsive to her as what it stood for. The choking sobs began, yet her hand seemed frozen on the doorknob. *"Snakes!"*

Conan had to wrench her hand free. He pulled her around, away from the door and into his arms, hearing her sobs muffled against his body.

"Dore, it's all right, everything's all right." He repeated the assurance over and over. The words didn't matter; only the sound of a familiar voice; a touchstone; reminder and proof that those horrifying illusions had no substance. And gradually, the trembling and weeping ceased.

And in reverse ratio, his rage grew.

Snakes. That was the key Milton Kerr had been seeking; the key to the amnesia. Someone had planted the delusion of snakes in her mind so that every remembrance of her father's death was associated with something she found unbearably abhorrent, and doubly so in the context of death; someone who was familiar with her phobia for snakes, who recognized its efficacy and used it to lock away a memory, letting her pay the price in terror.

Perhaps Dr. Kerr could make use of this key, yet Conan wondered if she could sanely tolerate walking into that garden of horrors again.

He heard a sound; footsteps. But when he looked up at

he top of the stairs, he saw no one. Catharine's door was losed.

Isadora looked up, too, but at him, and he smiled at her, nowing she was on the verge of an apology.

"It's too soon, Dore. You need more time."

She nodded, wiping her cheeks with both hands.

"I guess so."

"Come on." He put his arm around her and led her to the tairs. "What you need now is some sleep."

She didn't respond, only holding on to him until they eached the landing. It was part of the hall running at right ngles to the stairs. Closed doors met his eye in every direcion. At the head of the stairs was Catharine's room; next to , the one which had been John Canfield's; down the hall to ne left was Jim's room and three guest rooms, one of which ad been assigned to Conan; at the opposite end of the hall vas Isadora's room. The house was quiet; a silence weighted vith years.

She said, "I'd better turn off the hall light."

"I'll turn it off later."

"All right, but we leave that little lamp on the table there t night."

"The candle in the window?"

She laughed weakly. "Maybe the eternal flame."

When they reached her room, he turned on the ceiling ght and left the door open. As he looked around, he vas reminded of Jenny's poignant reference to Isadora s a princess. This was a room befitting a princess; Victorian princess. White wainscoted walls surnounted by rose-toned paper with a fine figure; the same ose hue in the carpet and damask draperies. The furniure was of dark wood, richly carved, the posts of the anopy bed exuberant spirals. The bed was curtained in filmy white cloth drawn back around the headboard in raceful folds.

Isadora, watching him, smiled faintly.

"This was originally my great-aunt Emily's room. She died here at an early age; a broken heart, I think. Or maybe it was typhoid."

He laughed and took her hand. "Not typhoid; not in this room. It had to be a broken heart."

"Conan, you're a hopeless romantic; I knew that when I looked through your tape library. All that Tchaikovsky."

"You expect sophistication of one of Pendleton's native sons?" Then he sighed; her eyes were still red. "Are you all right now?"

"Yes. It *does* help to understand why. I mean, these recurrences."

"Good. We won't talk about it now. Not unless you need to."

"No. But, Conan . . ." She looked up at him intently. "I wish I understood more about—well, about everything else; what's really happening."

"I've told you everything that's *really* happened since you went back to Morningdell."

"That's only facts. I want to know what you think."

He glanced out the door, keeping his voice low.

"You have the answers locked away in your head. I won't tell you what I think because when you unlock them, I must be sure the answers are entirely yours."

She accepted that, but only in part.

"And you're worried about how I'd react if you told me what you really think; what I might do."

"Perhaps. I wouldn't want to try to predict it. But the first reason still stands. Oh, Dore . . ." He reached out and ran his hand through her hair, and she smiled.

"I know, have faith. And I do, Conan."

"Thank you. Now, you'd better get some sleep; it's late. And don't forget to take your pill."

She frowned at that. "I really don't think I need it."

"Yes, you do," he said firmly. "Dr. Kerr's orders."

"I know, but I don't like to—"

"Dore, it's to prevent any recurrences, and you need ıe sleep without nightmares. Promise me you'll take ."

She paused, a little alarmed at his insistence.

"All right. I will."

"Now . . ." He pulled her into his arms and kissed er, intending for it to be only a brief, parting gesture, ut it seemed to get out of hand somewhere along the 'ay. Fear was part of it, he thought; they were both fraid. It was the remembrance of something else he had › tell her that finally made him draw away. His arms 'ere still resting on her shoulders, his hands clasped be- ind her head.

"By the way, your bedroom is bugged, and Sean Kelly is the next room on the monitor."

"In Dad's room? Conan, if anyone catches her in ere—"

"Sean doesn't get caught, so she tells me. She'll just watch ver you tonight, and in the morning creep out like the fog n little cat feet."

"Oh. I was hoping *you'd* be doing the watching over. A *ose* surveillance."

He laughed and kissed her cheek.

"It won't be too close; I might get distracted."

"Well, that's encouraging." Then she sobered. "Do you ally think I need watching over?"

"I don't know, but if you do, you'll be well watched. Now, ose the door when I leave. And take your pill."

She walked with him to the door, frowning absently.

"Conan, did Bob really . . . did he kill Jenny? And Dad? ɔu said the same person killed both of them."

He glanced out into the hall, then touched a finger to her ɔs.

"You're asking me what I think again."

"All right." She called up a smile and squeezed his hand. Good night. Thanks for being here."

"Good night, Dore. Good sleep."

He walked down the hall, pausing to turn off the ceiling lights, leaving the dim glow of the table lamp. He heard a door close. Not Isadora's. Catharine's.

CHAPTER 24

The Seth Thomas on the vanity chimed midnight. Isadora counted the tones, wondering if she'd really been asleep. It was warm; no breeze moved the curtains, dimly white in the darkness. Little of the city light reached the window through the trees, as little sound did; a distant murmur like the whisper of surf at the beach house.

She frowned at the memories that called up.

Still, she knew she could go back to the cottage in spite of the intense regret, even guilt, that shaped her grief for Jenny. It wasn't like the library.

Don't think about that. Not now; not in the dark.

She watched the tree shadows on the curtains, feeling a little guilty now about the sedative. She hadn't taken it, justifying her refusal as reluctance to become dependent on an artificial sleeping aid. But she admitted now that rebellion motivated her more than reluctance. She resented Conan's insistence and cautious reticence; it gave her an annoying sense of being manipulated.

Dr. Kerr hadn't been at all enthusiastic about releasing her from Morningdell, nor had she been anxious to come home. Home. The word was a mockery. Conan had engineered that, deftly evading her questions while seeming to answer them, just as tonight he had *seemed* to explain why the bedroom was bugged and Sean Kelly was on guard in the next room; why he was so insistent about the sedative.

She took a deep breath. Have faith. How many times had he asked it of her? And she knew that in some sense he loved her, as she did him. She was being childish, and perhaps she should get up and take the pill now. The memories—no, they were just vague feelings of memories—were lurking behind her thoughts, threatening any hope of sleep.

She turned over on her side, not even wondering why she faced the door, putting the windows, the only faint light in the room, behind her. She closed her eyes and thought about music. The Gershwin *Concerto in F*; she'd been working on it at the cottage. No, don't think about the cottage. That one passage—the accents had to be exactly right; a hint of jazz timing, yes, but the *Concerto* demanded as much restraint as any Beethoven sonata . . .

The clock chimed again; the half hour. She *had* been asleep this time but the dreams . . .

She stiffened, fear striking from some inner ambush.

The door was opening. It formed a rectangle of pale yellow; framed a dark figure that for a long time didn't move; that became almost an abstraction, shadow on light.

At length, the head turned, looking back into the hallway. She was only aware of how intense her fear had been when it disappeared.

Conan.

He'd changed his clothes; black pants, black sweater with a high neck and long sleeves. When his face was turned away from the light, he was only a shadow.

Then she closed her eyes, grateful for the dim light because of the rush of heat to her cheeks. The sedative. She hadn't taken it, and now she was embarrassed. He expected her to be soundly asleep.

Well, then she would be, or at least, seem to be.

A faint click. She opened her eyes into darkness, wondering if he'd gone. Then a few seconds later, another slightly different click, and she saw him kneeling by the wall near the door; saw him in the pale glow of night light in the electric outlet. He must have brought it with him; it hadn't been there before.

Then she closed her eyes again; he was coming toward her, and it seemed impossible that he wouldn't see the renewed flush of embarrassment in spite of the dim light. It was ridiculous, really, and when he left, she *would* take the pill.

For some time she heard nothing, then startlingly close, a soft rustling. How could he move so quietly? She had an impulse to laugh. That must be the Nez Percé coming to the fore. Or more likely, the G-2 training.

She felt a light touch on her hair, but didn't move. Now, she thought, he was sure she was asleep and he'd leave.

The next sound she heard wasn't the click of the door, but a faint thump directly behind her. Then a squeak; a familiar sound, and she knew exactly which of the two Queen Anne side chairs made it.

And she knew what it meant. Conan didn't intend to leave at all. He had settled himself to watch over her, hidden in the shadows behind the canopy curtain, and the only alternatives left her were to admit her deceit, or to make the best of it and try to go back to sleep without the sedative.

She was smiling to herself; he couldn't see her face. Perhaps she could sleep now with Conan watching over her. That should stave off the nightmares . . .

She was dreaming. Something about Jim. Yes, Jim wearing a pair of Catharine's sunglasses. There was a light, but it couldn't be morning. The night light.

The memory came into focus as she came awake. Conan was leaving. It wasn't the night light she saw, but the open door, the glowing rectangle broken by a silhouette.

But it *wasn't* Conan.

It was Catharine, wearing a floor-length robe of pale blue that had a spectral silver cast in the soft light.

Isadora shut her eyes. Hold on; just hold on. This is why Conan wanted her asleep, so he could be sure she wouldn't —what? Betray him somehow?

She concentrated on her breathing, and the anger seemed ironic in the context of the smothering fear. Anger at her body because the trembling was so hard to control; anger that she found it necessary to control it against all reason; and anger at Conan because somehow he was responsible for all this.

And he was. He had expected it, had prepared for it, even offering live bait. It all made sense now. Everything, including her release from Morningdell and this "homecoming," was carefully calculated. It was a trap, a trap for a killer, and she was the bait, supposedly lying in sedated helplessness, while he watched from behind . . .

What if he weren't there? She'd been asleep; he might have left the room, and she wouldn't have heard him.

No. He'd be there.

He might make her the bait for a trap, but not a sacrificial lamb. And if his trap needed a helpless, sleeping victim as bait, then that's what she'd be. She'd be anything to help him trap this killer.

She opened her eyes just enough to see between her lashes. Catharine was still at the door; this wrestling with fear and anger had occupied only a few seconds.

The anger wasn't entirely gone, but it was cold and subtle. The person who sprung Conan's trap would be her father's killer. Catharine. Was that something out of her memory? She watched her take a few hesitant steps toward her. No, there was no memory; still no memory.

What did she expect of a killer? Should a killer seem so wraith-like, so suddenly aged, every movement constrained as if it were painful, like an old woman leaning on . . .

Her eyes squeezed shut, head pounding with her pulse, the blackness turning around her.

The cane.

Where was the cane? And the dark glasses?

In all the years since the accident, she'd never once seen Catharine without dark glasses, never heard her footsteps without the tapping of the cane.

She listened now to her footsteps, muted by the carpet; listened to the rustle of her robe, like dry grasses in a wind. When it stopped, she knew Catharine was standing by the bed; standing there *looking* down at her, *seeing* her.

It was an act of raw will to remain still, to play at sleep when the fear was so stifling she couldn't breathe. If Catharine didn't move, if something didn't happen soon, in the next few seconds . . .

The rustling again, the footsteps moving away, and she was as stunned by that retreat as by the sense of imminent threat. But Catharine didn't leave the room when she reached the door. She only closed it, and ghost-like in the wan glow of the night light, sat down in a chair near the door, folding her hands in her lap, and Isadora realized with a dull shock that she intended to stay there; to wait.

But for what?

She heard something behind her; a stirring, or a whisper of a breath. Perhaps it was only something she felt. But Conan was there. She knew it as surely as if he'd spoken to her.

And across the room, Catharine waited and watched. All these years she'd been watching behind the dark glasses, and Isadora wondered at her own indifference to that. Emotional shock, perhaps. Real comprehension would come later for this whole paradoxical scene. Two people occupying the silent shadows of this room while she lay pretending sleep. Later she might even be able to laugh at that.

The clock struck. One o'clock and all's . . .

Hold on. She marshaled her mental resources, knowing she was close to weeping, and somehow she must find the strength to be still, to seem asleep until—what?

What was Catharine waiting for?

The chimes sounded twice more, the quarter and half hours, and she was grateful for their tangible demarcation of time; her own time sense had failed her.

She heard the click of the door, watched it open. It would be Jim. That was probably a logical conclusion. Who else could it be? Yet it hadn't occurred to her.

Catharine didn't move except to turn her head and look up at him. She *looked*, and that still seemed incomprehensible.

"Mother?" Jim's voice, a hiss of chagrin. "What are you doing here?"

"Waiting for you."

She wasn't whispering, but the words were soft, barely audible, making Jim's reply seem harshly sibilant.

"Are you out of your mind?" Then a quick glance toward Isadora.

"She won't hear you; she's thoroughly asleep. I suppose you've made sure Mr. Flagg won't . . . interfere."

Jim was still looking toward the bed, his response absent, nearly disinterested.

"Sure. Dore left her sweetheart a bottle of sherry by his bed. I just checked. The bottle's half empty, and he's dead to the world."

Isadora felt herself sinking into vertigo. That didn't make sense. It was like a nightmare, and she could almost believe it was only that, or an insane delusion, except for Jim's voice, a grating whisper, like a serrated blade.

"Mother, get back to your room."

"No. Not this time."

"Look, you're in this thing up to your matching sunglasses. Now, get out of here and let me take care of it."

"No."

"Then stay out of my way."

She asked softly, "What's that, Jim? Another 'tranquilizer' to make her forget?"

There was something in his hand; he looked down at it. "Yes."

"And that's all it is, just like the other time? You didn't understand the violent reactions; that was only shock and grief. Nothing to do with that drug or you. Jim, I'm a fool, but not such an ignorant one now. It can cause true insanity, can't it? Enough of it can destroy the mind. That's what you're hoping for."

He seemed to loom over her, to emanate a dark chill.

"Get back to your room, Mother."

"No. I made myself your accomplice once because I was afraid, and because I knew myself capable of what you'd done, but I can't let you go any further."

"You can't let *me* go any further? Listen, you're on this train, too."

"I didn't get on the train that ran Jenny down."

There was a brief, taut silence spaced by the sound of his breathing, and Isadora choked back a sick cry. Not Jenny; he couldn't. Not Jenny.

"You'd better talk to Bob about that train, Mother."

"How long did you have her—what do they call it? Hooked?—with the morphine? Since her illness? Is that when you got her addicted, because of the pain?"

"You're out of your skull if you think I had anything to do with Jenny's death. For God's sake, I was here in town. Chet can vouch for me."

"I suppose he's also one of your—your customers."

Another strained silence. When Jim made no response, she went on wearily, "Guilt engenders fear; I know because I lived with both so many years. If you hadn't been so afraid, you'd have known Jenny would never betray you."

"*Bob* killed her—I didn't!" Then realizing he'd let his

voice get out of control, he looked over at Isadora, and she closed her eyes, shivering, listening in frozen dread to Catharine's calm, dead calm, voice.

"Bob didn't kill her. He couldn't have."

A hesitation, then, "What do you mean?"

"Bob was here that night. We had a meeting; one he didn't want you to find out about because it was you he wanted to discuss. I lied to the police."

"Then you'd better keep on lying."

"Or what?" A laugh full of sadness. "Or you'll kill me, too? That's the fear, Jim. You're sick with it."

"And what are *you*?" His hand locked on her arm, but she didn't seem to feel it. "You nearly hung yourself playing your idiot game with dear old Dad, and you're going to hang us both whimpering around about Jenny. There's no way off this train till you get to the end of the line."

Isadora stared at him, too stunned for pretense, remaining still only because she was incapable of moving. The light caught on the object in his hand. It was small and transparent, but she didn't recognize it. She only knew there was terror in it; the same terror that was in his rasping whisper.

"And there's something else you'd better get straight, Mother. Dore's going to *remember*. I heard her down in the foyer tonight. With Kerr and Flagg working on her, she's going to remember what happened unless I do something about it. If you're too squeamish to watch, get the hell out."

"No." That quiet, yet obdurate syllable again, and Jim straightened abruptly.

"You haven't heard a word I've said. You're so—"

"Oh, Jim, I've heard every word and understood it. *You* don't understand. You learned ambition from poverty and from me; especially from me. But I won't let you destroy Isadora. Jim, it's finished. *This* is the end of the line."

"What are you going to do? Call the cops? True confession time?"

"There'll be no police and no confessions."

"Keep it in the family, huh?" He'd forgotten entirely to keep his voice down; there was a fevered, acidly cynical undercurrent in it. "So, how do you intend to stop me, mother mine?"

"With this, if I must."

She reached into the pocket of her robe; there was a brief, metallic flash as her hand came up. When Isadora realized it was a gun, she couldn't believe it was real. And Jim only laughed.

"Sure. You're going to put a hole in me, right? In *me*, your one and only love child. Oh, Mother, you're too—"

"My . . . what?" For the first time, there was fear in her voice.

"Never mind." He laughed again. "Damn, you missed your calling. You should've tried Hollywood."

"Jim! Don't—please! *Jim!*"

But he turned his back on her, and finally Isadora recognized what was in his hand. A syringe. And her last hold on sanity slipped.

Not again . . . not again . . . not again . . . not again . . .

The next split second she saw in a pulsing blur, apprehending it as perpetual, and the terror had a name now, madness, and it was contained in that looming shadow, the shadow that glowed incandescent red, shimmering, amorphous . . .

The explosion was blue-white, and the sheer agony of it made her scream.

Yet it drove off the encroaching madness, and when she found herself crouched against the headboard in a room suddenly filled with light and footsteps and voices, she could call it a recurrence and know what it meant; could recognize Conan and Sean Kelly and know why they were here.

But she couldn't comprehend Jim, lying face down on the floor, trying to brace himself on his elbows, head raised, strangely like an infant in its crib; there was a shining red smear on his back. Then Conan was bending over him.

"Jim, don't try to move!"

But he jerked away with a retching cry of pain, only succeeding in turning onto his back with a floundering lurch, and he offered no resistance when Conan eased his head down. He lay staring at the ceiling, silenced by some dreadful realization.

Conan looked up at Sean. She was standing behind Catharine, wary and ready, the gun in her hand, but Catharine only sagged into the chair, weeping soundlessly. She didn't even look at the man who appeared suddenly at the door, and Isadora didn't recognize him until Conan spoke to him.

"Carl, tell Steve to send an ambulance."

He went out without a word. Carl Berg, wearing a black wig. She understood now. He'd been Conan's sleeping stand-in.

When she moved, every muscle was stiff, resisting her commands. She pushed back the disarrayed covers, her steps unsteady as she crossed the short distance to kneel beside Conan at Jim's side.

He wasn't dead. He was in pain and mortally afraid, but not of anyone or anything in this room.

CHAPTER 25

Conan sat cross-legged on the floor beside Jim Canfield wondering vaguely how his hands could still be shaking when his muscles were flaccid with weariness. They were alone. He'd sent Isadora and Catharine downstairs with Sean and Carl; Catharine with her cheeks drowned in silent tears, Isadora still dry-eyed, mercifully numbed, asking, "Why can't I remember, Conan? I still can't remember."

It didn't matter now. She hadn't been the only witness to her father's death.

Jim could move his arms; his hands were clenched in the blanket Conan had covered him with. There was in his face a kind of mute beauty; pale, translucent skin drawn tight over the finely structured bones. Early Michelangelo in polished Carrara marble.

"How much longer?"

Conan knew what he meant. The sirens were audible in the distance.

"A few minutes."

"Mother's a lousy shot." He tried to laugh, but it turned into a grimace of pain.

"I didn't think she'd use that gun. Not on you."

"I didn't think she would, either, There's probably a moral in that. In this house, there's always a moral." He stopped to listen to the sirens, then laughed raggedly. "Tell them to give me a shot of morphine, will you?"

Conan only nodded. "Jim, what did you mean by calling yourself a 'love child'?"

His lips curled with a mocking smile.

"How about *bastard*? Ask Mother. It's too late to ask the old man, and he'd have denied it on a stack of Bibles. The Great White Father in the West stepping out on his ever-beloved and ever-bombed Anna? He didn't like to think about that."

"He adopted you, Jim; gave you his name."

"Sure, he did. Because Mother wouldn't get off his back. You know, when she married him—that was even before I found out—I used to think . . ." His eyes clouded out of focus. "Funny, I got so hung up on . . . on fishing. I used to think a father was supposed to take his kid fishing, like in the TV commercials. But he never did . . ." Then a wry grin. "Maybe I used the wrong toothpaste."

"When did you find out he was your father?"

"I don't know. Yes, I do. I was sixteen. I heard the servants talking back in the pantry, then I started checking a few records. And pictures. You ever see a picture of the old man when he was a kid?" A cold laugh. "I'm his spittin' image."

"Your mother didn't tell you?"

His head moved back and forth jerkily.

"And I never told her I knew. Family tradition, you know. Secrets. Always . . . secrets."

"He never recognized you as his son even in private?"

"Hell, no. I told you, he didn't like to think about—I was just some sort of extra baggage Mother dragged in." His ace twisted with pain or rage, or both. "Why did he ever marry her? He never really loved her. But, you know, she *did* love him; it went way back. I think the only thing she ever really wanted in this life was John Canfield."

"Is that why you killed him, his rejection of you and your mother?"

He looked at Conan and laughed.

"No. Because he was about to foul everything up. He finally caught on to Mother's little game."

"Foul what up?"

"Everything. The will. When he found out Mother had conned him all these years—well, he couldn't take that. Off with our heads. The vorpal blade went snicker snack, and . . . what's the rest of it?" He sighed, eyelids fluttering, nearly closing. "He was going to cut us out; Mother and her scruffy offspring. And ol' C. Bob, too. I just made up my mind I'd get my fair share one way or another."

"What about Carleton?"

"Well, C. Bob had the same idea, you know. Figured he and Mother'd ride off into the sunset hand in hand with the old man's money. But he was . . . useful." A sardonic smile flickered on his lips. "I kept him around; thought I'd let him put my father's house in order before . . ."

"Before you took over?"

He nodded slowly and closed his eyes, but opened them when Conan pressed his fingers under his jaw to check his pulse.

"I'm still here. Hey, are you—are you really going to marry Dore?"

"No."

"Just part of the game, huh? Okay. I've anted enough to see your hand. You set me up tonight. How . . . why me?"

Conan settled back, sorting the mixed threads of the sirens, resting one elbow on his upraised knee.

"Maybe because I knew something about LSD, Jim, and because Dore had two more 'attacks' the first week she was in Morningdell, and you were the only member of the family to visit her there. That was risky, too, but I suppose you had to reinforce the bad set and make sure the amnesia was holding. Then there were your electives in psychology and that chemistry course. You dropped it, but I'm sure you made some fruitful contacts in the chemistry department."

He laughed, his features contracting.

"You—you really did some research. Keep talking. Please. Just . . . keep talking."

Conan's mouth was dry, and it was an effort not to turn away from that pain-ravaged face.

"Yes, I did some research. I found out you'd almost been caught on a drug rap, and drugs were part of your entertainment, along with parlor hypnosis. That probably helped create the bad set for Dore and contributed to the amnesia. And I learned you had a talent for imitating voices. That's how you set Carleton up with Worth and Milly Weaver, and set Dore up with that call for help from Jenny. Then there was your choice in books. The blueprint for Canfield's murder is in *The Executioners*." He stopped. Jim wasn't hearing him any more; he was listening to the sirens, so close the old house echoed with their wails.

When they died, Jim took a long, rasping breath.

"They're here."

"Yes."

"What'd she have, anyway? Some damn pop-gun?" His words were getting slurred.

"A little .22. Saturday night special."

"Where'd she . . ." Then he shook his head. "Doesn't matter. You have *her* set up tonight, too?"

"No. I wasn't expecting her. I gave her a choice this afternoon, and she threw Bob Carleton to the wolves without a second thought. Jim, how much of an accomplice was she?"

His attempt at a smile produced a wracked grimace.

"A lousy one. Didn't want her in on it—the old man, I mean. Always took sleeping pills. But that night, she . . .

ıe came downstairs. That wasn't so bad, but then Dore—I ad to do *something*. She walked right in while—oh, damn, 'hy'd she have to come home then? I . . . never wanted to— ı hurt her.''

''And Jenny?''

At first, Conan wondered if he'd heard him; his eyes were xed on nothing, dull and glazed.

''Oh, Jen—she . . . she'd have spilled everything. I know er—I *knew* . . . she . . .''

A rattling thud of multiple footsteps was on the stairs, but 'onan didn't look up from Jim's grief-harried face.

''Doesn't even make sense now,'' he murmured. Maybe—maybe Mother's right . . . about the fear. You get ı . . . oh, God help me, I didn't mean to kill her. No, I *ıeant* to, but afterward . . .'' He had no words for after-'ard.

''It was Jenny who really pointed the finger at you.'' That asn't salt in the wounds of guilt; it was a salve of sorts ecause he was capable of guilt.

Jim's haunted eyes came into focus on him.

''The . . . painting.''

''Yes. She didn't intend it as an accusation. It was only a ındom reflection of what she was thinking of at the time. ou; her supplier. The Greek letters lambda delta.''

He nodded with a painful, jerking intake of breath. The ɔotsteps reached the door, but Jim didn't look around. His ves were closed. Two white-uniformed ambulance atten-ants came into the room, moving with grim efficiency. Steve ravers leaned against the doorjamb, equally grim.

Conan rose stiffly, watching the attendants.

''Be careful; he has a back injury. And for God's sake, ive him something for—some morphine.''

ravers stopped at the top of the stairs. The foyer was glaring 'ith light, swarming with policemen and relentless activity.

''How bad is it, Conan? I mean, Jim.''

"I don't know. I doubt he'll ever walk again."

After a brief silence, Travers started down the stairs.

"The ladies are in the parlor."

Conan followed him, flinching inwardly at the glare and noise. But inside the parlor, it was quiet; an irrational quiet that defied the open doors.

Across the room, Sean Kelly sat waiting and watching, clothed in slacks and a sweater, the role of domestic put aside. Catharine was sitting near the door, motionless and expressionless. He found Isadora standing at the front window, the bright yellow of her robe seeming incongruous. When he put his arm around her, she rested her head on his shoulder. Still dry-eyed, he saw; still numbed.

"Conan, how is he?"

"He'll live, Dore."

Travers began reading the litany of rights to Catharine, and Isadora turned, regarding her with no hostility; only an uncomprehending sadness.

"Will he ask her what happened?"

"Yes, I think so."

He took her hand, listening with her as Travers questioned Catharine. She seemed totally indifferent to both the questions and her answers, spelling out the story with no elaboration, nor any attempt at rationalization. It was a long recital, but the only time she showed any emotional reaction was when Jim was brought downstairs. She turned to watch the stretcher carried out, but asked no questions.

Finally, Travers said, "I guess that's all, Mrs. Canfield. Conan, anything else?"

"Yes. Two items you didn't cover, Steve." He waited until she turned, gazing at him with eyes that seemed truly sightless now. "Why did Carleton have Dore under surveillance? Whose idea was that?"

"Bob's. He was always so . . . anxious."

"But why was he worried about her? How much did he know about your husband's death?"

Her blind eyes shifted downward, fixing on the carved arm of the couch.

"Nothing. He was only worried about the notes John made on changing his will. They'd have left the will open to contest. Bob had my interests in mind, as well as his own; a contest would probably mean an investigation into his handling of certain trust funds, and he couldn't risk that. He was afraid Isadora had seen the notes, that John might even have said something to her about them before he died. Bob knew she wouldn't tell Jenny if she recovered her memory. He thought if she talked to the police or Hendricks, we'd at least have some warning."

"Did Carleton destroy those notes?"

"Yes, but all three of us were part of that."

"But not Jenny?"

"No," she said dully, "she wasn't part of any of it."

"Did your husband know Jim was actually his son?" Isadora tensed at that, but he was intent on Catharine, seeing a mordant regret in her lifeless eyes.

"No. Not until the day he . . . died."

"Why didn't you tell him before?"

She paused, her gaze shifting, and it was to Isadora the answer was directed, not Conan.

"At first, because I loved him. I hope you never have to learn the kind of hatred love turns into, Isadora. Hell hath no fury—and no agony. Jim was the result of a very brief . . . interlude. John loved your mother so much, I can't believe he was ever unfaithful to her before or after, and he was so consumed with guilt about it. That's why I didn't tell him; that and my own pride. Even when we were married, I couldn't tell him; not with Anna so recently dead. Then when our marriage began to go sour, I guess I was saving it as a sort of ultimate weapon. The day he . . . we had a confrontation that afternoon; he found out I wasn't blind. I told him about Jim, threw it in his face, but it only made him despise me more. It was too late. But I didn't realize Jim knew—

what it did to him all these years. I didn't *know* . . ." The words trailed off into an aching silence.

Finally, Travers glanced up at one of the policemen waiting at the door, then said quietly, "Mrs. Canfield, Lieutenant Sims will take you to headquarters."

She nodded and pulled herself to her feet hesitantly, as if she weren't sure she could walk.

"I'll go upstairs and get dressed."

Sean rose, sending Conan a quick, anxious glance.

"Maybe I should go up and help you, Mrs. Canfield."

Catharine knew who she was now, but there was no rancor in her reply; no emotion at all.

"Thank you, but I need no help, and I've no intention of trying to escape." Then she turned to Conan, and what he read in her gray-green eyes, so much like Jenny's, chilled him. A message; a plea she expected him to understand.

She had made a decision, and he knew he might stop her now, but she would carry it out eventually; one way or another. It was her choice; the only one left her.

He said to Sean, "You don't need to go up with her."

Catharine turned without a word and made her way into the foyer. Travers followed her, but only to the door to talk to Sims. When she ascended the stairs, she was alone.

"Dore, go get dressed." Conan was still watching Catharine. "We're going to the beach."

She stared at him, surprised and bewildered.

"Now? But can I leave now? I mean, the police, and—"

"We'll come back in the morning to finish up the loose ends, and Sean can look after the house tonight."

She sent Sean a questioning look that at her affirmative nod turned into a pale smile of gratitude.

"All right. I'll go get dressed."

"And hurry," Conan added.

When she was gone, he turned his back on the foyer.

"Sean, you'll get time and a half for this."

"At least. But get her out of here, Conan. She's had enough for one night."

He was vaguely startled at that. Feminine intuition, no doubt. She knew as well as he that Catharine would never leave her room alive.

Then Sean said, "Conan, someday you're going to see Isadora Canfield on a stage with the New York Philharmonic behind her, and then maybe all this will make sense."

He smiled at her. "I'd like to have you on my arm for that concert, Sean. Put it down in your date book."

"Thanks, but like they say, three's a crowd."

"Then there's already a crowd, and I'm the extra third."

She raised an eyebrow. "Oh? Who's the two?"

"Isadora and the Steinway concert grand." Then he added: "And I hope they live happily ever after."

ABOUT THE AUTHOR

M. K. WREN is a pseudonym for a West Coast writer of crime fiction and science fiction. In addition to her skills as the creator of Conan Flagg, Ms. Wren is also the author of the acclaimed science-fiction trilogy, THE PHOENIX LEGACY. As an artist, she has exhibited in numerous galleries in Texas, Oklahoma, and the Northwest. She has been lauded for her watercolor miniatures—detailed paintings with subjects tending toward Victorian houses and ghost towns. A MULTITUDE OF SINS is the second in the mystery series featuring Conan Flagg.